Calling the Shots

USA TODAY BESTSELLING AUTHOR
KARA KENDRICK

Copyright © 2025 by Kara Kendrick

CALLING THE SHOTS PLAYLIST

Firecracker - Josh Turner
Casual - Chappell Roan
What Could Go Right - Thomas Rhett & Lanie Gardner
Love Me Not - Ravyn Lenae
Happen to Me - Russell Dickerson
Change My Mind - Riley Green
I Love You, I'm Sorry - Gracie Abrams
Hell is a Dance Floor - Vincent Mason
If You Were Mine - Miranda Lambert & Leon Bridges
Sin So Sweet - Warren Zeiders

For the sidekicks who never feel like enough.
*You are **more** than enough.*

BLURB

A sexy small town, forbidden, football romance from bestselling author Kara Kendrick

One fake kiss with the coach next door changes all the rules of the game.

Mack doesn't give Prince Charming vibes. Sure, he's tall, ruggedly handsome, and the high school football team's defensive coordinator. But he's my mom's **brooding next-door neighbor—a decade older than me and absolutely forbidden.**

Friend-of-my-best friend's-dad kind of forbidden.

When I'm ditched on a date and losing aura points by the second, I salvage my pride in front of my archenemy the only way I can — I pretend Mack's my boyfriend. He plays along and seals our **fake relationship** with a kiss that sets my world on fire.

"Just one night" quickly spirals into secret rendezvous and heart-racing hookups. But then I discover the "blue collar" laid-back coach I've fallen for is hiding secrets of his own.

I'm certain we're doomed. What I don't count on?

Mack chasing after me—and this time, he's calling the shots.

CHAPTER 1
GRACELYN

should have stuck to my guns.

Stayed off *Blaze* and *Buzz* and *Soulmate.com* forever.

I managed just fine all summer long, while my bestie Sloane was back home here in Thunder Creek.

Living vicariously through her love life, everything was good.

Great, even.

But once she left for Florida with Cam and I was all alone again, I logged back in. Bored and lonely, I couldn't stop myself from swiping right. Like a freaking addict, desperate for excitement and ready for my next hit of oxytocin.

Flush.

The toilet whooshing in the next stall jolts me back to my miserable—and still very much single—reality. I have to sashay out there and bid the fondest adieu to Pixel Pete, the world's most boring IT guy. Why'd I even swipe right on the guy? We have nothing in common—I'm pretty sure his idea of a good time is writing code. The dude has zero game and may still be a virgin. Not that there's anything wrong with that, I just don't particularly want to walk him through the finer points of female anatomy.

Hard freaking pass.

With a heavy sigh, I wipe my sweaty palms down the thighs of my jeans and stand tall on my very-much-wasted-on-this-date stilettos. I slide the lock back on the stall and shove out into the dim restroom. Only to make eye contact with Jamie Ware, the biggest bitch in town. With her siren-red hair and matching lipstick staining her surgically enhanced pout, I couldn't miss her if I tried.

Fuck my life.

Now I have two choices. I can: a.) dip back into the stall and fake a violent retching episode. Or b.) waltz over to the sink and wash my hands like a normal person.

Much as I'd love to go with option A, I saunter over to the sink, head held high.

"Hey, Gracie. How are you?" Jamie trills, flipping her long scarlet hair over her shoulder.

I *really* hate when people call me Gracie.

I glare at her in the mirror, my right eye on the verge of twitching.

"All alone now that your little friend's shacking up in Florida?"

My gut clenches, bringing option A back into play.

"Great to see you too, Jamie. And not that it's any of your damn business, but I'm not alone. I'm on a date." I wrench at the faucet handle and water sprays out full-force, splattering out of the sink and turning bits of my gauzy white blouse sheer.

Shit.

I ratchet the pressure down, meeting her gaze in the dingy mirror. She arches a penciled brow and acts shocked.

"How nice for you. Another one-night stand in the books, then?"

My jaw clenches, hot anger bubbling in my veins. This bitch has been tormenting me since grade school and I am *over* it.

"You know a lot about those, I'm sure."

She unsnaps her clutch, pulling out a tube of lipstick. Popping the lid, she swipes the deep red color across her bottom lip.

"No, that's not really my style. I'm more of a long-term gal myself. And I'm not into the local dating scene, either. That's so, I don't know, passé, don't you think?"

Considering I told her five seconds ago I was on a date with someone who's most likely a local, no, I clearly do not think. But whatevs…

My cell vibrates in my pocket. Saved by the bell.

I quickly dry my hands, tapping the screen to life and reading the text.

> Pete: It was nice to meet you. I had to jet.
> Take care

This is a first, even for me. A shock rolls through my system, with cool relief following close behind. Aggravation squeezes in there, too, because what the hell?

Pixel Pete couldn't even wait for me to get out of the bathroom before he bolted. At least we can avoid the awkward end-of-date pleasantries and the "I'll call you later" lies.

"Lover boy texting you already?" Jamie angles her head, trying to read the message. I shove the cell deep into my pocket. No need for her to know Pete has left the building.

"No. Just Sloane, checking in with me. We always text each other when we go out, to be on the safe side. The old buddy system, ya know? Oh—you probably don't know because you don't have any close girlfriends."

Jamie purses her lips but doesn't take the bait.

"I'd love to meet your date, Gracie. Care to introduce me?" She smooths an imaginary wrinkle out of her satin top, thrusting out her perfect breasts.

Under ordinary circumstances, I'd say no to this request. Now that Pixel Pete is M.I.A., it's a hard fucking no.

"It's early days, Jamie. Maybe another time."

"Oh, right. I'm threatening, I get it. Happens to me a lot." She fans her long, delicate fingers over her chest.

Oh, brother.

"No, not threatening." I smooth my hair over my shoulder, locking eyes with her in the mirror. "More like aggravating as hell."

She scowls at me and a long second passes, neither of us backing down. I silently will her to walk out first because I have no plan, other than ducking out the emergency exit and calling an Uber.

The door to the restroom crashes open, banging against the wall, and two women stumble in. Still, Jamie doesn't budge as the ladies crowd us at the sink, giggling and talking loudly about the bartender. One of them turns on the faucet and water sprays me again, this time thoroughly dousing the lower half of my shirt.

"Ohmygosh, I'm so sorry." She grabs at a stack of paper towels and starts awkwardly blotting my midsection.

"It's fine, don't worry about it." I ease away from her and the geyser of a faucet, Jamie hot on my heels. She's so freaking close to me the heavy scent of her perfume stings my eyes.

Pushing out into the dim hallway, I frantically try to figure a way out of this jam. There's no way in hell I want to admit to Jamie my date bailed on me. I can't very well walk back to the empty table. That will be a dead giveaway.

Slowing my steps, I cast a quick glance over the crowd in the bar. Sure as shit, Pixel Pete is gone, our table sitting vacant in the corner. A large group of college-aged kids dance in the center of the room, high top tables shoved to the side of the makeshift dance floor. The bar's packed, but I don't see anyone I know.

Except Mack.

Sloane's dad's best friend and my mom's next-door neighbor. He's sitting alone near the end of the bar, drinking a beer and watching football on the television. A head taller than everyone else, with impossibly broad shoulders, he's easy to spot. His arm flexes as he casually lifts his drink, his square jaw outlined by the neon lights behind the bar.

With a deep breath, I straighten my shoulders and strut confidently in his direction, Jamie right behind me like a fricking drug dog. Hopefully she can't smell bullshit.

"Hey, babe." I sidle up close to Mack, resting my hand on his forearm as if we've known each other for years.

Which technically we kind-of-sort-of have, but not in a touchy-feely dating kind of way.

He stares down at my hand for a second, and I silently will him to play along.

"Hey, Gracelyn. Everything okay?" He cocks an eyebrow, a smirk dancing on his full lips.

"Yeah, bathroom was fine. Clean. All good. The

bartender didn't come back with my drink yet?" I wave at the server, leaning over the wooden bar in Mack's direction.

"Just go with it, okay? I'll pay you back," I whisper in his ear, the clean scent of his aftershave tickling my nose. I've never been this close to Mack before, never noticed how muscular he is, how he fills out his T-shirt in all the right ways.

"Ahem." Jamie clears her throat, and I glance over my shoulder.

"Oh, you're still here?" I wrinkle my nose and she stiffens, tipping her chin up.

"Hey. I'm Jamie." She purrs her name, popping her lips out in a sultry pout, and thrusts her hand in Mack's direction.

"Uh—hey." He shakes her hand, more out of politeness than true interest. "Mack. I coach over at the high school."

"Oh, I know. I see you at practice every day."

Really? This is news to me.

"You do?" I narrow my eyes at her. "You're stalking the high school football team now?"

Jamie lets out a high-pitched giggle, as if that's the funniest joke she's heard all year.

"No, silly. I took over as assistant coach for the dance team. We've been out on the field once or twice since school started. Most of the time the boys have it all to themselves, though, and we're in the stinky old gym. But I'm so happy to officially meet you, Mack." She flutters her false lashes at him and I swallow down the vomit, signaling to the bartender for another drink.

Luckily, he's a regular—and took my drink order with Pixel Pete—so he knows I need another tequila on the rocks, stat.

"How long have y'all been dating?" Jamie asks and the corners of Mack's lips tip up the teeniest bit as he takes a long slug from his beer bottle.

"Oh, a while." I stroke Mack's arm, trying to sell the story. His skin's warm and smooth, veins popping over his muscles.

"Like a month or two? Funny you never mentioned such a handsome boyfriend all summer long."

My cheeks heat under Jamie's stare, heart pounding hard in my chest.

"Only my close friends know. Like my inner circle. Oh —I forgot. You don't know about that sort of thing, I guess."

Jamie glares at me.

"We were keeping things kind of chill this summer." Mack snakes his arm around my hips and pulls me closer to him. I try not to panic as my ass brushes against his thick thigh and his fingers palm the round globe of my ass.

"Wow." Jamie stares at the two of us in disbelief, her thin brows raised.

For once, I may actually have the upper hand on Jamie Ware.

Halle-freaking-lujah.

"Well, Mack—I hope to see you again real soon." She flips her hair over her shoulder, locking her gaze on him.

"Yeah. See you around." He nods at her, then turns his attention back to me, a sexy smile playing on his lips. A fluttery sensation rolls through my tummy and fingers of heat lick at my skin.

I keep my eyes trained on Mack for a full minute, not daring to turn around and risk blowing my cover. He doesn't drop his hand from my ass, either, holding me in place against his hard body.

Now that I'm staring deep into his jade-green irises, I notice the laugh lines crinkling his tanned skin, the light stubble peppering his jaw, the line of perfectly straight white teeth, sandy curls peeking from beneath his ball cap.

The man is low-key hot.

Even if he is at least a decade older than me.

"Is she gone?" I mouth the words, trying to keep my voice low and barely audible.

"Not yet." He leans in closer, his breath warm on my face. "She's over in the corner, chatting with some people."

"Shit," I mutter. "Sorry, but could you just keep this going for like, a few more minutes, until she leaves? It's a long story."

Mack doesn't answer and panic flashes through me. If he bails now, Jamie will know I was lying and that will be a million times worse than Pixel Pete walking out on me. Because how pathetic am I, that I had to lie about having a boyfriend?

Without taking his eyes off mine, Mack sets his beer down on the bar with a clink. He grips my hips and pulls me into him, settling me right between his spread thighs. Then he leans in and presses his mouth to mine in a soft, slow kiss.

He tastes like beer and masculinity, his lips rolling over mine, teasing. My heart hammers, blood whooshing in my ears as my mind races over nothing and everything all at once.

I'm kissing Sloane's dad's best friend in the middle of Mustang's on a Saturday night.

And damn, it's good.

Very, very good.

This man knows how to kiss, a shiver of pleasure rippling through me as he squeezes my ass. He slides a hand in the back pocket of my jeans and wetness floods my panties.

"How was that?" he murmurs against my lips and I smile, trying to catch my breath.

"Good. It was…good."

"Okay, then." He inches away slightly, cutting his eyes toward the corner. "She's still looking over here, but she definitely bought it. Act natural."

He kisses me again, lighter this time, then the bartender slides a drink in my direction. Mack takes that as his cue to scoot back and I reach for the drink, knowing my entire body's flushed. The curse of fair skin, there's absolutely no way to hide my feelings. I'm a freaking walking mood ring.

"Cheers." Mack picks up his beer, clinking the bottle with my glass. I smile at him, happy I bested Jamie, at least for the time being. "Care to tell me what that was all about?"

CHAPTER 2
MACK

'**ve known of Gracelyn for a long time. Her mom's my neighbor and has been for the past decade, so of course I've seen her around.

But not like this.

Never like this.

Rosy cheeks, glossy lips, a nearly see-through white top and a slight tequila buzz. Her golden hair cascading over her shoulders in ringlets, wide blue eyes framed with thick lashes. She's snack-sized, too, petite with curves for days.

Kissing her should feel wrong, on so many levels. She's too young for me—shit, I met her before she could legally drink. Besides the whole next-door neighbor thing, she's also friends with my best friend's daughter.

His daughter.

Which probably makes me super creepy, I don't know.

Except that's not what this feels like at all.

Instead, that kiss a few moments ago felt natural. Like the universe set Gracelyn at this bar, her cute ass nestled in between my thighs, for a reason.

"So…" I lock eyes with her, a light pink flush creeping up her neck like a kudzu vine. "What was that?"

She takes a sip of her drink, those wide eyes darting around the room. Searching for Jamie, I assume.

"Long story, but the important detail here…" She leans in close, her face inches from mine. "The important thing to remember is Jamie Ware's been my sworn mortal enemy since the fifth grade. I was on a first date tonight—it wasn't going well, by the way—and the jerk bolted while I was in the restroom."

She huffs out a quick breath, flipping her golden curls over her shoulder before forging on. "Jamie stalked me, wanting to meet my date. Because that's the kind of asshole she is."

"Ah. Your date bailed, so you needed a cover. Got it." I swipe a hand over my jaw, surprised by the ripple of disappointment rolling through me.

"Yeah. Thanks for that. Put your beer on my tab. I owe you at least one."

"Nah. I got it. Pretending to be your date wasn't exactly a hardship."

Her cheeks tinge a shade darker and she drops her eyes down to my mouth, then flicks them back up again quickly.

Damn.

Gracelyn's all grown up and very much the kind of woman I go for. Soft curves and sass, with a tinkly laugh that sends all my blood rushing due south.

I should not get involved with her.

Horrible, terrible idea.

The only thing we probably have in common is our connection to the Carters. Coach Carter being my best friend and his daughter Sloane being Gracelyn's.

A cheer breaks out at the bar and several guys around us high-five. UGA just scored a touchdown to beat USC.

"Go Dawgs!" Gracelyn whoops, pumping her fist into the air.

I stand corrected. Apparently, we have friends and football in common. The makings of a solid relationship.

"You're a Georgia fan, too, huh?"

She grins, blonde curls bouncing over her shoulders. "Born this way, sorry."

"No need to apologize. It's my alma mater."

"I know."

I swallow hard, suddenly warm. The bar feels crowded now, and noisy. I very much want to leave—but not alone this time. I've had more fun in the last twenty minutes than I've had in a good, long while.

"Want to get outta here?" I cut my eyes at Gracelyn, surprised at how much I want her to say 'yes.'

Gracelyn tips her head, blinking at me, and I hold my breath. Damn, I'm way more nervous than I should be. It's not like I'm trying to take her home and get her naked or anything.

Not that I don't want to. But between the age thing and the neighbor thing, a casual hookup seems like a real bad idea.

After a long minute, she nods. "Sure."

Pulling a twenty out of my wallet, I toss the cash onto the bar and gesture to the bartender.

"See ya, Mack!" The bartender waves as I slide off the stool, my hand hovering over the sheer fabric covering Gracelyn's lower back.

We weave through the crowd and I pull her closer to me, the seductive scent of some exotic floral perfume drifting off her skin. She smells like a mistake I'd very much like to make tonight.

Awful idea, Mack. She's way too young. And that shit's gonna be awkward in the morning.

I hold the door, admiring her perfect peach of an ass as she swishes past me in sky-high heels and makes her way out to the parking lot.

"Well, thanks for the drink." She slides the tip of her tongue along her lower lip, drawing my attention straight to her mouth.

Look away. Don't do anything stupid.

"I'm going to grab an Uber before it gets any later." Fishing her cell out of her bag, her fingers tap on the screen.

"Don't. I can give you a ride."

Pausing, her crystal blue eyes fly to mine, pupils wide and dark in the pale glow of the streetlight. "You sure? I hate to put you out."

"It's fine. Probably not even out of my way."

"I live in the townhouses near the high school."

"See? That's like a five-minute detour. C'mon." I shove my hand in my jeans pocket and shuffle to my truck, unlocking the passenger side door for her.

"Wow. No key fob?" She cocks one brow up high, scrunching her nose.

"'Fraid not. This truck is old. Although I prefer 'vintage.' Sounds better."

She giggles, the airy sound floating through the quiet lot.

"It's cool, very classic. Love the baby blue color, too." She lifts her foot to climb into the truck, struggling with the height and the tiny, pointy heel of her shoe.

Being a gentleman—and itching to touch her again—I

slide in behind her. Gripping her at the waist to steady her, I guide her up and into the truck. I'm close enough to hear the hitch of her breath, her lips parting slightly. I grab the seatbelt and lean over, careful to avoid brushing any part of my arm against her voluptuous breasts.

"The seatbelt's a little tricky." I click the belt into place, winking, then pull back into my own space.

"Thanks." Her voice comes out a husky whisper as I close the door behind her.

Hustling around to the driver's side, I climb into the cab and crank the ignition, the floorboards rumbling with the effort. "This truck was my grandpa's. My mom hates that I still drive it."

"Why?" Gracelyn glances over at me, her smooth brow wrinkled in confusion.

"She claims it's about the lack of safety features. Plus the toxic emissions and saving the environment, blah, blah, blah. But it's really about status. She likes foreign cars. The more expensive, the better."

"Oh." Gracelyn's pink lips form a perfect 'O' and I flash back to our kiss in the bar, wishing we were doing that again instead of jawing about my mother.

"Anyway—" I lean back against the broken-in leather seat, my arm resting on the metal sill of the window. "What's the deal with Jamie? How'd she get to be enemy of the state?"

Gracelyn shakes her head, furrowing her brow.

"I told you. She's an asshole. Always has been."

"I'm gonna need examples." I flick on my blinker and head in the direction of the high school.

"For starters, she tripped me on the bus in front of my crush. I fell and busted my knee. Bled all the way home."

"Ouch."

"Yeah. Then the next year, she spread a rumor that I had a pet chicken."

I can't hold back my chuckle at this. "A chicken? So what? Who cares that you had a chicken?"

"I know, it's dumb. But I didn't even have a chicken!" She throws her hands into the air. "Sloane told me to brush it off, but do you know how hard that was? Every time I walked into the cafeteria, someone would start clucking and crowing at me."

"The horror," I tease, sneaking at glance at her. She's cute, all animated as she drops her face into her palms and groans.

"I know, right? Especially rough on chicken nugget day."

I snicker. "Brutal."

"Junior prom? That bitch wore the same exact dress as me. Like, how?" She almost smacks me in the face as she gestures wildly.

"Did you get your dress here in town? There aren't a ton of shopping options."

"No. That's the crazy part. Sloane and I went over to the mall in Lightning Ridge to avoid that very scenario. Jamie had to stalk me to buy the same dress. Then the yearbook did a Who Wore it Better spread and guess who won?"

She smashes her mouth together in a thin, tight line.

"Guessing it wasn't you."

"Correct. Apparently, she's a model now. Told everyone she was in Europe all last year. How can I compete with that?"

I stop at the red light, fingers thrumming on the steering wheel. "I'd say you're winning."

"Shut up!" She punches me lightly on the biceps and

shakes her head. "Get outta town! You're biased because I made a move on you. Or you need glasses. Because as much as I despise Jamie freaking Ware, I still freely admit that she's attractive."

I sneak a quick glance over at her. Moonlight bathes her face in a soft, white glow and I can't remember the last time someone pretty as her sat in my passenger seat.

"She's alright. Not really my type."

Gracelyn cocks her head, blinking. "Really? Tall, willowy, and gorgeous doesn't do it for you?"

"Meh." I shrug.

"Do tell. What is your type then? Because I thought all guys loved that look."

I suck my teeth, wondering exactly how honest I should be here. The events of the evening—coupled with a beer and the strong floral scent floating around in the truck cab—embolden me.

"Petite. Curvy." I keep my eyes fixed on the road, the motor rumbling loudly in the stretch of silence. "Bold, with a big personality and a good sense of humor."

"Huh. Jamie really isn't your cup of tea then. All she's got on that list is bold, but it's more brash. Like a bad dye job. In my humble opinion, of course."

I laugh at her analogy and she grins, teeth bright in the glow of the dash lights.

Before tonight, I hadn't spent much time chatting with Gracelyn. I'm surprised at how easy it is, how natural it feels.

I make a right at the next light, turning into the town-home complex, and Gracelyn points at the third door from the left. "Well, this is me. Thanks for the ride."

"No problem."

I pull into an empty parking spot and cut the ignition.

Gracelyn unbuckles her seatbelt and hops out before I can come around to get the door.

I hustle to her side and she swivels, blonde curls bobbing.

"You don't have to walk me to the door or anything. I'm fine." She waves her hand through the air, brushing off the gesture.

"Just to be on the safe side." I keep pace with her, matching her strides until we're standing on her welcome mat. She pulls the house key from her bag and slides it into the lock. I wait for her to go in, but she doesn't turn the key. Instead, she spins around and takes one step forward. Now we're toe to toe and she's pressing her body close to mine. Rising, she winds her hands around my neck and scoots even closer. Her mouth hovers inches from me and our breathing syncs.

With a slight tilt of her head, she presses her lips to mine in a soft, sweet kiss. So light I'm not even sure we're touching. Kind of like eating angel food cake. Heavenly air.

After a few long seconds, she breaks away, blue eyes glittering beneath the soft lamplight.

"Just wanted to test that out. See if it felt any different out here."

I stare down at her. "Did it?"

"Yeah." She nods, sucking at her lower lip. "It was better. Night, Mack."

Then she spins and disappears into her house, leaving me standing there speechless.

CHAPTER 3
GRACELYN

My back pressed against the door, I pull my cell out of my bag and the screen flashes to life.

Shit. It's almost midnight, but I need to talk to Sloane. There's no way I can sleep right now, not with the heady scent of Mack's aftershave clinging to my skin and every nerve in my body still tingling from that kiss.

I need to talk this out right now, try to make sense of everything that went down tonight. And Sloane's the only person in the world who will truly get it.

Gracelyn: BESTIE! You up?

I stare at the screen, willing a message to come through.

Bestie: Barely. What's up?

Gracelyn: You're never going to believe what happened tonight. Call me!

Not two seconds later, the phone trills in my hand and

Sloane's profile pic pops up. She always comes through for me, day or night. No matter how far apart we are, she'll always be my bestie, and the very thought fills me with warm fuzzies.

"Ohmygod, you are not going to believe this!" I breathe into the speaker, stepping out of the tight stilettos and ambling over to the sofa.

"What happened? Are you okay?" Sloane's voice tips up in concern and I feel a teensy bit guilty bothering her so late on a Saturday night. She probably was mid-coitus with her hottie football star fiancé, Cam.

"You're not busy, um, with Cam right now, are you?" I loop a curl around my index finger, twirling it round and round.

"No. You're okay, right?"

"Yes. Better than. Well, I did go on an epically bad first date with a guy from *Blaze*. He's the most boring guy on the planet and the jerk had the audacity to bail – via text – while I was in the restroom."

"Oh no. We talked about this, Gracelyn. I told you to stay off the dating apps. It literally never works out."

"Not true, Sloane. Like one in three long-term relationships start on the internet these days. But anyway—I'm at the sink in the bathroom of Mustang's and Jamie walks in."

"No! Shoot."

"I know! And she's sticking to me tighter than a burr on a sock, I swear. I cannot shake the bitch. She follows me out of the restroom, begging to meet my date. Who already left the building, by the way."

"No! So what did you do?" Sloane's voice fills with concern. She understands just what an awful predicament I was in.

"The only thing I could think of. I homed in on the one person in the room I recognized."

"Grace. Who was it? Not your ex, Troy?"

"Nope. You'll never guess. So, in the interest of time, we'll skip ahead to the good part."

"There's a good part here?"

I laugh, kicking my feet up on the sofa cushion and wiggling my toes to get the blood flowing back into my dogs.

"Definitely. I kissed Mack."

She sucks in a sharp breath and there's a long pause. So long I wonder if we've been disconnected.

"Sloane? You still there?" I tap on the screen. It appears I still have service.

"Mack? Mack-Mack? As in, my dad's best friend Mack? The coach at the high school who watches every sport known to man on ESPN? That Mack?"

"Yeah. That Mack."

"Oh. My. God."

"I know. Crazy, right?"

"You always surprise me, Gracelyn. Do I want to know the rest of the details?" She drops her voice low, all the way down to a whisper. "Is he there with you now? Did you sleep with him?" There's a mixture of horror and awe in her voice.

"No, he's not here. And no, I did not sleep with him. We kissed at the bar. Strictly out of necessity, to get Jamie off my back."

"Why do I feel like there's more to the story?"

"He pretended to be my boyfriend and really sold the whole dating thing. I never paid too much attention to him before—I mean, he's always seemed so much older than us, and he's my mom's neighbor and all."

"Right…" Sloane draws the word out.

"But he's low-key hot, Sloane. Like, built. I had no idea until tonight. The man's kinda gorgeous. Scruffy and laid-back, really manly. And he smells good. Did you know that?"

"No. I don't go around sniffing my dad's best friend. And do not start calling him Daddy. You do that and I'm hanging up right now."

I giggle, warmth flooding through me thinking about Mack and the kiss.

"What, you have something against Daddies now?"

"No. It's just, I don't know—weird. He's Mack."

"Well, Mack is hot. And he's not nearly old enough to be my daddy."

"I'll take your word for it."

"Hey, not all of us luck out and land our high school crush," I tease, and Sloane laughs.

"I don't think you had a high school crush, Gracelyn."

"You're right. I had about fifteen of them. Hard to narrow it down to only one loser."

Cam's deep voice rumbles in the background and I know I should let my friend go and get back to whatever she swears she wasn't doing when I called.

"I'll let you go. I miss you." A twinge of sadness pulls at my chest. "Love you, bestie."

"Love you, too. I'll be back in town soon. For Hoco."

"Good. I'm going to need moral support. Jamie's coaching the dance team."

"What? Although that tracks. She's perfect for the job."

"I know, she has the kind of hair you can really whip around. Okay, night."

"Night."

The line clicks and I toss my cell onto the sofa, staring up at the ceiling.

Mack.

I wasn't lying when I said I never thought about him in that way.

Until now.

I should have gone for it and invited him in. But I felt like I already pushed my luck pretty far this evening. The kiss was probably a one-time thing and I shouldn't read too much into it. Sure, he kissed me back with the exact right amount of pressure. And sure, his chest felt solid up against mine, my heart pounding as he stared down at me. And I'd be lying if I said his hand on my ass didn't send fire licking through me, wetness flooding my thong.

But Sloane's right. He's probably not right for me. And when things spiral downward—which, let's face it, they always do—I'll have to see him all the time. We'll run into each other constantly and that will be terrible.

Best to shut this down before anything really happens between us.

Even if that lip lock was the best kiss of my whole entire life.

I should one-thousand percent pretend it never happened and move on with my boring, safe, single life.

———

Mack stars in my dreams all night long. I can't stop thinking about the man and his beyond-kissable lips, the rough pads of his fingers as he brushed them across my cheek.

There's only one thing to do about this.

Morning comes around and I roll up to my mom's

house, hoping for a Mack sighting. Throwing my car into park, I drum my fingers on the steering wheel and crane my neck, searching for signs of life next door to my mom's bungalow.

Dammit. Nothing.

He's probably working out or something, sculpting those strong pec muscles for the next lucky lady.

Stop it, Gracelyn. Remember—Mack's a bad idea. He screams 'I've got Daddy issues.'

Which, to be fair, I kinda do.

But those have nothing to do with the Mack crush I've got going on right now.

Huffing out a breath, I stare at Mack's front door for a few more seconds. Nothing happens. The blinds don't open, he doesn't walk out wearing only his boxers.

A girl can dream, right?

May as well go say hi to my mom, since I'm here and all. Hopping out of the car, I traipse up the driveway as slowly as I can.

Still nothing.

Climbing the stairs, I rap on the door twice before letting myself in.

"Hey, Mom!" I take a quick left, bypassing the salon portion of the house where I work with my mother. She's an OG girl boss and together we're Thunder Creek's dynamic duo. Plumb Perfect is *the* place to get your hair done in this town and the surrounding counties. The only reason the dryers are off and the main salon is dark right now is because Sundays are the day of rest, the only day we're closed all week.

I love what I do, giving my clients new styles. Helping women look and feel their best. Bonus points for being up-to-date on all the latest gossip and the short commute. And don't tell my mom, but I really do enjoy working side-by-side with her.

Coming round the corner and popping my head into the bright kitchen, I about have a heart attack. My mom's not alone.

A man with broad shoulders and sandy, wavy hair's sitting at the small dining table. Even with his back to me, I recognize that thick neck, those corded forearms.

He swivels to face me, a smirk tipping up the corner of his full lips. Lips I know a lot better after last night.

"Morning, Gracelyn."

Face flaming, heat rushes through me as I choke out an acceptable greeting.

"Morning, Mack."

CHAPTER 4
MACK

Am I surprised to see Gracelyn here this morning?

A little.

Did a small part of me hope she'd show up? Maybe.

Okay, more than a small part of me.

Truth be told, I slept like shit last night. My mind kept circling back to Gracelyn and that kiss at the bar. How good she felt nestled in between my thighs, my palm cupping her ass. The way her lips felt against mine, soft and smooth and wanting. The memory of her curves pressing against me when we stood outside her door. The woman haunted me all night long and I woke up with a painful, achy hard-on.

I planned on going about my usual Sunday business. Getting chores done, doing yard work, catching some football on TV. But then I made coffee and ran out of creamer. Seemed like as good excuse as any to pop over to Mrs. Reynolds's house.

Could I have survived without creamer for one morning? Gone to the grocery store to buy more? Hit up the local coffee shop? Yes to all of the above.

But the likelihood of seeing Gracelyn again would have been much slimmer in those scenarios. Popping next door to her mom's house made bumping into her much more likely.

And this is the best-case scenario. Especially the way her entire body turns cherry red the second she spots me at the kitchen table with her mother.

Priceless.

Why am I such a dick?

I don't know. Genetic, probably.

Damn, she's cute as hell, getting all flustered. I've never seen her speechless before.

Until now.

"Uh, hey, Mack. Morning. What are you doing here?" she stammers, arching a suspicious brow at me.

"Outta creamer. Came to borrow some from your mom and she offered me a cup of joe. Real neighborly."

"Anytime, sugar." Mrs. Reynolds pats my forearm and Gracelyn's eyes light on the gesture, but she quickly draws her attention back to my face.

"Mack was just telling me about the Homecoming game coming up. Did you know we're three-and-oh for the season? Thunder Creek's undefeated!"

"Early days, Ma. And I know what three-and-oh means." Gracelyn sashays over to the cabinet, pulling a mug down from the shelf and pouring herself a steaming cup of coffee.

"Defeatist attitude, Grace. The team's gonna be the best in the state, you watch." Mrs. Reynolds wags her finger at her daughter, and I barely hold in the chuckle threatening to rumble from my throat. The only woman with more sass than Gracelyn is her mother.

"Hope so, Ma. That would be exciting." Gracelyn sidles up next to me, bumping her knee against mine as she takes a seat.

She's as pretty as she was last night, sunbeams streaming through the window and forming a halo around her golden curls. In the daylight, I notice the tiny pattern of cinnamon freckles streaked across her nose, the dimple in her right cheek when she smiles.

Gracelyn lifts the mug to her mouth and I catch the words etched on the cup: *Awesome Like My Daughter*.

Classic. I'm sure Gracelyn bought that as a gift for her mother.

"What?" She narrows her eyes at me, kicking my foot under the table.

"I was admiring your coffee cup."

Her face breaks into a wide grin. "Oh, this? I got it for my mom for Mother's Day a few years ago."

Of course she did. Called that one.

Mrs. Reynolds rolls her eyes. "Only my daughter would buy me a self-congratulatory mug."

"You don't like it?" Gracelyn pops her lip out, acting hurt.

"No, I love it. Exactly what I was hoping for."

"Geez, tough crowd." Gracelyn tsks. "What do you buy for a woman who has everything she could ever want? Sorry if I was stumped. Next year make a wish list."

"I think I will. Good idea. What are you up to today? And why are you here so early?" Mrs. Reynolds smashes her lips together and stares at her daughter.

"I wanted to pop in and say hi. And it's not that early."

"Please. You barely make it here for work on time. Anything before ten am is early for you, muffin."

"Harsh. I'll have you know that I was, uh, on my way to Pilates and thought I'd stop by to say hello."

"Hmm. You're going to Pilates in that?" She waves at Gracelyn's shorts and V-neck tee.

"Yeah. They let you in, even if you're not wearing lulu leggings."

"I'll take your word for it. Don't think I'm going to Pilates anytime soon. You had a date last night, right?"

The apples of Gracelyn's cheeks turn rosy. "Yeah, Mom. But Mack doesn't want to hear about it, I'm sure."

I work hard to keep a straight face as Gracelyn shifts uncomfortably in her seat.

"A date, huh?" I goad, nudging her foot under the table. "I wouldn't mind hearing about it."

Gracelyn swallows hard, the sound audible, her throat moving with the effort. She's off-balance as she searches for words.

"It was…fine." Her fingers glide up and down the black ceramic handle of the mug.

"Only fine?" I catch her eye and the skin on her chest flushes, giving her true feelings away.

She definitely thought the night went better than fine.

Her reaction buoys me—this thing between us isn't one-sided.

"The second half went better."

"Oh? Sounds promising." Mrs. Reynolds's voice tips up with hope. "Are you seeing him again?"

Gracelyn locks her gaze with me. "I'm not sure, to be honest. We left it kind of open-ended."

Wide open.

My muscles tighten under her stare, my body subconsciously flexing for her.

"Open ended?" Mrs. Reynolds cries, chiding her daughter. "Grace, you're not in college anymore. The clock is ticking! If you want to get married and start a family, you better get going." She taps her watch face for emphasis.

"Mother!" Gracelyn hisses. "Stop! I'm only thirty, for goodness sake."

"Only thirty." Mrs. Reynolds rolls her eyes. "By the time I was thirty, you were already in kindergarten. Y'all think you have all the time in the world these days. Flit about the globe, going on grand adventures, chasing careers."

"I'd hardly say I'm doing any of those things, Ma. Trouble is, I live in Thunder Creek. There aren't a ton of eligible bachelors sitting around."

I clear my throat, scootching back from the table. Now it's my turn to be uncomfortable.

"Thanks for the coffee, Mrs. Reynolds. It was good seeing you, Gracelyn." I nod in her direction and some type of emotion flashes across her face, but I can't quite place it.

"You're going?" Mrs. Reynolds presses her lips together. For a woman in her mid-fifties, I'm struck by how similar Gracelyn is to her mother. Same heart-shaped face, full bow mouth, even the same expressions.

"Yeah, I have yard work to do."

"Okay. Before I forget—would you mind fixing that chair in the salon? Probably needs a dab of wood glue."

"Sure. I can take it right now and get it back to you later today."

"No rush. But I don't want a client falling and breaking a hip." Mrs. Reynolds rises and shuffles out of the kitchen, gesturing for me to follow. Gracelyn shrugs and does the same, and I follow behind them down the hall toward the salon. I'm glad her mother's leading the way, giving me ample opportunity to appreciate the tiny shorts barely covering her daughter's ass, the gentle sway of her hips. Her blonde ponytail swishes back and forth and I can't help but think how it'd feel to wrap her hair around my fist and hold her tight, pressing my mouth to hers in a deep kiss.

Mrs. Reynolds flips on the overhead light, jarring me out of my fantasy. She points to an ornate violet chair in the corner. "That's the one."

The chair's going to need more than a touch of wood glue, I can tell by the lean from way over here.

"Got it. I'll see what I can do." I grab the offending chair and maneuver through the narrow doorway, brushing against Gracelyn as I walk by.

Sparks fly up my arm and I work hard to ignore them, especially on account of her mother being a foot away from us.

"Let me get the door for you." Gracelyn hurries around me, opening the screen door and holding it wide.

"Thanks."

"Mom, I'm going to help Mack with the chair. Be right back," she calls over her shoulder and I suppress my grin, happy my back's to Mrs. Reynolds.

"Not sure how you're helping me carry a chair, but okay…" I murmur, quiet enough that only she can hear.

That earns me a sharp elbow to the ribs.

"Open-ended, huh? Does your date know?" I tease.

"He does now."

I suck in a breath, digesting her words, rolling them over in my mind.

There are solid reasons not to get involved with Gracelyn, but none of them seem all that important right now.

Setting the chair down on the driveway, I punch in the garage code and wait for the metal door to lift.

"Well, aren't you going to say anything?" Hands on her hips, she stares me down, tapping her toe against the pavement and waiting for a response.

I carry the chair into the dim garage and she follows right behind me. Once she's over the threshold, I hit the button and the metal door rumbles back down, hitting the concrete with a loud thud. A small, dusty window lets in a few weak rays of light and the scent of sawdust and gasoline floats on the air. I haul the chair over to the back wall where I keep my tools and set it off to the side for repair. Then I spin around and take two long strides toward Gracelyn, stretching my arms out on either side of her face and pinning her back against the wall. I'm close enough to hear her breath catch, watch as her pulse flutters in her neck.

I lean in. "We shouldn't do this."

She presses her pink lips together, her face falling in disappointment. "Oh."

Her sweet floral scent assaults my nose, heat shimmering between us as her breath dusts my cheeks. The tip of her tongue trails along the seam of her mouth and every muscle in my body tightens.

This is a terrible idea.

Her curves brush against my chest with each shuddery inhale and I dip closer still. The crystal blue of her eyes darkens to a deep ocean, pupils wide.

I'm playing with fire and I damn well know it, but I can't stop myself.

Don't want to stop myself.

I smash my mouth to hers and every doubt, every hesitation, flies straight out the tiny garage window. Licking at her bottom lip, she opens to me and I slide in, tasting her. Our tongues roll together, tangling and fighting for dominance. Then her hands are at my chest, fisting in my shirt, pulling me up against her body.

"I thought we weren't doing this?" she mumbles into my open mouth and I shake my head.

"We shouldn't be." One of her hands finds the nape of my neck, her small fingers twining in my hair. Sharp bolts fly through me as her nails scrape my sensitive scalp, my dick twitching against the stiff denim of my jeans.

I cup her face with my palm, my thumb running along her jaw. "This is probably a bad idea."

"I've always been a fan of bad ideas." She locks her gaze on mine and my heart pounds harder in my chest.

Fuck me.

Gracelyn's exactly the type of bad idea I do not need. Young, perky, optimistic. We're nothing alike and I already know this is going to be complicated.

I should definitely walk away, not take this flirtation or whatever we have going on between us any further.

Make the right call, Mack.

For once in your damn life, make the right call.

CHAPTER 5
GRACELYN

"Same."

The word rumbles from his chest, a low, primal growl, and my body responds. Fiery sparks fly through me, racing beneath my skin. My nipples stiffen to tight peaks in my satin bra.

This man is beyond sexy. How have I never noticed him before?

With that deep voice, those large, rough hands. Hands I'd very much like to be all over my body right now, touching me and driving me close to the edge.

"Bad ideas always feel so good, you know?" I trail my fingers over his sculpted pecs, glide my hand down his chest, and rest my index finger at the waistband of his jeans. His eyes flick down and he sucks in a shuddery breath, his stomach caving slightly.

Arms dropping from the wall, he grabs me by the ass and lifts me into the air.

"Mack!" I grip his shoulders tight, wrapping my legs

around his waist as he carries me over to his work bench and sets me down gently.

Hands still resting on my rear and my legs spread wide, he leans in, closing the space between us. His warm breath a whisper on my face, a soft moan falls from my lips as he claims my mouth in a hot, possessive kiss. The kind of kiss that makes your toes curl and your thoughts drift away on a pink cloud of bliss.

The kind of kiss that leaves you panting and breathless.

The kind of kiss that lets you know who's in charge.

Nothing about Mack is timid.

He's strong, dominant, powerful.

I've never had a man take control like this. Guys my age defer to me and let me take the lead.

Not Mack.

He squeezes my ass and I inch closer to the edge of the bench, trying to get more contact with his tight torso. Wetness soaks my panties as he kneads and massages, caressing my curves. His hand dips beneath my shirt, the calloused pads of his fingers rough on my sensitive skin.

"Mack," I breathe, his palm on my breast. A ripple of pleasure washes over me as he thumbs the sharp point of my nipple. Pinching the sensitive peak, a bolt zips straight to my clit and I bite down hard on my lip to keep from crying out.

"You like that, don't you?" he murmurs, my eyes flickering up to his face. He's watching me intently, studying my reactions.

"Mm-hmm." I nod. I'm practically panting. It's been a hot minute since I've been with a man and I'm out of practice. Every nerve in my body's humming, strung tight and ready to snap.

"What were you saying about bad ideas?" His words

vibrate against the column of my neck, chill bumps rising from his warm breath skating over my skin. With the tip of his nose, he nuzzles against me and I shudder. He licks and nips and I swear I might come right there in his garage, fully clothed.

"Um…" Blood whooshes in my ears and I'm hot all over. "That I like bad ideas."

He sucks my neck and my body's melting into him.

Buzz.

I ignore my cell vibrating in my pocket, fully transfixed on what Mack's doing to me.

Buzz.

Damn, another text. Why now?

"Just a sec." I inch out of his grip and fumble for my cell. Of course it's my mother.

Cock block.

> Mom: Are you coming back?
>
> Mom: We need to talk about the game plan for Hoco

Annoyed as hell, I manage to suppress an eye roll and shove my phone back into my pocket.

"Everything okay?" Mack squints at me like he's trying to read a playbook.

"Yeah. It's just my mother, asking if I'm coming back."

That kills the mood.

Mack steps away, unwinding himself from me. The wild, hooded gaze from moments earlier vanishes and he's back to the laidback, casual Mack I know.

"You better get going then." He runs a hand through his hair, his T-shirt lifting slightly, revealing a glimpse of his abs and the bulge still visible in his pants.

"Just like that?" I try to squash the disappointment already bubbling up inside me.

"I don't want your mom to worry."

How can he be so calm and cool about this? Thirty seconds ago we were on the verge of banging and now he's acting like nothing's happened between us at all.

"Oh, for fuck's sake. I'm thirty years old and it's broad daylight. I'm fine!" I throw my hands up in aggravation and hop down from the bench, disappointed and pissed off at both him and my mother.

Mack chuckles, a low, throaty sound that sends my belly fluttering despite my irritation.

"Never said you weren't. But I don't want to be on the bad side of Mama Reynolds. Get going." He playfully swats my ass and I sigh.

"Fine. But we're not done here. We need to hash out this open-ended thing. If you're game." I hold my breath, waiting for his reply.

He scrubs his hand over the back of his neck, tips his head to the side. "You should think about it, Gracelyn. I'm a decade older than you."

"So?" I shrug. "Who cares?"

"People are gonna talk."

"I don't care."

He reaches out, tucking a loose tendril behind my ear, and my heart stops.

"Think about it, that's all I'm saying. This town can be real heavy on gossip."

"Don't I know it." I flip my ponytail over my shoulder, trying to act more in control and self-assured than I feel right now. "But I really don't give a flying fuck what people say about me."

Mack tilts his head to the side, a brow raised high.

"Really? So if your sworn enemy Jamie starts talking shit, calling me Grandpa or something stupid like that, you're not gonna care?"

"Nope." I fold my arms over my chest and stand up tall. "Not one little bit."

"Why don't I believe you?"

"Besides, Jamie's under the impression we're already dating. We have to pretend to be together for a few weeks, at least in front of her. Or I'll look like a total loser."

The corner of his lip quirks up. "Says the person who doesn't care what other people think."

Shit, the man has a point.

"Fine, maybe I care a teensy bit." I hold my thumb and index finger up, demonstrating just how little I care.

My cell buzzes again and I huff out an exasperated sigh. "I have to go before my mom sends out a search party. We can finish this conversation later, yeah?"

Mack scrubs a hand over the back of his neck. "Yeah."

Before I chicken out, I lean in and press my lips to his. He doesn't disappoint, wrapping his hand around the back of my neck and easing his warm tongue into my mouth. Tingles shoot straight through me as he rolls over my teeth, exploring.

Finally, he pulls away. "See ya, Firecracker."

With one last swat of my ass, he punches the button to the garage door and bright rays of sunlight pour into the space.

"Bye." I wiggle my fingers at him and race out of the garage, pulling my shirt down as I head back to my mother's house, acting like nothing happened.

———

I think about Mack the rest of the day. His muscular body, the clean scent of pine and sawdust wafting from his skin, the way his lips felt on mine.

The man is a fantastic kisser.

I want that mouth all over my body, not gonna lie. Want to feel his tongue tracing lazy circles on my thighs, licking me in all the right spots, making me squirm and writhe for him.

So what if he's older than me? Just means he's got more experience and knows what the fuck he's doing with his life. It could be refreshing to date someone with life goals and shit.

Buzz.

I pause *The Bachelor* episode I'm watching and check my phone. I don't recognize the number.

Hey, Firecracker

Mack.

Holding my breath, I text back, my fingers shaky over the keyboard.

Hey. What's up?

I re-read the text and decide I can do better. Delete and try again.

Hey. Can we finish what we started this morning?

Mack: That's what I'm texting you about. I thought about it and I don't think it's a good idea

My stomach sinks, reading and re-reading the words, right there in cold black-and-white.

I don't think it's a good idea.

Mack's rejecting me.

Dammit.

I stare up at the ceiling, disappointment weighing heavy on my chest. This thing between us has been going on for less than twenty-four hours. Why does it feel as bad as a real break up?

Sucking in a breath, I gnaw at my lower lip, weighing my options. I could do what I usually do and cut my losses. Agree with him and keep things firmly in the friend zone. I close my eyes and visualize what that would look like.

Working right next door to him and acting like his lips never touched mine, his hands haven't caressed my breasts, my ass.

That scenario doesn't feel great, leaving me with a hard pit in my stomach.

Or, I could take a big-ass risk right now and actually go for it. Because the thing between me and Mack feels different. Rare and special. I've never felt like this before in my entire life. Light and airy, an electric spark burning bright from deep inside me.

And dammit, I don't want to back down and run away from that.

Again.

Not this time.

I decide to go for it.

> Gracelyn: Stop thinking so much

Mack: That approach typically gets me in trouble

Gracelyn: Trouble's my middle name

Mack: That's what I'm afraid of

Gracelyn: You're scared of me?

Mack: I didn't say that

Gracelyn: Are you busy right now?

Mack: This is where I should probably say yes

Gracelyn: So you're not...

Mack: Watching ESPN. I'm not not busy

Gracelyn: ESPN 1, 2, or 3?

Mack: Actually 4

I laugh, then take the risk, fluffing my hair and snapping a selfie. I try my best to look devastated, making an exaggerated sad, pouty face, and sending the photo to Mack.

Gracelyn: Come over

I stare at my screen, watch the bubbles swirl, then disappear. My gut churns, heart hammering as I wait for a response.

He leaves me hanging for a long minute, then finally I get an answer.

Mack: That's a bad idea

Disappointment washes over me, a frigid tidal wave dashing my hopes. I shouldn't keep pushing. He's not into me, despite his show last night and this morning. I should leave him alone and move the fuck on.

I toss my cell onto the ground and hit play, resuming *The Bachelor*. But after another ten minutes of the show, I have no idea what's happening, nor do I care. I'm not really into it anymore, my mind fixating on the rejection.

Mack's right. The two of us don't make sense. Sure, he'd be a fun distraction, but the relationship wouldn't go anywhere. Best to stop here, before anyone gets hurt.

Knock, knock.

I jerk my head up and stare at the door. Am I losing my mind? I'm so delulu now that I'm hearing things?

Knock, knock, knock.

Harder, more insistent raps vibrate the door. Nope, not losing it. Someone's definitely at the door. I pause the TV again and tiptoe warily across the room, peering out.

My heart skips a beat as I stare through the tiny peephole. Straight into jade green eyes, fringed with dark lashes that make me jealous.

Mack.

With a quick inhale, I ease the door open a crack. "You really are into bad ideas, aren't you?"

CHAPTER 6
MACK

've lost my damn mind.

All I've thought about for the last day is Gracelyn.
Her luscious curves, the quick wit flying out of her smart mouth, the way she wrapped her arms around me and held on. Like I grounded her.

This is insane.

I shouldn't be here.

But every inch of me wants to be.

I lean against the doorframe, one arm outstretched, acting way more casual than I feel.

"Guess I am, Firecracker."

The corner of her mouth tips up in a slow smile, her eyes twinkling in the porch light. Gracelyn opens the door wider and reaches for my arm, dragging me inside.

She wastes no time. Slamming the door behind me, she stalks forward and boxes me in like I did to her this morning.

"Thought you weren't coming?" Her tone tips up, challenging me.

I shrug. "I wasn't going to."

The tip of her tongue darts out and glides along her lower lip and I'm transfixed, staring.

"Then why did you?"

I swallow hard, my Adam's apple bobbing in my dry throat. No sense lying about it.

"I wanted to see you again."

"And finish what we started?"

Damn. Cutting straight to the chase.

"If that's what you want. Or we could sit around and talk about it, dissect and diagram out all the possibilities, the different ways this thing could go sideways."

She shakes her head. "No, thanks."

Inching closer to me, her body brushes up against mine and my muscles coil tight, nerves springing to life. Her floral scent winds around me, tickling my nostrils and lighting me up inside.

This woman does something to me, waking up a part of me that's been sleeping for a very long time.

Her hand glides over my chest, those bright blue eyes wide and questioning. Daring me to lean in and kiss her, break through the barrier between us.

And damn if I don't want to.

All the reasons why I shouldn't do this race through my mind at warp-speed, a blurry jumble of 'no' and 'this is wrong' and 'you're going to regret this.'

"Fuck it," I growl, grabbing her by the ass and pulling her soft, warm body into me.

Smashing my lips to hers, I kiss her with everything that's been building up inside me all day. The want, the longing, the desire, like she's the last woman I'm going to kiss in this lifetime.

I urge her mouth open with my tongue and she lets me

slide in, rolling around and tasting her. She's sweet like vanilla as I lick and suck, a tiny moan vibrating low in her throat. I grip the nape of her neck and trace light circles with my thumb, applying subtle pressure. She leans into me, her hands winding around to my ass, sliding into the pockets of my jeans.

"Have I told you you're a great kisser?" she murmurs and I smile into her open mouth.

"Now you have. I have other skills too, you know."

"Mmm, sounds promising." She leans back slightly, gazing up at me through lowered lashes. "Show me."

Without hesitation, without thinking, I peel her leggings down and drop to my knees.

"Step." It's not an ask, it's a command, and she does as I say.

I toss the pants aside and work my way up her body, massaging first her calves, then her thighs with open palms. Her eyes flutter shut as she leans back against the door.

Inching toward the apex of her legs, I cup her sex. The silk of her panties is smooth on my skin as I trail my thumb over the fabric, finding her clit. Rubbing the sensitive spot, a moan slips from Gracelyn's parted lips. She arches her hips forward into my hand, seeking more pressure, more friction.

"Greedy girl," I tease, my voice low and husky.

I move my thumb back and forth over her clit, dampness soaking through the tiny scrap of fabric. Pressure builds in my lower torso as I watch her respond to my touch, her fair skin flushing pink. Head thrown back and eyes closed, she spreads her thighs wider, granting me better access. I hitch my thumbs in the sides of her panties and drag them down her legs. She kicks them off to the side and I dip my head, her scent filling my nose.

Flattening my tongue, I lick through her wetness, tasting her for the first time. She's sweet and juicy as I suck at her pussy. I flick her clit, then pull the bean deeper into my mouth.

"Mack—" Her voice is strangled, breathy, her fingers twining in my hair. Pulling me in closer to her.

"So fucking sweet." Tangy fluid floods my mouth as she bucks against my face. "I could eat you out every day, you're so delicious."

Another long, low groan as I drive my tongue into her tight pussy. Her fingers grip my shoulder hard and I snake my hands around to her bare ass, holding her up and supporting her as she shudders and cries out.

"Oh my god, Mack!" Her orgasm rips through her, and I ease the pressure, her body humming in my hands as she comes fast and hard. I rock back on my heels, a smug smile tugging at my lips and my cock pulsing in my pants.

"Wow – that was quick." I swipe at my mouth, coated with her juices. Her gaze drops to mine.

Gracelyn's sexy as hell, a few loose strands of her golden hair falling onto her shoulder as she leans back against the door, panting.

I did that. Made her cry out and explode in pure pleasure.

"You were right. About your skills." She strokes my hair absently and pride fills my chest.

"Thank you. I aim to please."

Rising, I lift her chin with my finger. Her cheeks pink and pupils blown wide, she's absolutely stunning. I drop my lips to hers and urge her mouth open with my tongue.

She sucks hard and deep, pulling me into her and tasting her own sweetness.

After a long moment, she pulls away. "I have skills, too, you know."

She flutters her lashes at me and I feel myself giving into her magnetism, the attraction between us crackling and raw, animalistic.

I should give her an out, stop this thing before we go any further.

My dick twitches in my pants, chiding me. Telling me what a dumb fucking idea it would be to walk away now, with this beautiful woman in front of me, practically begging for more.

I want to fuck Gracelyn. Hard and fast and deep. Make her come so fiercely she screams my name, begging for more.

Right now, age is just a number, a concept that I don't give two shits about. All I want is her pretty bow lips wrapped around my cock, sucking me deep into her warm mouth. I want her choking as she takes all of me down her throat, swallowing every last drop of my cum.

Then I want to climb on top of her and show her what a real man feels like. Driving so hard into her she remembers me tomorrow, every time she takes a step.

"Mack?" The way my name rolls off her tongue, her voice low and sultry.

No fucking way am I walking out of here now.

Her fingers skim over my chest, then she reaches for my hand and leads me down a dark hallway into her bedroom.

CHAPTER 7
GRACELYN

Anyone who knows me can tell you I've done a lot of crazy things in my lifetime. Jumped off the top of a boathouse buck naked?

Check.

Drank seven tequila shots in a row to win a bet with a bunch of frat boys?

Check.

Ate three grapefruits a day to try to lose ten pounds in a month?

Also check.

But hooking up with Mack like this—without any kind of plan, just following my instincts and out-of-control hormonal urges—is probably the craziest.

Nothing about the two of us makes any sense. On paper, we're the most unlikely match of all time.

The way he makes me feel, though? Alive and electric, bubbling over with needy desire. Like I will literally die if he doesn't kiss me, touch me, hold me, right now.

That makes perfect sense.

So I link my fingers with his and lead him to my bedroom, not daring to look back.

I'm taking a risk, so I may as well enjoy it.

Especially if this is a one-time thing.

My bedroom's dark and I purposely keep the lights off. Don't want to scare Mack away before things even get going. Curvy is the polite way to describe my figure, the word I always use on my dating profile. But I have more *curves* than I would like, no matter which diet I try. Plus, the bonus twins, cellulite and stretch marks. I'm not tall and thin like Jamie or perfectly proportionate like Sloane.

All things being equal, I prefer to have sex in complete darkness. Figure it's better that way for all involved.

I guide Mack to the bed and hold my breath, waiting for him to say something. To agree with this plan or stop things before we drop more clothing and inhibitions.

"You gonna turn a light on?"

"It's better if I don't." I'm glad the room's dim, hiding my flaming cheeks in the shadows.

"Yeah? I wholeheartedly disagree." Mack snakes his hand up the inside of my shirt and palms my breast, squeezing. "I want to see these luscious tits while I ride you."

Shimmery heat ripples through me, my belly swooping at his dirty words.

"You don't."

He pulls me up against his hard body and squeezes my ass, pressing his lips to the shell of my ear.

"Don't tell me what I want, Firecracker. I'm a grown-ass man and I know what I like. Know what I want. And I very much want to see you, watch your pretty face as I make you come for me and scream my name. But if you're more comfortable in the dark, I'll live with it. For now."

Pleasure skitters across my skin as his warm breath tickles my face, my neck. My thighs clench and I quickly debate the merits of lights on versus lights off.

Taking the scary leap, I unwind myself from him and move over to the nightstand, clicking on the light. "Fine."

"Ah, there she is." He stares at me like I'm a real-life supermodel and a bit of my self-consciousness fades away.

With two large strides, he's in front of me, caressing my face with the rough pads of his fingers. Tracing down the line of my jaw to my chin, he tilts my head up to meet his gaze.

"You okay?" His eyes search mine, waiting for an answer.

Heart pounding and throat dry, I nod. "Yeah, I'm good."

Nervous as hell, but good.

He doesn't wait for further reassurance. Instead, he reaches around and grabs the back of his shirt, pulling it over his head. I suck in a breath as his T-shirt hits the floor, taking in his broad chest and the ridges of his abs.

Mack is all man. I've never hooked up with anyone as rugged and handsome as he is. Not that my exes were duds or anything, but they sure as hell weren't Mack.

The hard lines, the stubble, the spicy masculine scent wafting from his skin. The way he's staring at me right now, like he's had his snack and that was cute and all. But he's still hungry and ready for the main course.

Heat unfurls low in my belly under his smoldering gaze. This man is doing things to me and we've barely even begun.

He unbuttons his jeans and kicks his pants off. Matter-of-fact and unceremoniously. Like it's no big deal.

Meanwhile, I'm over here all up in my head, worrying about lights on or off.

Fuck it.

Following his lead, I shimmy out of my oversized sweatshirt and drop it on the floor. Reach behind my back and unhook my bra, letting the silky fabric fall on the pile of clothing.

"Fuck me, Firecracker." Mack lets out a low whistle, his eyes widening in appreciation as he takes in my naked body. "You are absolutely stunning."

Every inch of me flushes at the compliment and my confidence buoys.

"Thanks. You're not half bad yourself." I run my palm over his broad chest, appreciating the hard lines, the wall of muscle beneath the light smattering of hair.

"Not too shabby for someone my age?" He tips his head, flexing his pecs.

"I didn't say a word about your age. In case you haven't noticed, I'm not all that concerned about numbers right now."

Winding my arms around his neck, I press my mouth to his. Kissing him long and hard, getting lost in the moment. Everything falls away—all the reasons why we shouldn't be doing this, our relationships outside of this bedroom, the boundary we're about to cross.

The only thing that matters, right here and right now, is what's happening between us.

I want this man.

I want him to touch me, kiss me, do dirty things to me until I can't take any more.

And then I want him to do it all over again.

His hands slide from my hips to my ass and he squeezes.

"I love your ass." His deep, husky voice makes me believe him. "I've been thinking about it all day. So round and juicy."

Warm happiness blooms inside me, all those cycling and bootcamp classes I skipped suddenly validated. He squeezes hard and gives my backside a light slap, then rubs the spot tenderly.

A soft moan escapes my lips, wetness slicking my thighs. "Mack—" His name comes out strangled. I barely recognize my own voice, so desperate and needy.

Dropping a hand between my legs, he trails a thick finger through my pussy. "So wet for me."

He pushes inside me and I groan. "Oh my god, that feels amazing."

Sliding another finger in, he thrusts gently in and out. I spread my legs wider and he adds a third finger, moving faster and harder. Pressure builds in my core and I'm bucking against his hand, seeking more.

More friction, more heat. More Mack.

"I love how ready you are, baby," he murmurs, nipping at my earlobe. A hot bolt of desire zips through me and I shudder, nipples peaking.

His lips quirk up as he watches the effect his words and actions have on my body. He's in total control right now, pushing me closer and closer to the edge of bliss. Thumb brushing lightly against my clit, he slows and pulls out. I bite back a whimper, my pussy throbbing.

"Lay down." Mack hooks a thumb at the bed and I quickly do as he asks, getting comfortable against the mountain of pillows.

Bending down, he retrieves a foil packet from his pants

and rips it open with his teeth. Then he casually drops his boxer briefs, his hard shaft springing free.

"Wow." I take in the length and size of him, doing mental gymnastics trying to decide if he's going to fit inside me. "That's, um…you're…big. Not that I'm not game, it's just…do you think you're going to fit?"

"Don't worry, Firecracker." He strokes his dick a few times before rolling on the condom. "It'll fit."

It's gonna be a tight squeeze, that's for sure.

Grinning, he straddles me. Laugh lines crinkle around his eyes and up close I notice a sprinkling of gray in his sandy curls. Other than that, I'd guess he was my age or maybe even younger.

"You're really gorgeous." I stroke his chest, taking all of him in.

"Thanks, baby." He smooths his thumb over my cheek, leaning in and kissing me. "You're beautiful."

Trailing from my face to my chest, Mack caresses my breasts with both hands. His light touch sends flutters straight to my belly and my nipples pebble. He rolls the sharp points with his thumbs and a fiery bolt rips through me.

"Mack…" I moan, my eyes drifting closed. Bright lights dance behind my eyelids as I get lost in the sensations. Heat and desire and pleasure mix together, pushing me closer to ecstasy.

Mack spreads my thighs further apart, then he trails the tip of his cock through my wetness. Testing, teasing.

"Yes," I whisper, opening my eyes. I roll my hips, urging him to keep going, and he follows my lead. Pushing in, slowly, oh so slowly.

"Fuck, you're tight—" he hisses, sinking in further. "So damn tight. You feel so good, baby."

I breathe out a long exhale, focus on relaxing and taking him all the way. My hands move from his shoulders down his back, every muscle tight and defined. One more deep breath and he pushes in the rest of the way, our bodies joined together.

"Are you good?" He strokes my cheek and I nod.

"Yes. Better than."

"Good. I knew you could take me. Such a good girl."

His words, his husky voice, wash over me and I melt for this man. He could do anything to me right now and I would like it.

With a slow rock, he moves inside me and I almost die from ecstasy, it feels so fucking good. I match his rhythm and soon we're moving together, back and forth, in and out, the only sound our ragged, shallow breathing.

He picks up the pace and I keep up, rolling my hips against his taut body and gripping his ass. I'm hot and panting, white dots dancing in my peripheral vision. I know I'm close to tumbling over the edge.

"Fuck me, Mack. Harder."

Clutching my hands above my head, Mack hammers into me. Harder and faster, my muscles coiling and ready to explode.

"Yesss!" I cry, ripples of pleasure rolling through me as I crash, riding the wave of my release.

"Come for me, baby. That's it, let it all out." Mack keeps thrusting, not slowing down as I shudder beneath him. "Fuck—"

He explodes inside me, pumping out his own release. I squeeze my thighs together, riding him and milking his cock until he finally slows.

"Fuck, baby—" Mack rolls off me, collapsing on the pillows, breathing hard. "That was fantastic."

He pulls me onto his chest, stroking my hair as we both come down.

"When's round two?" I tease, feathering my fingers over his chest, his heart still pounding hard beneath my hand.

Growling, he squeezes my ass. "Whenever you're ready for it, Firecracker."

CHAPTER 8
GRACELYN

I should go."

Mack's husky voice startles me out of my sleepy, blissful state.

"What? Why?" I trail my fingers in light circles over the ridges of his abs, each muscle defined, and try to hide my disappointment.

I mean, of course this was just fantastic sex between two consenting adults.

I was foolish to think this time might be different. That Mack might be different.

Still, I feel a little bit stupid, a little bit used and bruised.

"Work tomorrow. I need to get some shut eye." He rubs my back up and down in a calm, soothing motion. Like he's trying to take away the sting of his words.

It's not working.

"You can get that here." I point out the obvious. "This bed is great. Very comfy. I upgraded my mattress last year and sleep like a baby now."

"Nah. Probably not a great idea."

I lift my eyes to his, glancing up at him through lowered lashes. "I thought we established we're both fans of bad ideas?"

He chuckles, a low, throaty laugh vibrating his chest beneath my cheek.

"You got me there, Firecracker."

Still, he unwinds his body from mine and slides away, leaving the warm nest of the bed. Moving quickly, he gathers up his discarded clothes. Boxers, jeans, T-shirt. All I can do is stare is at his muscular bare ass in the air, shocked into silence. He throws on his pants and a familiar flash of panic shoots through me.

This always happens.

I'm a love-'em-and-leave-'em type of girl. Not the spend-all-night-together girl I always longed to be. I can count on one hand the number of times I've actually spent the night—the whole night—with a guy.

Zero.

Technically, I guess that's no hands. No one ever stays the night with good time gal Gracelyn.

I don't know why I thought Mack would be different. Naivete, I guess. Or perhaps misguided optimism. Either way, I feel like an idiot right now.

For ever believing Mack might not be like all the rest of the male population. That he might actually be different.

My cheeks burn and tears prick at the corners of my eyes. I blink rapidly, willing the liquid to dissipate and not spill over, giving me away.

"Hey—you good?" His deep voice jolts me out of my swirling obsessive thoughts and back to shitty reality.

I force a tight smile, swallowing hard over the lump of

disappointment in my throat. The last thing I want—or need—is Mack to feel sorry for me.

"Yeah, sure. I'm great." I attempt to infuse cheerfulness into my voice and it seems to work because he drops the subject.

Pulling his shirt on, Mack runs a hand through his messy hair then makes his way back to the bed. He leans down and presses his lips to mine, kissing me softly.

"Thanks for tonight. It was fun."

Fun.

Super. I hold my eyeroll in check and chalk this evening up to another mistake. You'd think I would've learned my lesson by now, but apparently not.

Mack's mouth moves against mine and, despite my regret in how things are ending, I have to admit it's still a fan-fucking-tastic kiss. Just the right amount of heat and pressure.

Eventually, he breaks away. Tucking a stray curl behind my ear, he stares down at me.

"Make sure you lock the door behind me."

"Okay, Dad," I tease, pursing my lips together.

He grips my chin with his thumb and forefinger, forcing me to meet his gaze. "Hey, I'm not kidding."

"Fine. But this is Thunder Creek and I've lived alone for years. I'll be okay."

"I'll sleep better knowing you locked the door."

"Geez, if it's that big of a deal..." I swing my legs over the edge of the bed, ready to follow behind him.

"It is, baby. I need to know you're all tucked in, safe and sound."

If he really cared, he'd stay the night. But I don't mention that little tidbit.

"Okay, okay." I hold my hands up in surrender, palms in the air. Bending down, I scoop up my sweatshirt and toss it over my head, uncomfortable being naked in front of him right now. Way too vulnerable.

Together, we pad to the front door. I shift awkwardly from foot to foot, not really sure what to say.

See you around?

Thanks for the sex?

Luckily, Mack swoops in and saves me from saying anything embarrassing. Instead, he grips me by the hips and kisses me one last time.

"Night, Firecracker."

Then he lets himself out and I sink my forehead against the cool wood, deflated.

"Lock the door, baby." His muffled voice drifts through the door and I do as he asks, sliding the deadbolt into place. Only then do I hear the shuffling of his footsteps as he walks away.

A few seconds later, a chirp sounds from across the dark living room. I saunter over, picking up my cell.

Mack: Good girl

Despite my disappointment, those words ooze through my veins like warm, reassuring honey. Some warped primal pleasing instinct I wish I didn't have, but clearly do.

I'm one twisted sister, that's for sure. The man didn't even stay the night with me and deep-down, I still care what he thinks of me.

So much for feminism.

Just to fuck with him, I tap out a teasing text back.

Gracelyn: Thanks, Daddy

Mack: You trying to get me to come back
right now?

Mack: Because you're turning me on
again

I smile down at the screen. Good, I hope he has a raging hard-on the whole drive home and regrets leaving very, very much.

Gracelyn: Perfect

Gracelyn: Remember me when you're
alone tonight

Mack: Like I could forget you, baby girl

I squint at the words, trying to figure Mack out. If I'm that memorable, that desirable, why didn't he stay? We could have chatted late into the night, learning about each other. Sharing funny stories, cuddling and kissing. Maybe fucking again.

Instead, he left, chipping away a tiny piece of my already-tender heart in the process.

Deciding to let it go for tonight, I tap out one last quick flirtatious text before plugging in my phone.

Gracelyn: Night, Daddy

Mack doesn't let me down. Five seconds later, my phone dings.

Mack: Night, baby girl

Smiling, I skip to my bedroom and toss my phone on

the nightstand, peeling my sweatshirt off and climbing back into bed naked. I burrow into the pillows, the spicy scent of Mack and sex clinging to the rumpled cotton sheets. A few seconds later, I'm fast asleep, dreaming of a particularly sexy carpenter.

CHAPTER 9
MACK

amn, Gracelyn lived up to her nickname. When I called her Firecracker, I had no idea just how accurate that title is. She's absolute fire, alright. Wild and responsive, fucking without restraint. Her body lighting up everywhere I touched. The woman's sexy as hell, with those luscious, creamy tits and that perfect peach of an ass. The way her ivory skin turned pink with the slightest smack, her breath catching as I squeezed the soft globes of her cheeks.

She's an amazing woman. Someone I'd very much like to be with again.

And when she called me Daddy? Yeah, that did something to me too.

A new kink unlocked.

Good god, Mack. She's your next-door neighbor's DAUGHTER.

This is a very bad idea. A terrible idea.

I should one thousand percent delete her number and pretend nothing happened between us last night. Let her down easy and never go there again. Leave it as a one-time thing, an itch we had to scratch and get out of our systems.

Find someone my own age to play kinky games with. Not a hot, curvy woman ten years my junior. Everyone in town's gonna talk, and I don't much care for being the subject of gossip.

Mack: How'd you sleep, baby girl?

My thumb hits send before good sense kicks in. Clearly thinking with my smaller head this morning.

Silence.

She's probably still sleeping. I roll out of bed and stretch, my spine cracking like it always does these days. That's what happens when the game of football's been your life for the better part of almost twenty years. Lots of creaking and groaning—much like the vintage furniture people hire me to repair—especially first thing in the morning.

I lumber out to the kitchen and pour myself a cup of coffee, add a splash of creamer. The sun's barely peeking over the horizon, the first golden rays of light filtering through the old oak in the yard. The tree's still green, but the leaves are starting to think about changing. In a few weeks, all of Thunder Creek will be ablaze in reds, oranges, and golds, the air moving from hot and humid to crisp and cool.

Fall is upon us.

The busiest season, with football taking up most of my free time. Another good reason to stop this situation with Gracelyn before it gets going.

I don't have time to date.

Kinda bullshit, but seems like as good a reason as any.

Buzz, buzz. I stare at my cell, vibrating on the table. Much as I'd like to deny it, my heart's beating faster than normal, and it's not from the caffeine in one lousy cup of coffee.

Blowing out a breath, I pick up the phone and read the text.

Firecracker: Fine. Probably a good thing you left last night

Mack: Why?

Firecracker: I bet you snore

Chuckling, I shake my head in disbelief. This woman's something else.

Mack: For the record, I do not snore

Firecracker: How do you know? You're asleep

Mack: No one's ever mentioned it before

Firecracker: Probably didn't want to hurt your feelings

Firecracker: Guess you'll never really know…

Damn, now she has me second-guessing my own sleeping habits.

Mack: Are you volunteering as tribute?

> Firecracker: IDK. Can I afford to miss a
> night of beauty sleep?

> Mack: 100%

What the hell am I doing? I left Gracelyn's house last night, vowing to not go there again. Now here I am, less than twelve hours later, flirting with her and talking about sleeping over. I'm a confirmed bachelor, the type of man self-help books label a commitment-phobe.

Yet it's easy to slip into this thing with Gracelyn. She's fun to banter with, witty and clever. The kind of woman I could really fall for.

Except I can't, for all the reasons. Age. The next-door neighbor thing. The fact that she probably wants to get married and have babies and I've been alone for over twenty-odd years. I'm perfectly content on my own and I'm pretty sure that I'd just screw a kid up. Fatherhood's never been on my radar and I doubt I'd make all that great of a dad.

Still, my fingers hover over the keyboard. Extremely interested in finding out what exactly Gracelyn's doing tonight.

> Mack: You busy tonight?

I hurry and hit send before I talk myself out of it. There's a long pause and my heart's pounding a mile a minute as I stare at the phone like it's a freaking crystal ball.

> Firecracker: Yeah, late night at the salon

My chest stiffens as regret washes over me. She's busy. I should let it go. Move on, like I planned.

> Mack: What about after? You'd be pretty close by

What am I doing here? Sure, I'd love to see her, be with her again. Kiss that pretty mouth of hers, run my hands up and down her body, and see where the night takes us. But I need to be a logical, responsible adult here.

I stare at the screen, waiting.

Buzz, buzz.

> Coach Carter: Pizza at my house after practice? We can catch Monday Night Football

> Coach Carter: My fantasy team's kicking your team's ass 😊

It's a sign. The universe does not want me to see Gracelyn tonight. I should play it safe and hang out with my friend. Watch football, drink a beer, and forget all about my neighbor's sexy daughter.

Buzz, buzz.

Another text comes in, this time from Gracelyn.

> Firecracker: Sorry, but I can't make tonight work

I huff out a deep sigh, frowning down at the screen, jaw tense. I took a risk and it didn't pan out.

Happens to the best of us, but it still fucking sucks. I'm

surprised at how sharp the sting is, stabbing me in the ribs. Perilously close to my heart.

I shove that disconcerting thought away and text Coach back.

> Mack: Sounds good. See you later

After chugging the rest of my coffee, I fire off a quick text to Gracelyn.

> Mack: Too bad. Have a good day, Firecracker

Hitting send, I try not to dwell on the fact that I got rejected. I head to the shower to get ready for the day.

———

The best part about owning my own business, Made by Mack, is all the glorious alone time. Plus, the bit about playing with power tools and building shit. Also pretty amazing.

I started Made by Mack the day after I moved to Thunder Creek ten years ago. The period of time my mother affectionately calls my quarter-life crisis, which she's pretty certain I'm still in the throes of.

I fervently disagree.

Getting my carpentry business up and running was one of the best decisions of my life. I have the triple gifts of time, money, and freedom, and I don't take any one of those for granted.

And typically, I thoroughly enjoy each of those blessings. But today, the solo time stretches and yawns like salt-water taffy baking in the sun. Long and drawn-out, hot and sticky and never ending.

Everything Gracelyn runs through my head on loop. Her wide smile, her infectious laugh, the musky scent of her sex. The way her eyes fluttered shut when she came all over my cock.

I saw and sand, measuring and remeasuring the Sanderson cabinets. But still, she's there. Right here with me, rubbing her luscious curves up and down my body. Begging for more.

I check the clock. Minutes tick by, but not fast enough.

Time doesn't matter anyway, because I'm not seeing her again. So who cares? It's not like I have something to look forward to later tonight. Much as I love the guy, pizza with Carter is not the same thing as seeing Gracelyn.

I won't have her hair wrapped around my fist as I drill into her tight pussy. She won't giggle at my jokes as we banter back and forth. Her fingers won't lace through mine as we cuddle on the sofa.

I turn back to the cabinetry plans, double-checking the dimensions, then measure again. Make a cut, sand the edge, measure, make another cut.

Finally, the work day is over and I can escape the confines of my garage. I unplug the wood saw, toss the safety goggles on the back counter, and change into my coach's uniform for practice.

Walking out to my truck, I catch sight of Mrs. Reynolds launching a lumpy garbage bag into the trash can at the side of her house.

"Afternoon, Mrs. Reynolds," I call out, waving across the lawn.

"Afternoon, Mack. You let me know when you're done with the chair and I can send Gracie over to pick it up."

My mind flashes back to Gracelyn's glistening pink pussy last night, how sweet she tasted as I knelt between her thighs and feasted.

I shove the thought away as I stare across the yard at her mother, hand over her brow shielding her eyes from the sun.

"Don't worry about it, Mrs. Reynolds. As soon as I'm finished, I'll bring it over."

She shakes her head, her dark curtain of hair swishing on her shoulders. "You're too good to me, Mack. Thank you."

Doubt she'd think that if she knew what her daughter and I got up to last night. Guilt gnaws at my gut and I hold back a grimace, forcing a smile.

"Welcome." I wrench the truck door open and hop in, eager to shut down this conversation.

Turning the key in the ignition, I fire up the engine and gun down the driveway. The scent of Gracelyn's perfume lingers in the cab and my dick springs to life, stiffening in my shorts.

Not the time, dude.

How am I so hung up on this girl after only a few days? This is madness.

I coast through town, finally pulling into the lot of the high school. The sharp tweet of a whistle sings through the air, and I grab my playbook out of the backseat.

Sauntering onto the field, I join the other coaches on the sidelines.

"Glad you could make it, Mack," Coach Baker calls from the end of the bleachers.

"Y'all started early." I check my watch, noting it's only five minutes after three.

"No, we started on time. You're late." Baker chucks a

football at me and I shoot my hands out, catching the ball before it hits me square in the chest.

"You two quit bickering. You sound like old married people." Coach Carter strides over to me, adjusts his ball cap. "Boys are warming up. Baker, you'll take the offense and run drills, then the plays we're gonna use on Friday night. Mack, take the defense and do drills, then practice blocking. Sandalwood's got a tough offense this year."

I nod, knowing he's right. I've seen the film from the last few games. They have a wide receiver on the roster rumored to be getting recruited by Alabama—fastest kid in the state. Stopping him is going to be a challenge if he gets the ball in his hands.

"Got it, Coach." I twirl a finger in the air, signaling to the defense to follow me to the opposite end of the field.

"Okay, boys. We're going to start with drills this afternoon. First up, the redirect drill. Remember we did this last week. Get into your lines and let's go."

The boys fall into their three lines, one behind the other, and I stand five yards ahead of the first line.

"Now, first row—I expect to see y'all exploding off this line. Keep your eyes on the ball. Ready?" I snap the football off to the left and the front row moves, chasing the ball down the line.

"That's it! Yes, Griffin, just like that. Take the shortest route possible. Next line!"

The second row moves up, taking position, and I fire off the football. This time I snap the ball to the right and a few of the players scramble.

"Some of y'all guessed wrong," I chide. "Watch my eyes. Next!"

The third row steps up and I snap the ball to the far

right. None of the players misstep, all moving toward the ball this time.

"Good work, third line. First line—again!"

We run the redirect drill five or six times, then I move the players down the field to the blocking stations. They practice tackling with the dummies and I scribble notes for Friday's game. Sweat beads on my low back and my polo sticks to my skin, although it's nearly five pm and the sun's quickly sinking.

Finally, Coach Carter blows his whistle, signaling the end of practice.

"Good work today, boys. See you tomorrow!" He waves everyone off and Baker and I walk around, collecting equipment.

"Baker, you coming over for pizza?" Coach Carter asks, tossing a football into the mesh gear bag.

"Can't. I promised Lindsey I'd work on the nursery this week. She's starting to panic that the room won't be ready in time."

"Dude. Don't you have a few months still?" I frown over at him, wondering when my friend transformed.

"Yes. Four months, most likely. The doctor explained to her that she probably won't deliver early, since this is her first pregnancy and all. But she said she'll feel loads better once the nursery's ready." Baker throws up his hands in defeat. "Whatever. I just want to make her happy right now."

Coach Carter chuckles, shaking his head. "The old mantra, 'I just want to make her happy.' Words to live by, Baker."

"Whipped," I mutter under my breath, teasing, and Baker punches me in the biceps.

"One day you'll understand, Mack. Sometimes the path

of least resistance is better. Happy wife, happy life." Baker fishes his keys out of his bag, throwing the duffel over his shoulder. "See y'all tomorrow."

He hustles off the field and I stare at his retreating backside.

"Tell me that doesn't happen to everyone." I turn to Coach Carter, searching for reassurance, and he just laughs.

"Wish I could, Mack. But happens to the best of 'em. Come on, let's drop off the equipment and go watch the game."

Two hours later, the pizza's devoured and I'm two beers in, my max on a weeknight. We're sitting in his living room at opposite ends of his ancient sofa, the television blaring.

"I thought this game would be closer," Coach Carter grumbles, stretching his legs out. Carter's tall, six-three at least. A former football player himself, he seems oversized in the tiny space.

"Yeah, it's not very riveting, that's for sure." I pick at a callous at the base of my hand, wondering how much longer I need to stay. Normally, we watch the entire game including the recap. But tonight, I have other things on my mind.

Namely, a certain curvy blonde I should stay away from.

"You check your fantasy? Looks like you're back in good standing after tonight." Carter taps on his cell phone, scrolling through the fantasy football points.

"Not yet. I had total faith."

That's a lie. I purposely kept my phone in my pocket to avoid the temptation of texting Gracelyn.

"You okay? Baker get you worked up tonight? You

seem distracted." Carter narrows his deep blue eyes at me, like he's reading the field. I try not to squirm under his stare.

"Me? Yeah, I'm good. Why wouldn't I be?" I take the last slug of my beer, set the bottle on the coffee table.

"I don't know. You just seem off is all."

"Nah, I'm fine. Busy day today."

If you count building one order of cabinets as busy.

The only thing busy today was my mind, dirty fantasies of Gracelyn playing in my head.

"I'm gonna go." I stand and stretch, then gather up the bottles and take them into the kitchen. Chucking them into the recycling, I shuffle out to say goodbye.

Carter's gazing at the screen, his lips moving as he watches the next play. I swear, that man is perpetually coaching football. Even when no one's watching.

"Night, Carter. See you tomorrow."

He shoots me a wave, but doesn't move from the sofa. We've been friends long enough now to skip the formalities.

"See ya."

I let myself out, the air much cooler than inside the house. A shiver rolls through me, but it's not only from the change in air temperature.

No, every inch of me's suddenly wide awake and fully alert.

All day long I tried to stop thinking of Gracelyn, but I can't. I don't know what it is about this girl, but I want to —need to—see her again.

I have one last stop I want to make tonight and I'm almost positive it's gonna be the highlight of my day, assuming she'll let me in.

CHAPTER 10
MACK

"What are you doing here? And how'd you know I'd be home?" Gracelyn narrows her eyes at me, hand on hip.

She's clearly suspicious of my little visit and I'm not sure how to play this. Chasing after women isn't my typical M.O. I'm in uncharted territory here.

"I wasn't sure. But thought I'd stop by on the way home and check on you. Make sure you locked your door." I point at the doorknob, catching her eye.

"I did." She casually leans against the doorframe, the sparkly purple polish on her toenails drawing my eyes down to her bare foot resting on her calf. She's wearing only a sweatshirt, no shorts or leggings, and my fingers itch to reach out and touch her. Instead, I shove my hand in the pocket of my jeans.

I should go.

Yet my feet stay rooted to the spot. Hopeful.

"It's unlocked now, though." The tip of her tongue

darts out as she gnaws at her bottom lip, and that tiny bit of hope surges through me.

"You gonna invite me in?" I tip my head, waiting and praying for a yes.

She drops her gaze, fiddling with the cuff of her sweatshirt. "I probably shouldn't. It's late and it's a school night."

Heavy disappointment slams me hard in the chest. "You're right. You shouldn't."

Gracelyn steps aside, waving her arm at the empty living room. "Come in."

The pressure lifts off my sternum, hope filling up my lungs. This woman is a mystery, that's for sure.

I move inside and she closes the door behind me.

"So, what were you up to? How come you're out and about on a weeknight?"

"I was at Coach Carter's watching football. We have a fantasy football league going. Baltimore beat Pittsburgh, so I scored some points. Good thing, too, because Carter was beating me something fierce before tonight."

"Yeah, you wouldn't want to lose a make-believe football thingy."

"Football thingy?" I arch a brow, my lips quirking.

"I don't know. Tournament of champions or something?" She waves her hand around in the air and I laugh.

"It's not *Jeopardy*, Gracelyn. You don't know much about fantasy football, huh?"

"I don't know all that much about real football, boss, let alone make-believe football."

"It's not 'make-believe football.'" I air quote the phrase. "The football's real, the teams are not."

"Ri-ght..." She stretches out the word, nodding. Her

hair bounces around on her shoulder, a sliver of skin peeking out where the roomy sweatshirt slid down.

She's sexy as hell right now and every inch of me wants her. Wants to lay her down on the sofa right now and make her cry out with pleasure, come all over my cock.

"So—what do winning fantasy football coaches do to celebrate?" She twirls a curl around her finger, gazing up at me through a fringe of thick lashes.

Fuck me.

"I have a few ideas…" I inch closer to her, drawn to her curvy body like a magnet, the very air between us charged.

"And how do I figure into those ideas?" She tilts her head, toying with the hem of her sweatshirt, and I take a chance.

Closing the gap between us, I splay my hands over her hips and pull her up against me.

"Up to you, Firecracker."

Her breath hitches, the apples of her cheeks turning rosy as she stares up at me.

"Well, Coach—I do believe a win should be rewarded." Eyes twinkling in the glow of the lamp, she wraps her arms around my neck and presses her mouth to mine in a soft, slow kiss.

A kiss so sweet and tender it takes my breath away.

This woman does something to me, unlocking a part of me that's been buried for years. I want more of her, need more.

Sliding my tongue along the seam of her mouth, I urge her to open. Rushing in, I explore and taste. She's minty and sweet as she tangles with me, both of us trying to dominate.

Her hands rove over my chest, down my abs, tiptoeing to the waistband of my pants. My cock twitches, straining against the fabric, and Gracelyn strokes me through the cotton.

"Football must be really exciting," she whispers and I snicker.

"Don't think that has much to do with football. More to do with the woman I'm holding right now."

She pulls away, one brow arched. "Nice line."

"Not a line. Just the simple truth."

A light flush creeps up the ivory column of her neck and I dip down, nipping at her earlobe. I suck on the tender flesh, and she moans softly.

"If I would have known this is all you were wearing, I would've come over at half time." My hand drops from her hip to her ass, palming her cheek and squeezing.

I massage her ass, working the tender flesh. Trail kisses down her neck, licking along the smooth skin. She's soft and sweet, like a ripe piece of fruit.

Snaking my hand underneath her sweatshirt, I cup her bare breast. "You're killing me, Grace."

She giggles, a sweet, melodic sound that has my lower body coiling tight. I roll her nipple in between my finger and thumb, tweaking the sharp point. Caress her full tit, then move to the other side and do the same.

Reaching down, she glides her hand over my hard cock, once, twice. With deft fingers, she unbuckles my pants and I hurriedly pull them down, kicking off my shoes at the same time. Dropping my boxer briefs and ripping off my T-shirt, I'm naked in point-two seconds.

"Okay, Jackrabbit. I've never seen anyone drop trou that fast before."

"You did say it was a school night. Don't want to keep you up past your bedtime."

She laughs, pushing me over to the sofa. The backs of

my knees hit the edge and I sink down, sitting bare assed on the fabric cushion. Dropping to her knees in front of me, she wets her lips with the tip of her tongue before taking my length in her hand. Encircling the shaft, she glides up and down my cock a few times before licking the tip. She swipes up the droplets of pre-cum, gazing at me through lowered lashes.

Damn. She's beyond sexy—sultry—kneeling at my feet with my rock-hard dick in her small hands.

"Damn, baby. That feels good."

With a sly smile, she laps along the length of my dick, licking me like a freaking lollipop. Her tongue's soft and wet and perfect as she moves up and down. Then she parts her lips and sucks me all the way into her warm mouth. My hand loops around the nape of her neck, fingers fisting in her hair as she sucks me off.

She has no idea how much power she has over me, this golden-haired siren with the wide, beautiful eyes.

"Fuck, baby girl, you're so perfect." I stare down at her as she hollows out her cheeks, taking me in deeper still. I'm almost all the way in, my hips thrusting of their own accord as she works me in and out of her mouth. I've never felt like this before, been so far gone for someone in such a short time.

She's wild and beautiful, holding my balls in her hand. Stroking the tender, velvety skin, tingles zip up and down my spine and everything coils in my gut. The pleasure's intense and exquisite as she takes me all the way in. I'm dancing on the edge, tight and ready. Much as I want to hold back, I don't think I can. Not with Gracelyn licking and sucking, her lips wrapped around my cock and her curls bouncing around, wild and free.

"I'm gonna come, baby, unless you stop right now."

Shaking her head 'no,' I shove deeper into her mouth, hitting the back of her throat. Tears shimmer in her big blue eyes, but she doesn't let up, maintaining pressure. Fisting her hair, I thrust one last time, exploding my release.

She swallows hard and fast, the delicate column of her throat moving as she drinks me down.

"You're so fucking gorgeous, baby girl." I stroke her hair as she pulls away, swiping at her mouth.

"Thought I'd return the favor." She winks up at me, still on her knees.

"Such a good girl." I take her hand, pulling her up onto my lap.

Straddling me, she winds her arms around my neck and kisses me on the lips. I taste the salty brine of my cum as she swirls her tongue in my mouth.

"And good girls are always rewarded." I smooth my palm over her ass, giving her a light smack.

"Oh yes, Daddy," she murmurs, her voice breathy. And damn if that doesn't have my cock already swelling again. I haven't had this kind of response to a woman in a long damn time.

She squirms on my lap, rubbing the tiny scrap of her panties against my bare skin. I run my palm up and down her thigh, inching toward the apex.

"Fucking soaked," I murmur, rubbing the wet spot on her panties. She shimmies beneath my touch and I brush her clit over the silk before kissing her hard on the lips.

Flicking her sensitive spot, she grinds against me and now I'm rock hard.

"Take these off." I pull roughly at her V-string, working them off her body. "I want your bare pussy on me."

She doesn't hesitate, scrambling out of the V-string and

flinging it to the ground. Then she climbs back on my lap, running her fingers through my hair.

"You're so sexy, you know that?" She smashes her lips to mine in a hot kiss and all rational thought flies out the window. The only thing on my mind right now is slamming my dick into Gracelyn's tight pussy and making her scream my name.

"Oh shit—I don't have a condom. I used it last night and didn't restock." I sigh, leaning back against the couch cushion. I can't believe I forgot that critical detail. Although, to be fair, I had no intention of doing this again. Was only planning on talking and sorting things out.

"It's fine," Gracelyn murmurs, stroking the stubble on my jawline with her thumb. "I'm on birth control. And had a check-up before my last epic fail of a date."

"You sure?" I raise a brow, assessing the situation. I mean, I know she's fine with me. Bare's not my usual style. Too risky and I'm not one to throw caution to the wind, even in the heat of the moment.

But Gracelyn makes me want to take that chance, consequences be damned.

"Yes." Her tongue darts out, gliding along her bottom lip, and that's all the encouragement I need.

"Okay then." Reaching down, I tug the sweatshirt over her head and my breath catches as she loops her arms around my neck.

"What?" She stares up at me with wide, innocent eyes.

Eyes that scream *Fuck me,* even when my rational brain's shouting the exact opposite.

"You're a vision, baby girl." I run my hand up the underside of her full tit, thumbing her rosy nipple. "Fucking breathtaking."

I tweak the tip into a sharp point and she sucks in a

breath, her eyes drifting shut as she sways into my touch. Leaning down, I kiss and suck at her breasts, massaging the flesh. I could get lost in these tits for days, they're so damn perfect.

With an open palm, I slap the side of her right breast lightly and she rolls her hips, wetness slicking my skin.

"Oh, baby girl likes that."

She moans and I slap her other breast, giving her more of what she likes. Her skin mottles, pink and creamy splotches, and my dick's a steel shaft. Ready and waiting for her.

Dipping down, I finger her and she takes me in, ready and willing. I add a third finger, scissoring and stretching her. She rolls her hips, seeking more, and I know she's ready.

I grip her ass, lifting her slightly and lining her up with my dick. Then I sink into her wet heat, spearing into her tight pussy.

"Fuck, baby. You feel even better bare." I thrust all the way into her and she cries out, her nails digging into my shoulders.

"Yes! Fuck me, Mack."

Her wish is my command. Gripping her hips, I piston in and out, hard and fast. Her creamy tits bounce against my chest, her head thrown back and eyes closed as she rides me.

"You're so fucking beautiful, baby, riding my cock like this. Fuck!" I hiss, watching as she scrunches her eyes shut tight. Her nipples tight pink points, cheeks flushing, her breathing ragged. She's milking my cock, sucking me into her with everything she's got.

"Oh god, I'm coming…" she whimpers, squeezing my dick with her muscles.

I slap her hard on the ass. "Come for me, baby girl. Be a good girl and come all over Daddy's cock."

That's all it takes to send her crashing over the edge, crying out. I keep moving, in and out, not slowing down as she rides out the waves of her orgasm.

"Fuckkkk…." I shout, gripping her ass tightly, squirting ropes of hot cum into her. She slumps against my chest, panting, as my dick convulses inside her.

"Mack—" She says my name reverently, a soft whisper on my skin. "That was amazing."

"You were amazing." I stroke her hair, press a kiss to the top of her head.

"Thank you, Daddy."

Fuck me.

This girl's going to be the death of me.

And I'm gonna love it.

CHAPTER 11
GRACELYN

"That was fun." I brush my hair back from my face, unwinding myself from Mack. Standing, I pluck my sweatshirt from the ground and throw it back over my head. Covering myself up in the cozy cotton.

"Yeah." Mack leans back against the cushions, his long legs kicked out. The man's a vision, his chest and abs defined as he lounges on my sofa.

"Thanks." I toss him his pants and T-shirt, a not-so-subtle hint. This time I'm getting the jump on him. Better to guard my heart from disappointment and protect myself from the sting of rejection.

He catches the clothing with one hand, his eyes narrowed.

Definitely picking up what I'm laying down.

"I'm guessing this is good night then." His voice is low and husky as he stares across the room at me.

I shrug. "Like I said, it's a school night."

"Too bad." There's a hint of regret in his tone as he

pulls his pants on, shimmying into the denim and zipping up. My stomach flutters, my heart warring with my wind. Much as I want him to stay, long to wake up in his strong arms, I'm not going to take that risk again. Put myself out there like I did last time.

I don't want to wind up looking like a sappy fool, my feelings smushed like a lovebug on a car grille.

Nope.

"Okay then." He stands up, runs his fingers through his messy waves before pulling the T-shirt over his head.

Bye-bye, abs.

Sadness twinges low in my belly, but I push it away. I can't dwell on feelings right now, not while Mack's still here. So close to me, the scent of pine and sex floating through the living room air. My body still warm in all the places he touched me, my thighs slick and sticky.

I need to get him out of here before I break down and cave, give in to my desires.

"I have to be up early tomorrow." I throw his words right back at him, although I don't sound very convincing.

"Right." He presses his lips together, a vein popping in his neck.

The air shifts between us, both of our guards up now. I don't know where I stand with him, his expression blank and jaw tense.

Wrapping my arms around my stomach, my shoulders slump as he gathers his phone and keys without a word.

"Well, thanks for tonight, Gracelyn." He spins to face me, his eyes flicking to my face. My breath hitches as he locks his gaze on mine for a long second.

"Welcome," I murmur, my voice barely above a whisper.

Everything about this feels wrong.

I want him to stay.

Want him to say something—anything—to give me hope for the future, for us.

But he doesn't.

Instead, he tips my chin up and presses his lips to mine in a tender kiss.

A kiss that feels very much like goodbye.

Tears sting my eyes and I'm happy they're closed. I'm not going to give Mack the satisfaction of witnessing me cry over him.

What we have going on is clearly a fling, nothing serious.

"Night, Gracelyn."

"Night, Mack."

He lets himself out this time and I stare at his retreating backside, a lump in my throat. The door clicks closed and then there's silence.

Tap, tap, tap.

"Lock your door, baby." His muffled voice carries through the wood and one hot tear slides down my face as I hurry to the door and slide the deadbolt into place.

"That's a good girl."

I brush the tear away along with the strong feeling of déjà vu.

I'm not going to do this with him again.

As much as I like Mack, I can't keep putting myself out there. I want to be the cool, casual girl—so much—but I don't have it in me. Not this time. I've been the casual fuck before, but I know I'm worth more that that.

With shaky hands, I tap out a text that I very well may regret in the morning.

Gracelyn: It's been fun, but I can't keep doing this with you

I hit send before I overthink the entire situation, knowing deep-down in my heart it's the right thing to do. Then I stare at my phone, waiting and willing him to text something good back. Tell me what we have is real, I'm not just a fuck-and-roll.

Stalling, I get ready for bed, throwing on my pjs and brushing my teeth. I floss, rinse with mouthwash.

Nothing.

Finger comb through my wild curls, trying to detangle my golden mop.

Nothing.

Apply lip mask treatment and hand cream, including cuticle oil.

Damn it. Still no response.

I crawl into bed and slip under the covers, scrolling through social media for a few minutes to kill time. Finally, I give up and plug in my cell, shut off the light, and stare at the ceiling.

Focusing on my breathing, I try to forget all about Mack and his stupidly handsome face. That square jaw, with just the right amount of stubble. His full lips as he kisses me, licking and sucking and bringing me to the brink of ecstasy. The way his hands brush over my skin and light me up inside. His gravelly voice as he whispers sweet, sweet compliments in my ear.

I squeeze my eyes shut tight, knowing full well that guys like him don't pick girls like me. I'm not the most beautiful woman in the room. I'm not thin or athletic. I'm short and curvy, with a big mouth and an even bigger personality.

I'm the sidekick, the good-time gal. I don't give main character energy and I'm certainly not the heroine in a romance. Never have been, never will be. Those roles go to women like Sloane or our friend Lindsey, even Jamie.

But not me.

So why would Mack want anything more than a hookup? I was dumb to entertain the concept, the very idea laughable. He's probably relieved I let him off the hook.

CHAPTER 12
MACK

Tonight didn't go as planned, that's for damn sure. For once, I wasn't going to bail.

For once, I wanted to stay. To lay down with Gracelyn, wake up tomorrow morning holding her beautiful, curvy body in my arms. To kiss her soft, warm lips as the sun beamed into her bedroom, worship her like she deserves.

I wanted to be with her.

But clearly that's not what she wants. She practically kicked me out before I pulled on my pants, before I could even protest.

And I'm sure as hell not going to beg.

Ego bruised, I'm letting myself into the dark house when my phone lights up.

Firecracker: It's been fun, but I can't keep doing this with you

Ouch.

Been fun.

Past tense.

I read and re-read her text, a dull ache in my gut. She let me down easy, I guess.

She's one hundred percent right. It's been fun, but we have no business being in a real relationship together. A go-on-dates, meet-the-parents kinda thing. We wouldn't work.

Gracelyn's too young, and I'm not the right guy for her. It'd be messy and complicated. We're all wrong for each other.

We had a fun fling, but we absolutely need to leave it at that.

Much as I hate seeing the harsh words there on the screen.

And hate the feeling I have right now even more, loneliness creeping in and filling the empty house with deafening silence.

I want to hear her laugh, see her bright smile light up the room, feel her soft breath on my skin as she lays peacefully beside me.

It'll never work, though. Both of us know it. She was just the first to admit it.

I delete the text I typed out on my phone before I pulled out of her lot: **Want to go out Saturday night?**, the letters disappearing one by one.

Tossing my phone onto the counter, I head to bed, working hard to ignore the bitter disappointment weighing heavy on my chest. After all, Gracelyn and I had a casual hookup, nothing to carry on about.

But laying alone in my bed in the dark, all I can think about is her.

Her big, blue eyes, pupils blown wide as she gazes up at me through a fringe of dark lashes. Golden curls spilling over her shoulders, the creamy skin of her chest turning pink as she bounces up and down on my cock. The sweet sound of her voice as she cries out my name, panting. Her thighs squeezing me tight, nails clawing at my skin as she unravels.

God, she's beautiful.

It's going to be tough seeing her car next door, knowing she's *right there* and I can't talk to her, see her, touch her. I mean, technically I could do all those things, but I shouldn't.

Not after she sent me the old *It's been fun* text.

No matter how good her body felt in my hands, how right everything between us is when we're alone together. Just the two of us, without any preconceived notions or small-town bullshit.

Leave her alone, Mack.

Not bothering to turn on the light, I rip my clothes off and flop into bed. I'm more than happy to leave the last hour of today behind me.

The brush off always sucks, but this one hurts a little bit more than usual.

As the days roll by, I expect to forget about Gracelyn. Put what happened between us in the rearview and move on with my life.

Turns out, that's easier said than done.

I spend more time thinking about her than I'd like. Doesn't help that I live next door to her place of employment. I catch myself glancing out the window more than is strictly necessary, hoping for a quick glimpse of the sassy, curvy blonde.

Guess I'm a masochist or something.

But surprisingly, I hardly ever see her. She must sneak in while I'm working and by the time I'm home from football practice in the evenings, her car's already gone.

Probably for the best.

Much as I'd love to pursue her, she made it pretty damn clear she's not interested in anything more from me. I need to let the spark between us fizzle like a Fourth of July firecracker dunked in a bucket of cold water. Keep us both safe from combustion.

So I go about my normal life, waiting for the memory of Gracelyn—the way she lit me up inside—to fade.

After a long and grueling practice, I pull into the lot of the grocery to grab something for dinner. Thunder rumbles off in the distance. Thank goodness the weather held out and we made it through drills this afternoon. We have a big game on Friday night and the team needs every repetition we can get.

Head down, I hurry into the brightly lit store on a mission. Soft rock plays over the speakers as I make my way over to the deli in search of a rotisserie chicken. I'm in luck—there's one left, sitting all by it's lonesome in the metal warming tray.

Homed in on the target, my hand darts out to grab the food. Stomach growling and mouth watering, the delicious scent of salty, spicy chicken floats through the air. I'm downright starving and cannot wait to dig into that bird. Hell, I may even feast in the parking lot.

"Hey!" A familiar, tinkly voice stops me in my tracks, my fingers brushing against hers as we both grip the greasy paper bag.

Gracelyn.

And she's every bit as beautiful as she is in my dreams, wearing tight jeans and a satin blouse, her hair pulled up in a messy bun. Bright, blue eyes shining beneath the fluorescent lights of the grocery, she stares straight at me, hand on her hip.

"I was gonna buy that." She points at the chicken we're both clutching, her pretty bow lips scrunched up.

I shift my weight, not loosening my grip on the bag. "Me too. How about a sub instead?" I tip my head in the direction of the meat counter and she frowns.

"Not really feeling it tonight."

"Huh. Could be a problem. Maybe they have more chicken in the back."

Gracelyn waves at the woman behind the counter and she sidles up behind the display.

"Yes, honey?" The woman squints at the two of us from behind her oversized glasses. "What can I do for ya?"

"Do you have any more rotisserie chicken?" Gracelyn asks in the sweetest voice possible, not a trace of aggravation in her tone.

"Sorry, sugar. It's late. What's out is all we've got."

Gracelyn blinks once, twice, exhaling a tiny sigh. "Well, shoot. Thanks, anyway."

She glances over her shoulder at me, not loosening her grip on the bag. "Looks like this is the last chicken."

"Appears so." My lips quirk in amusement as Gracelyn's foot taps double-time on the linoleum.

"How about we play Rock/Paper/Scissors for it?" She tips her chin up at me.

I quirk a brow, somehow managing to hold in a chuckle. "You want to play a game for the chicken?"

"Yeah. Unless you're willing to cede to me right now."

"Don't think so."

"Okay, then. Let's go." Mouth set in a tight line, she has on her game face now and it's fucking adorable.

"I didn't say I'd play." I lick my lip, stringing her along.

"Oh, c'mon. It's only fair."

I exaggerate a sigh, shrugging. "Fine. I'll play the damn game."

"Best out of three."

"Okay." I nod at the bag. "But you're going to have to let go of the bird."

She narrows her eyes, debating the wisdom of that move. Like I'm going to steal the chicken when she lets go or something.

"You are too."

"Obviously." I loosen my grip and she follows suit, both of us backing away from the warming display.

"Alright, on the count of three—" Gracelyn squeezes her fist, ready for battle. "One, two, three!"

We both shoot our hands out, Gracelyn's palm flat and mine squished into a tight ball.

"Yes!" She pumps her fist in the air, victorious. "Paper beats rock. Let's go!"

"Lucky try. It's best out of three. Your rules, remember?"

"Yeah, dammit," she mutters, taking position. "Let's go again. And if I win, that tasty chicken is all mine." She rubs her hands together, eyes gleaming. "One, two, three!"

This time I make a fist and she throws out two fingers.

"Crap!" She stomps her foot and the corner of my lip tips up.

"Bummer. Rock beats scissors." I point out the obvious. "Guess we're going with a tiebreaker."

Gracelyn rolls her shoulders, stretching her neck side to side.

"You ready there, Rocky?" I tease, smirking at her pre-game routine. She's cute, all animated over this rotisserie chicken.

"Yeah, yeah. Don't rush me." Squatting down a little, her brow creases in concentration. "One, two, three!"

She throws out two fingers again and I make a last second decision, laying my palm out flat.

"Yes!" She jumps up and down, beaming. "I win!"

Judging by the celebration, you would have thought she just brought home the gold at the damn Olympics.

"Looks like you did, Firecracker."

"Fair and square." She beams up at me with rosy cheeks and my gut clenches—and it's not from hunger. She's so damn beautiful. The fact that I can't have her, can't be with her, physically hurts.

Gracelyn grabs the lone bag from the display with one hand, inching closer to me. The scent of rosemary mixes with her sweet perfume as she moves into my space, one hand reaching up and patting my chest.

"Better luck next time, Mack." She winks at me, then spins on her heels, bag of chicken in hand.

I stare at her gorgeous ass, swaying back and forth as she trots up to the front register. The soft rock's drowned out by the thudding of my heart directly below the spot where Gracelyn's hand rested a few seconds ago, the skin still burning.

Hope she enjoys that chicken at least half as much as I enjoyed watching her win the stupid game of Rock, Paper, Scissors. Letting her beat me was one-hundred percent worth it, even if I have to eat a frozen pizza tonight instead.

———

Football season Fridays are my favorite. There's nothing quite like the vibrant energy of the crowd sitting on the metal bleachers at Thunder Creek High on a crisp autumn evening, cheering on their home team. Most folks in the stands are alumni, making each victory that much more special.

And we win—a lot. Coach Carter's the winningest coach in the entire state of Georgia. I like to think Baker and I have a little something to do with it, too. But most of the credit should go to him. The man's a legend. A football star here himself, and now he's coached the school to the state championships each of the last five years.

I expect this year to be no exception, given how strong our team is. But that's the thing about football—you never really know what's going to happen.

"Listen up, boys." Coach Carter claps his hands once and the entire locker room falls silent, waiting to hear what he's about to say. "I know y'all have heard the rumors about the Sandalwood team and the wide receiver already getting recruited. Yes, he's good. But we're better. We train harder, longer, and more often than any other high school team. I have absolute faith in each and every one of you. Now, huddle up—Mustangs on three."

Everyone puts their hand into the tight circle and counts down: "One, two, three, go Mustangs!"

The deep roar of the chant echoes off the metal lockers and it's go time. Helmets fastened, mouthguards in, the athletes run out of the locker room and the coaches follow quietly behind.

We're each lost in our own thoughts, thinking about plays and the lineup. None of us speak as we make our way out onto the field, bright white lights blaring down on the grass, the band playing the school fight song. I block out all the background noise of the crowd and thumb through the playbook as I take my usual position on the sideline. Baker's next to me on one side and Coach Carter's on the other, huddling with the offense.

"Sandalwood won the coin toss, so we kick off. Mack, what you got?" Coach Carter elbows me and I call out my starting line. The players take the field and the game's on.

Within five minutes, Sandalwood scores. The quarterback finds the infamous wide receiver and it's all over, my guys totally blowing it. They somehow manage to forget every defensive play we practiced all week, and the ball's in the end zone before the stands fill up.

"Shit!" I mutter under my breath, crushing the pages of the playbook as the kicker launches the ball through the uprights to score an extra point. I wave my arm through the air and my guys jog off the field, shaking their heads in disbelief.

Taking a deep, cleansing breath of cool air, I work on keeping my temper at bay. Not an easy feat, hot anger burning my chest.

"Boys, have a seat." I motion at the wooden bench and they slump down one by one, helmets dropping to the ground.

I smash the playbook into my back pocket and press my lips together in a tight line, trying to figure out the nicest way to say this.

"Respectfully, what in the heck was that?" I catch each player's eye, shaking my head in disbelief. "I'm going to forget about what I just saw and we're going to hit refresh, 'kay?"

They all bob their heads, gazes downcast. I spin and

face the field, arms crossed over my chest as I watch our offense march the ball down the field. But we fail to score and the defense is back out on the field, the score still seven to zero.

Shouting the play, my guys take their positions. Griffin's lined up with the wide receiver and he's squatting low, like we talked about. But damn if the kid doesn't cut the opposite direction and outrun Griffin, spinning to catch the quarterback's perfect spiral.

"Dammit!" I growl, shaking my head as the demon sprints into the end zone again. The scoreboard flips to thirteen-zero and beads of sweat form under my ball cap. We're too early in the season to suffer a loss like this. These kids need to get it together right the fuck now.

Unfortunately, they go for the two-point conversion and we fail to stop them—again. Now we're down fifteen-nothing.

The second quarter doesn't go much better. We look like a pee wee team compared to this Sandalwood lineup, and the once-rowdy crowd's stunned into silence as they roll up the score. By halftime, we're down twenty-two to eight.

"Locker room, now." Coach Carter points down the field and the boys file off the turf, helmets hung low. Carter doesn't say anything to the other coaches, either, and by the time we hit the fluorescent lights I have a pounding headache and a pit in my stomach.

The room's quiet, no one daring to speak. That phrase about being able to hear a pin drop? You definitely could in this space.

"Y'all are playing like toddlers out there tonight. Langley, I don't know what's going on in that head of yours, but whatever it is, figure it out. And defense—you're getting beat on every play. You can't get beat off the line! You hear me!" He raises his voice, face flushing. Very atypical of him. He's usually calm, cool, and collected.

Not right now.

"Defense—get with Coach Mack and figure out what the hell you're doing. Special teams—talk to Coach Baker because we need to do something different if we're going to win this game. Offense, huddle up."

We all take our respective boys and regroup. I try my best to give them a pep talk, buoy their spirits after Coach Carter tore them down. Feels weird because I'm hardly ever the good cop in the locker room.

"We're going to try a different formation, guys. Cover 2 zone defense. Deep safeties and double coverage on that kid. Let's get out there and stop 'em!" I pump my fist and determination flashes across their young faces.

With halftime over, we jog back onto the field. The Sandalwood cheerleaders are hyping up the crowd and our squad's doing their best, although our stand is unusually quiet.

Langley manages to launch the ball down field and we score a big touchdown. Baker high-fives me and Carter's shoulders relax a touch, now hovering only halfway to his ears. We go for the two-point conversion and we're back in the game.

"Alright, boys—remember the new coverage. Go get 'em!" I slap the defenders on the back as they hustle out to the line.

The ball's hiked and the quarterback searches for the wide receiver, but for the first time all night, he can't get open. He's jammed up by my guys and the QB has to find another target. He hands off to a running back, who's immediately tackled.

Sandalwood can't get anything going and the ball's back to us. The offense doesn't execute like the defense, though, and we don't manage to score. The whistle blows and it's already the fourth quarter.

I huddle quickly with my guys. "Fourth quarter and it's a close game. Stop them here and don't get beat. Understand? We are not giving up any more plays."

They all nod, blue-and-white helmets bobbing up and down in unison.

"Get 'em, boys. Scootch and slant. Got it?"

"Got it, Coach!"

Defense takes the field and I hold my breath, willing them to stop the ball. The first play goes nowhere, the cornerbacks doing their job and holding the wide receiver at bay. But the second play connects and they get a first down.

I lift my ball cap, run my fingers through my hair. The pressure's on as I work through the team's options.

"Press!" I shout as the team lines up again, tension sitting in between my shoulder blades.

The quarterback has the ball and miraculously, the defense presses. The receiver scrambles, but the timing's messed up and I clap my hands as Sandalwood doesn't make forward progress.

"Two more like that!" I yell and we go again. Same execution, same result.

"One more, boys!"

The hike and the quarterback's scanning, trying to find an open receiver. He's got nothing and throws the ball away.

With four minutes left, it's a six-point game. But at least we have the ball.

Coach Carter and Coach Baker huddle together. I pace

the sideline and try to think positive. I know we can do this, Carter's pulled off tougher feats than this before. But our team's young, and this is Langley's first season as starting quarterback. The kid's still green, even if he is talented.

Sandalwood blocks the first two passes and Langley's shaking his head, his fingers flexing around the ball. Coach Carter calls a timeout and waves Langley over, giving him a quick pep talk. The cheerleaders pump up the crowd during the brief delay and I scan the stands. Tons of people I know fill the seats, but only one stunning blonde catches my attention.

Gracelyn.

Wearing a Thunder Creek High T-shirt stretched tight across her ample breasts and a pair of ripped denim shorts that barely cover her upper thigh, she's gorgeous. And surrounded by a big group of guys I don't recognize. Of course I don't, seeing as how she's a decade younger than me. I force my gaze back to the field, gut churning.

I have no right to be upset she's hanging out with other guys. She called it off.

Still, jealousy rips through me, white flashes of light dancing in my peripheral vision, neck burning.

Focus, Mack. This is definitely not the time.

The whistle blows and Langley walks back out on the field, his mouthguard moving up and down as he gnaws it nervously. He catches the snap and lobs the ball twenty yards down the field to an open receiver. The kid runs for ten more yards and we have another first down.

Two minutes left to score and win the game. I hear the tick of the clock in my head, the red numbers counting the seconds down one by one. Langley throws another good pass and we move down the field, but we're still twenty yards away from the end zone with one minute and thirty seconds left to play.

We have to score here or the game's over.

Langley winds up and tosses the ball to the far right. The wide receiver catches it and the crowd goes wild, the band starting the school's fight song and everyone cheering.

The kicker takes the field and I hold my breath as he makes contact with the ball.

"And it's good! Thunder Creek beats Sandalwood!"

The cheerleaders chant, the band plays, the dance team runs onto the field, and our players high-five as the other team hangs their heads in defeat.

I spin my head around and stare up at the stands. Part of me hopes Gracelyn waves or smiles at me, acknowledges my presence somehow. But she's chatting with the guys next to her, oblivious to my presence.

Chest tight, I turn my attention back to the happy whoops of the team and try to block out the hollow feeling in my gut.

I've never been less excited about a win in my life.

CHAPTER 13
MACK

Despite my crashing mood, I hit Mustang's with Carter and Baker. More out of a sense of duty than an actual desire to celebrate our win, but I'm here.

We press through the thick crowd, making a beeline to the bar. People stop Coach Carter every two seconds, congratulating him on the hard-won victory. A few of the men offer up coaching tips, which is something else considering I know a few of them never played one second of football in their damn lives. Carter takes it all in stride, and I'm reminded again why I have no desire to be the head coach.

After what seems like an eternity, we finally make it to the bar. There are two open seats and I magnanimously offer them to Baker and Carter. I'm too amped up after the game to sit down, anyway. Although I have a sneaking suspicion a good portion of the buzzy energy churning through me has more to do with seeing Gracelyn and less to do with football. But I'd rather not dwell on that right now.

The bartender takes our drink order and Carter and Baker settle in, with me hovering behind them.

"Good game, Carter," Baker says, cracking his knuckles. "I was nervous there for a second, but we somehow pulled it out."

Carter rolls his shoulders, adjusts his Thunder Creek ball cap. "It was a close one. But I knew we could do it. Good zone coverage strategy at the end there, Mack."

"Thanks." I nod, accepting the beer bottle from the bartender and take a long slug. "That kid from Sandalwood's real good. I see why he's already getting picked up."

"We'll be playing that team again in the playoffs, I'm betting," Baker says. "And now they'll know our plays. We're going to have to keep getting better if we want to win state."

Carter shrugs. "We will, boys. Keep the faith." He lifts his drink and scoots back in his seat, giving me a clear view down the length of the bar.

And there she is, laughing and talking with the same guys from the football stadium. Gracelyn, the neon lights from the bar lighting her up and making her glow even brighter. The beer swirls in my stomach as she smiles at the man next to her, throwing her head back and laughing. The familiar, high-pitched tinkle floats across the room, hitting me hard in the chest.

I want to be that guy.

Tearing my gaze away, I pick at the edge of the label on the glass bottle. Anything to keep my focus off Gracelyn and the dude she's talking to.

"Mack—do you have plans this weekend?" Baker rams

my elbow, knocking my arm so hard a few droplets of beer slosh onto the wooden bar.

"Working in the yard. Tons of leaves to rake." I swipe at the spill with my knuckles, my eyes wandering back over to Gracelyn. Now she's looping one of her long curls around her finger and fluttering her lashes at the dude. He moves in closer, boxing out the other guys.

I don't like the way he's staring at her tits. Or his aggressive posture, chest all puffed out. Like he's some modern-day caveman ready to haul her out of the bar over his beefy shoulder.

In fact, I don't like anything about the guy. Jealousy pings through me like a silver pinball trapped beneath the glass of an arcade game, bouncing off my taut nerves. I take another chug of my drink, the cool liquid doing nothing to ease the scratchy tightness in my throat.

"I'm gonna use the john. Be right back."

Setting my bottle on the bar, I shove a hand in my pocket and move through the crowd toward Gracelyn, who's conveniently located near the restroom. I slow down as I get closer to her group, unsure if I should say anything to her.

What are you going to say?

Ducking my head and avoiding eye contact, I step into the bathroom. Surprisingly, there's no line and I do my business, debating what to do as I stand over the urinal. Part of me wants to sidle up to her and see what happens. An even larger part of me wants to tell the fuck boy to get lost.

Zipping up, I wash my hands and shove out of the restroom. Gracelyn's still standing in the same spot and now the guy's inched in tighter, his fingers dangerously close to my girl.

My girl.

Except she's not my girl.

Scrubbing a hand over my tight jaw, I stalk back to our spot at the bar. Last thing I want is to make a scene and embarrass myself. In a town as small as Thunder Creek, everyone will hear about it by tomorrow morning. The story may even hit the local paper, and I'm pretty keen on keeping my coaching position. A bar fight would definitely put that in jeopardy.

Baker and Carter have their heads together, fully engrossed in putting together a Special Teams offense for the next game. They don't loop me into the convo—I'm uncertain they know I'm back from the bathroom.

Leaving me more time to fixate on Gracelyn and the frat bro at the other end of the bar. Now he's leaning down, whispering something in her ear. I bet he's sniffing her floral perfume and wondering what she'd smell like rubbing up on him. Anger surges through me as his meaty paw strokes her arm.

Hell, naw.

I can't stand here and watch this. But I can't bring myself to look away, either. It's like witnessing a slow-motion car crash, knowing something grisly's about to happen and there's not a damn thing you can do to stop it.

Frat bro reaches out and tucks her hair behind her ear and that's all I can take. Black spots flicker at the corner of my vision and I'm hot all over. Pulling my phone out, I tap out a text.

Mack: If that dude touches you one more time, he's going to have a few broken knuckles

I smash the send button and glare over at the corner, waiting for Gracelyn to read the message. A few seconds later, she picks up her cell and glances at the screen. Then her head pops up, her gaze wandering over the crowd until her crystal blue eyes land on me.

She holds an index finger up to frat bro as her hands fly over her cell.

> Firecracker: Seriously? You don't have a claim on me, Mack

Accurate. I have no claim on her at all. And that's burning me up, from the inside out.

> Mack: I know. But I can tell from here he's not right for you

She flips her hair over her shoulder and shakes her head at her phone.

> Firecracker: You don't know anything about this guy. Maybe he's Mr. Right

Now it's my turn to shake my head, my right eye twitching. Surely, she's not falling for his amateur moves.

> Mack: He definitely isn't

> Firecracker: How do you know?

I glance up, locking eyes with her for a long second. Then I shoot her another text.

> Mack: I told you I can tell

Firecracker: Tell what, exactly, from way
over there?

She pops a hand on her hip and glares down the bar at me. Pressing my lips together, I don't hesitate with my response.

Mack: Tell that he's not me

Her cheeks turn pink as she reads the message, so I go for broke.

Mack: You should be sitting on my face right now while I play with your beautiful tits and make you scream

Mack: Not getting loved up by some overgrown frat bro

Lips forming a perfect 'O,' her neck and face brighten.

Mack: Ditch the bro and come home with me

I hold my breath, waiting for her answer as she stares down at her cell. Although the bar's noisy, all I hear is the blood whooshing loudly in my ears, heart hammering. If she didn't know how I felt about her before, she sure as hell does now.

Gracelyn turns to the frat bro, patting his forearm and smiling. Time flips to slow-motion as she sips her drink and leaves me hanging.

My cell buzzes again.

Firecracker: As lovely as that offer is, I
can't keep doing the casual thing

I frown at the screen, my insides swirling as I quickly debate showing my hand here. But fuck, who am I kidding? All I think about is Gracelyn—what she's doing, how she's feeling. If she's having a good day or not. I haven't felt this way about anyone in years.

Take the chance, Mack. Tell her how you feel.

Mack: Who said anything about casual?

She rattles the ice in her glass, then lifts her wide baby blues to mine.

Questioning.

I tip my head toward the door with a slight nod.

Answering.

Smiling up at frat bro, she gives him a finger wave and my chest fills with relief, my entire body lightening.

"I'm gonna get going. See you boys later." I lean over and toss a twenty onto the bar to cover my drink.

"What? You're leaving already? It's barely eleven pm," Baker says, tapping his watch.

I shrug. "Yeah, it's too crowded tonight. I'll see y'all later."

Carter doesn't protest, waving me off while Baker grumbles something about me being a boring old man.

But right now I could give two shits what Baker thinks. I have a much better offer on the table than hanging with my two buddies, talking football and drinking beer.

I'm about to have my face buried in Gracelyn's sweet pussy, lapping up her juices and making her scream my name.

CHAPTER 14
GRACELYN

My nerves hum louder than summertime cicadas as I sashay out of Mustang's. I'm trying to play it cool, but inside I'm a mess.

What am I doing?

Mack didn't text me, he didn't call. Now I'm going to go home with him and do the same thing all over again.

I'm pretty sure that's the definition of insanity.

My head's screaming no, but my pussy's throbbing yes. And the pulsating yes gets louder and more insistent when I hit the parking lot. Mack's leaning against his truck, acting all cool and casual, looking sexy as hell in his coach's uniform and backward baseball cap.

God, I'm a sucker for a backward baseball cap. His sandy hair curls over his ears, muscular arms crossed over his chest. The man's veins pop out when he's standing still—I can't imagine how hot he is when he's working out.

And he's standing here, waiting.

For me.

"Hey." My voice comes out breathy in the relative quiet.

"Hey." He tips his chin at me as I approach the truck, his pupils dark and wide.

I shouldn't be doing this again.

But I know myself and there's not a chance I'm turning back now. Not with this giant hunk of a man ready and willing to do dirty, nasty things to me.

"So—what is this?" I wave my hands in the shrinking space between us, moving closer to him. Close enough to smell his spicy cologne mixing with hoppy beer, see the light sprinkle of stubble peppering his jaw.

He swallows hard, locking eyes with me. "I know you gave me the brush off. But seeing you with that guy in there—" He glances away for a second, takes a shuddery breath before meeting my gaze again. "It didn't feel good, Firecracker."

My heart thunders at his words, breath hitching in my throat.

God, I want this man.

But I can't go there again, blindly trust him. I need more from him before I put my heart on the line.

I shrug. "Sorry. But you didn't even text me back. It's pretty obvious what we had was a fling. Nothing serious."

I huff out a breath, my hair feathering up, then down on my forehead as I try to work all this out in my mind. If Sloane were here, she'd tell me what to do.

But she's not.

She's down in Florida with Cam and I'm here on my own. Well, just me and Mack.

Digging deep, I find the courage to tell Mack exactly how I feel. "I don't want to be your fuck buddy, someone you only call when you're horny."

"Is that what you think you are, Gracelyn?" Mack furrows his brow, his green eyes serious.

To my horror, hot tears spring to my eyes and I will them to stay put with everything I've got.

"Yeah, kinda."

"Oh, baby, no." He shakes his head, his gaze darkening. He trails his thumb over my cheek, then drops his mouth to mine. Lips moving fervently, he kisses away all my doubts, one by one. His hand wraps around the nape of my neck, the rough callouses of his fingers tracing light circles on my skin.

This is what I've been waiting for, hoping for, longing for. Him.

"You're so much more than that," he murmurs. "Let's give this a shot, for real."

I pull away slightly, staring up at him. "You want to date? Me? Out in the open?"

"Yes, you. Out in the open, as you put it. I'm not going to hide someone as incredible as you away."

Heat rushes to my cheeks and I'm positive I'm blushing. "You sure you can handle that? Even if there's gossip?"

"I can. I'm a big boy, Firecracker. Promise."

"Oh, I know you're a big boy," I tease, running my hand over his broad chest. "You've proven that a time or two."

Mack laughs, a low, throaty rumble vibrating through the night, and my heart soars. *I could get used to this.*

"Now are you going to take me home and make good on that dirty text or what?" I ask, arching a brow.

"You better believe it, baby. Get in the truck."

———

We don't even make it home. Instead, Mack takes a detour down the nearest dirt road and we wind up in a field on the side of town.

"Pretty sure this took as much time as driving straight to my house," I point out as he kills the ignition.

"Nah. Besides, this is more romantic. Wait till you see." He hops out of the truck and jogs around to my door, wrenching it open for me. The creak of metal screeches, loud out here in the quiet of the night.

Stepping out and looking around, I realize just how right he is. The entire field is dark, except for a path of moonlight cutting through the grass, the green blades tipped in silver. Twinkly stars form a sparkly canvas above us and the cool fall breeze licks at my overheated skin. A symphony of wildlife sounds from the trees, an owl hooting somewhere in the distance.

The entire scene's magical, way better than a boring old bedroom.

More than that, I'm touched that Mack thought to bring me out here, to show me this special spot.

He grabs my hand, pulling me around to the rear of his truck. Lowering the back, he lifts me up into the bed by the hips, tossing me around like I weigh nothing. Then he spreads out a quilt and pats the center of the blanket.

"Get comfy. I have a promise to make good on."

With a grin, I undo my shorts and shimmy out of them as gracefully as possible.

"Lose the panties, too. I don't want anything in my way now that I have you out here."

"Yes, sir," I tease, giving him a salute and I swear he growls, pupils dilating.

Tossing my clothes to the side, I lay back on my elbows

and wait. Fizzy excitement bubbles through my veins, the night air cool on my hot, exposed center.

"Fucking gorgeous." Mack's eyes rake over me, lingering on my chest, my bare pussy. Then he pushes my legs apart gently and ducks between my thighs, licking all the way down.

"Fuck, that feels so good." I lift the baseball cap from his head and chuck it next to my clothes, running my fingers through his soft curls as he kisses my most sensitive spot. Shimmery pleasure rolls through me, cascading from my shoulders all the way to my belly. He dips his tongue inside me and I throw my head back, biting my lip. The pressure builds as he eats me out beneath the glittering stars.

The breeze blows through the trees, kissing my heated skin, and I'm close to falling over the edge. Mack slides two fingers inside me and I roll my hips to get more friction.

"Mack—" I whimper and he lifts his head for a second, grinning.

"You taste so good, baby. I could do this all night."

"I can't…" My body trembles as he sucks at my clit, flicking his tongue at the swollen skin.

"Oh, you can. Come for me, baby girl."

His words, the vibration on my pussy, send me careening over the edge. I shudder as he moves his tongue along my slit, kissing and sucking up my juices.

"Oh my god, Mack—" I cry out. He holds my hips and keeps me locked into place, trembling on his face.

Finally, the last waves of my release subside and I lay there, staring up at the sky, breathless.

"That was amazing." My voice is strangled, barely above a whisper.

"You're the best thing I've eaten all week." He smirks up at me, his face breaking into a shit-eating grin. Like he just won a state championship or something.

My chest swells with happiness and I grab him by the collar, pulling him on top of me. Now we're face to face, the musky scent of sex rolling off him.

"God, you're sexy," I purr, tracing the strong line of his jaw. His stubble's prickly beneath my fingertips, his skin tanned from the sun.

"You have no idea what you do to me, Firecracker. I want to bury myself in you." He unzips and slides his boxers down low enough to free his cock. Then he strokes himself, long and slow. My mouth waters watching him lengthen and harden.

"Do it then." I spread my legs for him, wiggling my hips.

Mack wastes no time, kicking out of his pants and positioning himself above me. He glides his tip through my wetness and I arch up to meet him.

"Eager little pussy," he teases, one hand sliding up my arm to my neck. Splaying his strong fingers around the delicate skin, slight pressure emanating from the rough pads. A pulse zips straight to my clit as his thumb strokes the divot in the center of my throat, breath hitching.

"Even after I just got you off. Here you are, wet and ready again." He pushes in, just barely, giving me only the velvety crown.

My pussy throbs, wanting more. I grind on him, but he pulls back.

"We have all night, baby. Relax."

I bite back a groan. At this rate, it's going to be dawn before he's all the way in.

"Fine." I breathe out a sigh, leaning back. He tightens

his grip on my neck and heat pools in my belly. I'm certain he can feel my rapid pulse racing beneath his fingers.

Pushing in further, I gasp as he releases the pressure on my neck. Light flashes in the corner of my eyes and I'm hot all over.

"Beautiful." Easing back out, he kisses me on the lips. Slipping inside my mouth, swirling around, I taste myself on his tongue. Tequila and sex.

Thrusting, he buries himself inside me and I gasp in shock. My muscles tighten around his cock, instinctively gripping him.

"Such a good fucking girl." His fingers wrap around my neck, squeezing lightly, cutting off my breath. All my senses focus on him and how he's making me feel—like I'm floating, my core hot and tight.

He loosens his grip, sliding out, and I instantly miss him. Tension low in my belly, the heat from his body on mine, his spicy scent winding around me.

"More," I pant, nails digging into the tight muscles in his shoulders.

He pistons back into me, harder this time, pressing against the sides of my neck and cutting off air. My eyes flutter closed as I milk his steel shaft, my hips moving of their own accord. Thrusting in and out, his fingers open and close, allowing me to get air, then cutting it off again. I've never had anyone take charge like this, commanding my body to his will.

It's erotic as hell.

His hand releasing, I cry out. "Mack—"

Voice high-pitched and shrieky, I shudder and tremble against his body as my orgasm crashes through me hard and fast. Grabbing my hips, he drives into me, over and over again.

Finally, he explodes. Hot cum shoots inside me as he chases his release. His face contorts as he pounds into me, then finally relaxes.

"Fuck me..." He slumps down on the blanket, chest heaving. "You're tight as fuck, Gracelyn. You took me so good."

He pulls me onto his chest, the cotton of his shirt soft on my cheek. Warm happiness trickles through me as he strokes slow, lazy circles on my back.

This is what I want.

A lump lodges in my throat and my chest tightens. I take a deep breath and relax into his strong body, trying not to worry about what comes next.

We're not casual. I made myself clear on that.

I let my worries about the future float away on the wind and get lost in the moment with Mack.

This is good. We're good.

"Gracelyn..."

Mack's deep voice rumbles, his chest vibrating.

"Hmm..." I murmur, eyes still closed.

"I'm not a stay-the-night kind of guy."

A surge of panic rushes through me, my muscles tensing.

I shouldn't have trusted him.

"It's been a long time since I dated anyone and I'm horribly out of practice. You're going to have to be patient with me."

I let the air out of my lungs, relief whooshing through me.

He's not bailing.

His fingers slide up and down my back and I lift myself up on my elbows, gazing down at him.

"I'm not universally known for my patience, Mack. But

I'll try." I drop my mouth to his, trying to kiss away all his doubts.

About us, our relationship, the future.

He kisses me back with a ferocity that takes my breath away. Off in the distance the owl hoots again, our very own aviary cheerleader. I take the sound as a good omen.

"And for the record, I don't snore. I'll prove it to you tonight." He squeezes my ass and happiness surges through me, tingling all the way down to my toes.

"Whatever you need to tell yourself, Mack," I tease, kissing him again.

This could be it.

I'm falling hard for this broody bachelor, the man whose been my mother's next-door neighbor for years.

I just hope I don't end up regretting it.

CHAPTER 15
MACK

I stay the night with Gracelyn.

The whole night. Lying next to her in bed, listening to her quiet, peaceful breathing. Watching her chest rise and fall, white moonlight spilling through the blinds and bathing her in an angelic glow.

Fuck, she's beautiful.

Every once in a while, she stirs. Curling up closer, her arm flings over me. A leg twines with mine, her foot tickling my calf. By dawn, she's got me in a tight grip, climbing me like a tree.

Surprisingly, I don't mind at all. In fact, I like it. Although I'm gonna be tired today since I spent most of the night watching her sleep.

"Morning, Firecracker." I brush a golden curl off her forehead as she blinks her eyes open.

"You stayed."

I nod. "Told you I would. So I did."

Her neck bobs as she swallows, cheeks tinting a soft shade of pink.

"Besides, I didn't have much of a choice. The way you have me pinned down here." I pretend to try to wriggle out of her grasp and she flexes her arm muscles, squeezing me like a boa constrictor.

She giggles and the sound washes over me like a gentle ocean wave. I'm more relaxed than I've been in ages.

I didn't think I could do this again. But here we are.

Her delicate fingers feather over my bare chest, sending tiny sparks over the entire surface of my skin, and my dick twitches beneath the sheets.

"Well, good morning." Gracelyn reaches down and strokes me, her eyes glimmering as she teases me. "This is the perk of the sleepover, you know."

"In that case, you've convinced me to move in," I joke, caressing her round ass.

I really could get used to this.

"Whoa, there, cowboy. Nobody said anything about moving in." She pops up and straddles my hips, dipping her head down and kissing me on the lips. Soft and slow, her mouth moves over mine as I massage her bare bottom.

Beep. Beep. Beep.

Gracelyn breaks away to silence her alarm. "Shit, it's late. I have to get to work."

"Too bad. Because I had much better plans for you." I squeeze her ass and she shakes her head.

"Sounds more promising than Mrs. Humphries's full color I have scheduled. But my mom will be pissed if I'm late. Would you mind giving me a ride to work? My car's still at Mustang's."

"Sure. You want to pick up your car?"

"No time." She rolls off me, already buzzing around the room getting ready. "I'll worry about it later. I'm supposed to be there in ten minutes."

"Ten minutes?"

"Mm-hmm."

Her head disappears into the closet, so I take that as my cue, climbing out of bed and gathering up my clothes.

Remarkably, she only takes eight. I pegged her as more high maintenance, seeing as how she always looks stunning. But she flits around and gets ready in record time. She locks the front door and I loop my arm around her waist as we walk out to my truck.

The movement's natural, instinctive, and the realization hits me hard straight in the chest. Much as I've been fighting all things relationship, she's a perfect fit beneath my arm.

"What's on tap for you today?" She glances over the console and something inside me shifts, unlocks.

I want to be with this woman. Spend time with her, find out what she likes, what makes her tick.

I want to make her laugh and smile.

I want to make her happy.

But instead of going sappy on her, I drum my fingers on the worn leather steering wheel and play it cool.

"Not much. Figure I'll work on fixing the salon chair."

Her full, glossy lips break into a smile. "Okay, good. My mother will be happy about that. She's super concerned we don't have enough seating. Not sure why, considering I book the appointments and make sure we never need to use the eggplant throne—that's what I call it ..."

Her hands fly through the air as she explains the situation and I can't help but chuckle.

"What? Why are you laughing?" She scrunches up her nose, scowling.

"Nothing. You're cute is all. Did you always want to be a hairstylist?"

She nods. "Yeah. Well, mostly. I went through a phase in the fourth grade where I was obsessed with animals and wanted to be a veterinarian. Then a kid told me about his dog having cancer and taking him to the vet to get put down. Changed my mind real quick."

"Oh. Yeah, that's a tough one." I sneak a quick glance at her, the apples of her cheeks rosy, a beam of sunlight dancing across her thigh.

"What?" She knocks me in the arm.

"Just admiring you."

"St-op." Gracelyn draws out the word, rolling her eyes and blushing. "What made you get into carpentry? Your love of drilling, pounding, and screwing?"

I chuckle. "Something like that. I always loved working with my hands and building stuff. I used to woodwork with my grandpa. Seemed like as good a job as any and I was pretty good at it."

"I saw the bookshelf you built for Josh and Lindsey in their nursery the other day. It was lovely."

"Thanks." Pride fills my chest as I pull up to the curb, dropping her off directly in front of the salon. "I wanted the two of them to have something special. For the baby."

She reaches over and squeezes my hand. "That's so sweet, Mack."

I shrug, playing down my emotions. "Don't tell anyone. Can't have my tough guy reputation getting tanked." I wink as she hops out of the truck, slamming the door closed behind her. "How long you working today?"

She pauses on the sidewalk to check her calendar. "My last client's at five. Should be done around seven."

"I'll call you after work then."

In one quick step, she leans through the open window of the truck and kisses me on the mouth. She tastes like vanilla, her lips soft and warm.

"Have a great day, Mack," she murmurs.

"You too, Firecracker."

Then she sashays up the stairs and disappears into the salon, leaving me wanting more for the first time in as long as I can remember.

———

The weekend passes by in a blur of Gracelyn. We talk, watch television, eat some food. Mostly, though, we spend a lot of time kissing and naked in bed.

It's the best weekend I can remember.

Monday rolls around and I feel like I have a Gracelyn hangover as I settle into the work week. I slog through the day, finally finishing the cabinets I've been working on for what feels like months. Then I go over to the high school for football practice. We're wrapping things up when Carter asks Baker and me about our plans for the evening.

"You boys in for the game tonight?" Carter ties the mesh equipment bag and peers in our direction.

Nine times out of ten, at least one of us joins him for Monday night football. But hanging with the boys isn't on my agenda this evening.

"I have tests to grade, sorry. Wish I could. See y'all later." Baker jingles his keys and waves goodbye, not looking overly apologetic.

"Mack? You in?" Carter cuts his eyes at me, adjusting his ball cap.

"Can't. I have to make a delivery after practice." I scrub

my hand over the back of my neck and avoid eye contact. Last thing I want here is an interrogation.

"That shouldn't take too long. You could always head over once you're done." He shoves a hand in his pocket and waits.

Shuffling from foot to foot, I try to figure a way out of the situation. I don't want to bring up Gracelyn yet—the whole thing's too new, too fresh to be a topic of conversation. Not to mention I still feel weird dating the best friend of his daughter.

"May take a while."

"Hmmm…" Carter presses his lips together, searching my face for answers.

I squirm under his intense stare, kick at a loose patch of grass with the toe of my sneaker.

"Where's the delivery?"

"The salon. Plumb Perfect."

"That's next door to you." Carter points out the obvious, and my gut churns as he waits for a logical explanation.

Because he's correct—normally, a delivery to the salon would take five minutes. But now, with Gracelyn in the picture, I doubt that's how things will go down.

At least, I really hope not.

"I might be getting a haircut." I pull the lie straight out of my ass.

"Really? Interesting. Mrs. Reynolds paying you in haircuts?"

Heat creeps up my neck and I can't make eye contact with Carter. "No, don't think so."

"Hmm. I didn't think she'd be working this late."

Damn, this guy's not letting it go.

"Not her. Gracelyn." I keep my voice neutral, not giving anything away.

"Gracelyn? Sloane's friend?"

I nod. "Yeah."

"Interesting." The corner of his lip curves up and I'm grateful Baker already left. Carter's discreet and probably won't ask any more questions. Baker would never have let this go.

"We can catch the game on Sunday night, probably."

Coach nods, picking up the equipment bag. "Okay."

He starts walking away from me, toward the office. After a few steps, he calls over his shoulder. "Better check with Gracelyn."

Then, smirking, he walks away.

Jackass.

That's why I love the guy, though. He's smart as hell, picking up on every little detail. But he doesn't pry and minds his own business, which I appreciate.

The man's a legend in my book.

Chuckling to myself, I hustle to my truck and drive home to pick up the chair.

CHAPTER 16
MACK

Twenty minutes later, I'm hoisting the "eggplant throne," as Gracelyn calls it, and carrying the oversized chair next door.

I climb the stairs, gripping the arms of the chair tightly and ignoring the hammering of my heart.

Relax. You're making a delivery, nothing special.

Except that's not strictly true. The last time I was in this space, I hadn't been sleeping with Mrs. Reynolds's daughter.

Everything's different now.

I only hope the woman doesn't have a sixth sense or something. Because if she does, this is gonna be real awkward.

I hesitate at the door. *Should I ring the doorbell? Knock? Will anyone be able to hear over the blow dryers and all the noise in the salon anyway?*

Probably not.

Making a split-second decision, I yank open the screen door and let myself in.

"Hello? I brought the chair," I yell down the hallway toward the salon, but there's no response. A loud whirring noise vibrates the floorboards, and I assume Gracelyn and her mom are still hard at work.

Grabbing the chair, I haul it down the narrow hallway, being careful not to nick the walls with the ornate wood.

"Knock, knock." I raise my voice before entering the bright salon space.

"Oh, the chair's back!" Mrs. Reynolds's voice rises up over the whoosh of the dryer she's wielding on her client's head. "You can set it over in the corner." She motions to the far side of the room and I haul the furniture over to the designated spot.

"Wonderful!." Mrs. Reynolds clicks the dryer off and sidles over to me, leaning down and stroking the seat of the chair like a beloved pet. "Perfect. Thank you so much, Mack."

"Mom, can you squeeze Lucy in tomorrow afternoon?" Gracelyn swoops into the room, phone in hand, and I suck in a breath.

Her hair's pulled into a high ponytail, leaving her creamy neck and chest exposed. The round apples of her cheeks tint pink the second she spots me, and my lower body coils and tightens in reaction.

"Hey." Her voice is breathy as we lock eyes with each other, desire sparking between us.

"Hey." I practically grunt the word, my throat dry. Her mother glances from me to her daughter, then back to me again.

"I can fit Lucy in tomorrow, Gracie. Mack, you look like you could use a trim." Mrs. Reynolds's hand hovers above my ear and prickly panic sets in.

I cannot get a haircut from Gracelyn's mother.

"Gracie, why don't you give Mack a haircut?" She arches a dark brow and Gracelyn's full lips part slightly.

"Oh, I'm sure he doesn't want a haircut right now. Do you, Mack?"

I run my fingers through my hair, which is admittedly kinda long.

"Actually, a trim would be great. If you don't mind."

Gracelyn swallows hard, fiddling with the tie of the black stylist apron protecting her clothes.

"Fine. Come on." She waves her hand, motioning me into another room.

"Thanks again, Mack. For fixing the chair." Mrs. Reynolds smiles as I move past her. I tip my head in acknowledgment before following Gracelyn's perfect ass down the hall, swishing side to side.

"You really want a haircut right now?" Gracelyn hisses as soon as we're out of earshot. "I could do this for you at your house, you know. Without my mother watching."

"I couldn't very well turn down the offer, then have your mom see me tomorrow with a fresh cut."

"True. And she would notice. Sit." Gracelyn pats the chair in the dimly lit converted bathroom, and I sink down into the supple white leather.

Water splashes behind me as she tests the temperature on her wrist before pressing on my shoulders.

"Lean your head back."

I follow instructions, resting my head on the cool indentation of the sink and staring up at the ceiling.

"Nice tiles."

"You like those? I picked them out. Thought clients might want something pretty to look at while they're getting their hair washed."

"They already had something pretty to look at. Before

the tiles." The words slip out of my mouth and I should be embarrassed by the blatant rizzing. But they're the damn truth and I don't mind her hearing it.

She blushes so deep, the red flush on her skin's visible even in the low light.

"You don't have to flatter me. I'll sleep with you again."

"Looking forward to it. But it's not flattery—it's the God's honest truth."

Warm water sluices through my hair as she squirts shampoo into her palm. A lemon-mint scent tickles my nostrils while she works the suds into my scalp.

Not gonna lie, I'm loving the view.

Gracelyn's standing at my shoulders, bending down and rubbing my scalp, her luscious tits directly at eye-level. Although the massage is relaxing as hell and I'd love to close my eyes, I can't bring myself to do it—not with her round, full breasts in my face. My mouth waters with each scrub, every jostle.

She rinses the shampoo from my hair, then rubs a towel vigorously over my head.

"When's the last time you had a haircut?"

"It's been a while."

"I can see that."

Wrapping the towel around my neck, her fingers comb through the damp waves and a shiver rolls down my spine.

"Come on."

I follow behind her to the main room of the salon, my eyes squinting as I step back into the shocking brightness. Everyone's gone now except me, Gracelyn, and her mother, who's sweeping the floor.

This could get real uncomfortable, real quick. I decide

to take Gracelyn's lead and say as much or as little as she does.

"Sit." Gracelyn pats a tall swivel chair in front of a large mirror and vanity.

I lower my body into the seat and she whips out a black cape, waving it through the air before wrapping it around me. Then she lifts a comb from the glass dispenser and runs it through my damp hair.

"How much do you want off?" Lips pursed, she tips her head and studies me.

I shrug. "I dunno. What do you think?"

She runs her fingers through the front of my hair, tousling the curls. "I like it kind of long. But it's your hair."

"I don't spend too much time worrying about my hairstyle."

"Yeah, I didn't figure. I'll trim it up, okay?"

"Sure."

Scissors in hand, she pulls my hair through her fingers and snips. The first lock falls and I watch her face in the mirror. A tiny V forms between her brows as she concentrates, the tip of her tongue darting out between her glossy lips. She's cute when she's working, all her attention focused on the task at hand.

"So, Mack—" Mrs. Reynolds startles me out of my trance. "I heard y'all had a good game Friday night. Everyone in town's talking about the defense. Good job."

I go to nod, but freeze when I remember Gracelyn's holding scissors an inch away from my ear. Best not to be bobbing my head at the moment.

"Thanks. Had to mix it up a bit to get by their wide receiver."

"It worked. We're all looking forward to the Homecoming game coming up."

Gracelyn pauses, the scissors stilling above my head. "We are?"

"Yes, of course we are." Mrs. Reynolds grins at her daughter and Gracelyn blanches.

"You're going to the game, Mom? Since when are you a football fan?"

"Since forever. I'm usually busy on Fridays, but I thought Layla and I could go together this time. With you."

Oh boy.

My eyes meet Gracelyn's in the mirror and I try not to laugh at the sheer look of horror twisting her pretty face.

"Well, I'm planning on hitching a ride with Cam and Sloane. They'll be in town for the game." Gracelyn pops a hand on her hip and taps her toe in agitation.

"Oh, right. I'll tell Layla to find another ride then and tag along with you three. Then you won't be a third wheel."

Gracelyn's nostrils flare, and I'd love to duck out of the conversation right about now. But unfortunately, I'm stuck here, trapped by the cape and a half-cut head of hair.

"Actually, I'm not going to be a third wheel."

"Really? You're taking a date?" Gracelyn's mother narrows her eyes at her daughter.

"Yeah, I have a date."

I suck wind, almost choking I inhale so hard. *This is how Gracelyn's going to tell her mother we're dating?*

"Gracie, you've been holding out on me!" Her mother squeals with delight, beaming. "Who's the lucky guy? Have I met him? You need to have him over here for dinner."

Gracelyn snips the scissors closed with a decisive snap,

the sound loud in my ear. One hand rests on my shoulder as she locks eyes with me.

"Mack, do you want to stay for dinner?"

CHAPTER 17
GRACELYN

Well, that was one way to break the news to my mother. Direct and to the point.

I catch a quick glimpse of Mack in the mirror, his expression blank.

Maybe I should have run this by him first.

It's fine, my mom was going to find out anyway.

"Uh…" Mack stammers.

I've never seen him at a loss for words and if I wasn't low-key freaking out inside, it would be kinda funny.

"Sure, I can stay."

"Great." My mom rubs her hands together with delight, her face lighting up like it's Christmas day. "I'll get started on dinner then."

She beams at the two of us one more time before spinning and gliding out of the room, humming softly.

I huff out a long breath, shaking my head. "Sorry about that. We probably should have discussed if and when we were telling people about us. I don't even know if we're exclusive…" My voice trails off, heat flaming my face.

"Probably should have talked about it, yeah. But it's absolutely fine, Gracelyn. Better to get everything out in the open." Mack's deep voice is calm and steady, the low timbre soothing my amped-up nerves. He locks eyes with me in the mirror. "And I'm exclusive, at least. I'm too old to play games. Other than football."

Whew. I didn't just blow it. Everything's fine.

Warmth spreads through me at his reassurance and my entire body feels lighter with the weight of sneaking around lifted off my shoulders.

"Good. We're on the same page then. Because I'm not seeing anyone else, either."

"So no more frat bros for you?" Mack teases.

"Why? Were you jealous?" I run my fingers through his hair, resuming the cut.

"Hell yeah, I was. I don't want anyone flirting with you —touching you—besides me."

His eyes flash, then darken, and my belly gets all fluttery. I don't think I've ever made anyone jealous before.

"Okay, Daddy," I joke, fluttering my lashes, and his hand darts out from beneath the cape and grips my ass. He squeezes and my body instantly responds, my core throbbing.

"If you want me to make it through dinner with your mother, you better not call me that right now." He growls the words and dampness floods my panties as his hands work my curves, caressing me.

"Fine." I pop my lip out in a pretend pout. "I'll save it for later, how about that?"

"Deal."

"Now stop feeling me up so I can finish cutting your hair. Especially if you value your ears."

With a throaty chuckle, he slides his hand away from

my body and beneath the cape and I get back to work on his hair. A few minutes later, I'm all finished and dusting the strays from his neck.

"How's that?" I offer him a hand mirror before spinning the chair around so he can inspect the back.

"Looks good, Firecracker. Thanks."

Mack lowers the mirror and shakes the cape, sandy hair floating to the ground. Then he pulls me onto his lap. I squeal and slap at his broad chest, laughing and kicking my feet.

"What are you doing?"

He answers with a hot kiss, cupping my chin and claiming my mouth with his. I sink into him and get lost in the moment, his strong arms holding me tight against his body. After a long minute, he pulls away and runs his thumb over my lower lip, his gaze serious.

"Kissing my girlfriend."

My stomach swoops.

Girlfriend.

It's been a hot minute since anyone's referred to me as his girlfriend. And it's never been someone as gorgeous as Mack.

Be careful, Gracelyn. You're not girlfriend material, not really.

A warning voice chides, but I silence the inner bitch. I'm tired of listening to her. Everything about this—about us—feels right. So, so right. Better than anything I've ever known.

Now's not the time to stop taking chances.

"Oh, I like the sound of that, Daddy."

Mack growls, his pupils growing wider and impossibly dark as he squeezes my upper thigh. A bolt of pleasure zings straight to my clit.

"What did I tell you about that? Pretty sure your mom's gonna notice if we don't make it to dinner. But if you keep it up, I'm not going to be able to resist burying myself in your sweet little pussy."

Heat unfurls in my belly as a soft groan falls from my lips.

"Right, dinner. Let's eat fast, okay? No need to play twenty questions with my mother. Besides, I'd much rather skip to dessert." I trace my tongue along my lower lip seductively and now it's Mack's turn to groan.

"You really don't want to get to dinner, do you, Fire-cracker?"

I giggle, wiggling out of his grasp and standing. "Not really. But I'll never hear the end of it from my mother. C'mon, let's get this over with."

Unclasping the cape, I free Mack from the salon chair and sweep up as quickly as I can. Then I take him by the hand and lead him through the salon to the kitchen.

Rounding into the bright room, I immediately regret the impromptu invite.

My mother's set out my grandmother's good china and a bottle of champagne's chilling on the counter.

Tell me it's been forever since you've had a boyfriend without telling me it's been forever since you've had a boyfriend.

"Mom, you didn't need to go to all this trouble." I motion at the decked-out table, the white linen napkins and the champagne flutes.

"What? Of course I did! It's not every day that your only daughter brings home a handsome boyfriend!" My mom bats her eyes at Mack, and hot humiliation washes over me.

"Thanks, Mrs. Reynolds. I didn't mean to put you out,

though. Anything I can do to help?" Mack tips his head toward my mom standing at the stove, his voice sincere.

"No, no, definitely not. Have a seat and Gracie will get you a drink." My mom waves her hand in my direction, not-at-all subtly directing me to open the champagne.

Good gravy.

This is beyond embarrassing. Honestly, I'd love to melt into the wooden floorboards right now and disappear until after dinner's over.

Since that's not a feasible option, I grab the wine from the counter and peel off the foil wrapper. Wedging the bottle against my stomach, I aim away from Mack and my mom and try to pry the cork out.

It doesn't budge, not even a little bit.

"Shit," I mutter, yanking at the stopper. I struggle for another solid thirty seconds and sweat beads at my hairline.

"Let me." Mack stands and takes the champagne from my hands, wiggling the cork from side to side before popping it off. A tiny sigh escapes from the bottle along with an exhale of white mist.

Damn. He made that look easy.

I snag the flutes from the table, and he pours each of us a glass of sparkly champagne.

"Thanks." I accept the beverage gratefully, downing half of the wine before he sets the bottle down. Figure I'm going to need the liquid boost to sit through this meal.

"So…how long have you two been together?" My mom screws up her lips and gives me a pointed stare.

Mack clears his throat and takes a big slug of his drink, so I field question number one.

"A little while. Not long really. Although if Jamie Ware

happens to mention it, we've been together since this summer."

"This summer?" My mom's brows crush in confusion. "What?"

"It's a long and twisty story." I shake my head and Mack chuckles. "Don't worry about the details."

"Hmmm." My mother shoots me a disapproving look, then pivots back to the saucepan. "Dinner is ready."

Turning off the heat, she brings the spaghetti sauce and pasta over to the table. I grab the salad and a basket of garlic bread, and the three of us settle in for dinner.

"Smells great, Mrs. Reynolds. Thanks for cooking." Mack spreads his napkin over his lap, perfectly at ease sitting down to a semi-formal dinner with my mother.

"Oh, my pleasure. I'm always happy to entertain Gracie's friends." She puts special emphasis on the word *friends,* beaming at him, and a tiny part of me dies inside.

This is so fucking awkward. Reminding me exactly why I don't introduce guys to my mom and I sure as hell don't have them over for dinner. Well, that and the fact that no guy ever sticks around long enough to get invited.

"Please, go ahead and start." My mother slides the salad bowl across to Mack, and I reach over and pluck a piece of garlic bread from the basket. Shooting me the evil eye, she snatches the basket away and offers it to Mack instead. "Fresh bread?"

Oh geez. Now she's acting like the perfect Southern hostess, which couldn't be further from the truth. Dinner with my mom typically involves the microwave and some frozen entrée we shovel straight out of the plastic container onto paper plates.

Holding in my eye roll, I chug the rest of my champagne and pour another glass.

"Want some?" I slosh the bottle in the air at Mack.

"I'm good for now."

"Suit yourself." I sip at the golden bubbly and wait until Mack's plate is full before I attempt to serve myself.

"So Mack, tell me about your future plans." Mom twirls spaghetti on her fork as I turn the same shade as the tomato sauce.

"Mom—" I hiss, kicking her foot under the table.

Mack ignores the kerfuffle and the rattling plates, taking the interrogation in stride.

"What do you want to know?"

"Oh, anything. You're planning on staying in Thunder Creek, right?"

He nods. "Yes, ma'am. I have no intention of moving anytime soon. Business is good and I'm happy at the high school."

"That's great." Mom beams at him, her head bobbing up and down like a plastic bobblehead figurine on the dashboard. "And what about family?" She cocks a brow at him and it's official. I'm literally dying. Call 911. Actually, please don't. I'd rather not be resuscitated after this. I'm way too mortified.

"My family all lives in Augusta." Mack dodges the question my mother intended—the one about *his* plans for a family—instead focusing on his parents.

Well played, Mack. Well played.

"Lovely area down there. Who all's down there? You mom and dad? Any brothers or sisters?"

"One younger sister, a few years behind me."

"Older than Gracie, though."

Oh for fuck's sake.

"Yes, older than Gracelyn. But only by a few years."

"And do you want children? In the future?"

"Mother!" My fork clatters to my plate at her audacity. "Leave him alone."

"It's fine. I never seriously considered having a family before. But I'm not ruling it out."

My mom's mouth tips up into a slow smile. "Good to hear. Gracie's my only child and I've been patiently waiting for a grandbaby."

"No pressure..." I grumble, staring at my spaghetti. My stomach churns as I wilt with humiliation, way too stressed to eat. I thought the baby talk would be postponed at least one dinner, but I guess I overestimated my mother.

"I wanted more children..." Mom gazes wistfully into space. "But then Gracie's father got sick and passed."

"I'm sorry." Mack shifts in his seat. Probably regretting his acceptance of the dinner invitation. We went from babies to death in one quick zigzag.

This is way more than he bargained for.

Mom waves her hand, the fork zipping through the air. "What's done is done. It wasn't meant to be. But I am looking forward to some baby Gracies running around."

"Oh-kay..." I interrupt before she flat-out asks about a wedding date. "Mom, I saw Mrs. Gillingham at the drugstore. She told me the two of you were going to be playing pickleball together."

"Yes, we are! She's starting up a Ladies League. You should come—it's great exercise and we have a nice group."

A vision of chasing around after a yellow ball, sweating my ass off with my mom's friends pops into my head.

"Thanks for the invite, I'll keep it in mind." I set my fork down, shoving my plate away. "Dinner was great, Mom. Can I help with the dishes?"

"No, no. You and Mack relax. I'll put on some coffee and we can have dessert."

"Oh, I'm stuffed, Mrs. Reynolds. The pasta was fantastic, but I can't eat another bite." Mack folds his napkin into a tidy square.

"Same. I hate to eat and run, Mom. But I've got to get going." I shove away from the table and start stacking plates.

"So soon?" Mom pops her lip out in a full-on pout.

"Yeah. It's been a long day."

"Alright. Leave the plates, I can clean up. It was wonderful seeing you, Mack. Don't be a stranger!"

To my horror, my mother pops out of her chair and gives Mack a tight squeeze. He clumsily pats her shoulder with his huge hand.

"Great seeing you as well, Mrs. Reynolds. Thanks for having me."

I rush to his rescue before my mother starts stroking his chest or doing something else equally embarrassing.

"Hate to break this up, but I've got to get going. C'mon, Mack." I untangle the two of them and drag Mack out of the kitchen, saving him from the lovefest.

"Sorry about that," I murmur as he laces his fingers with mine.

"It's fine. I like your mom." He squeezes my hand and I feel slightly better about the dinner.

"She can be a lot."

"Y'all are so different." Mack glances at me, chuckling, and I elbow him hard in the ribs.

"Not funny. You giving me a ride home or what?" I stare out at the street, remembering my car's still in the lot at Mustang's.

"Can you drive?" Mack asks and I remember the half bottle of champagne I chugged at dinner.

"Good point. Probably not."

"You can stay over." His voice is low, his pupils wide. Almost like he's nervous to ask me.

Heart pounding hard, my stomach flip-flops.

Mack invited me to stay the night with him.

"You sure?"

"I wouldn't have offered if I wasn't sure, Firecracker. Or you can stay with your mom, if you'd rather."

"I'll stay with you."

"Good. For a second there, I thought I might lose out to your mother."

His lips quirk and I laugh, my chest light and my heart lighter. Despite my mom's best efforts, Mack doesn't seem like he's changing his mind about us.

Us.

I really, really like the sound of that.

CHAPTER 18
GRACELYN

Homecoming week in Thunder Creek is a holiday, just like Christmas, Thanksgiving, and Easter. Stores close early and everyone in town has Friday off, except for students, teachers, and hairstylists.

The week's super busy for me, what with all the ladies wanting to look their best for the big game and then the Hoco dance the following night.

No rest for the weary, I swear.

But this year, there's a double silver lining brightening up hell week. For one, Sloane's back in town with Cam, which is amazing and I can't wait to squeeze her. And second, Mack and I are hard launching our relationship.

I'm excited and nervous about it at the same time.

Of course, Sloane already knows everything. From the first kiss to the embarrassing spaghetti supper with my mom, she's been in the loop every step of the way. She told Cam, too, so at least I won't have to backtrack and fill in all the details.

But other than Sloane, Cam, and my mom, I'm not sure

anyone else really knows about the two of us. We've stayed home most nights, preferring sexy time over dinner dates.

That all changes tonight.

For the first time, Mack and I will be together. In public. Legitimately, not in an impromptu fake dating scenario to save face.

I hope I don't throw up, I'm so nervous.

Spritzing anti-frizz spray on my hair, I run my fingers through the curls and pray it doesn't so much as mist tonight. Even though we're deep into fall, it's still Georgia. Humidity's high here practically year-round.

Satisfied with my efforts, I apply blush to the apples of my cheeks, then contour and highlighter. I swipe a taupe shadow over my eyelids and add a smoky effect with a slightly darker shade. Shaking my hand to dispel the nerves, I pencil on black eyeliner. Two swipes of waterproof mascara, a coat of pink lip gloss, and I'm good to go.

I smile at myself in the mirror, happy with the reflection. Hair and makeup are on point, and I don't have to worry about my outfit tonight. I'm wearing my Thunder Creek T-shirt and my favorite pair of jeans with sneakers, just like everyone else.

Knock, knock, knock.

Hurrying to the door, I swing it wide open and there's Sloane. She's absolutely radiant, her face lightly tanned from the Florida sun. Her long brown hair cascades over her shoulders in loose waves and I've never seen her look happier.

"Eek!" I scream, jumping up and down and hugging my bestie with everything I've got. "Sloane! I'm so happy to see you! You too, Cam." I pop my head around to acknowledge the handsome hulking football star of a fiancé standing beside her. He's equally tan, every inch of him fit and muscular. They're a picture-perfect couple, right down to the matching Thunder Creek T-shirts.

"Same, Gracelyn." Cam shoves a hand in his pocket and waits patiently for the two of us to get all our hugs out. The man's perfect, I swear.

"You ready to go?" Sloane asks when we finally stop squeezing each other.

"Yep. Let's go." I grab the keys and lock the door, then we all clamber into Cam's Range Rover and head toward the high school.

"So, how's Florida?" I lean forward, popping my head over the center console.

"Hot," Cam says, rolling his window down. "But you can't beat the beach."

"Do you like the new team, Cam?"

He nods. "I do. The coaches are great and the guys are solid. So far, so good."

"That's awesome."

Sloane swivels to face me. "Enough about us—what's going on here?"

A blush creeps up my neck and I'm glad it's dark outside. "Not too much."

"Not too much?" Sloane squeals. "Except you're dating my dad's best friend!"

"Yeah, I didn't have that one on my bingo card," Cam says, sliding into the parking lot. "Mack's a cool guy, though. Helluva a baller, back in the day. And he's a great coach."

I forgot that Cam worked with him this past summer. Mainly he trained with Coach Carter, but Cam practiced with the entire high school team before he got the offer from Fort Lauderdale.

"The team's having a great season so far." My heart rate picks up as we weave our way through the nearly full parking lot.

A few people spot Cam and we're instantly surrounded by a throng of people fawning over him, asking questions about the new team.

I lean close to Sloane. "Does this happen everywhere you go?"

"Mm-hmm. We don't go out that much, to be honest, unless we're with the team. It's easier to stay home than deal with fans."

"Ohhh, fans," I tease and she giggles.

"I know, it's weird to say that out loud."

Sloane and I wait patiently while Cam signs autographs, then Sloane whispers something in his ear and he breaks away. Together, we make our way toward the endless queue in front of the stadium. We're standing in line when one of the boosters spots us—I don't know if it's Sloane as the coach's daughter or Cam the football star that catches her eye. Maybe both of them, the power couple of Thunder Creek. Either way, the nice booster mom pops over and grabs us out of the line, ushering us through the crowd.

"Nice perk, guys." I tag along behind them, thrilled to bypass the mile-long queue and be inside the stadium.

"Every once in a while, Cam comes through." Sloane beams up at him, and I swear the two of them have hearts in their eyes like freaking emojis.

Normally, I'd feel a tiny bit jealous of the two of them and what they have going on between them.

But not tonight.

Because tonight I have a man of my own and I'm sure I'll have matching heart eyes soon enough.

We wait in yet another line for concessions, buying big bags of popcorn and cold bottles of water before climbing the metal bleachers. After a solid seven minutes of searching, we find a spot. Tonight's especially tough because everyone in town's here and the three of us get stopped a million times on the way up. Finally, we take a seat next to Meg, the quarterback's mom.

"Hi, Meg!" Sloane leans over and gives her a hug.

"Hey! I was hoping y'all would make it. Hi, Cam, Gracelyn." Meg waves at us. "Langley will be so glad you're here."

"Heard he's having a great season." Cam smiles over at her and she beams, tucking her hair behind her ear.

"He's doing good. Coach Carter's amazing." Meg's cheeks flush when she mentions Sloane's dad, her voice going breathy with admiration.

I swear she also has heart eyes.

Damn, it's contagious around here.

"He's a fantastic coach. Best out there." Cam squeezes Sloane's thigh and she grins at him.

If I were still single, I'd be gagging at the way the two of them are so head over heels for each other.

"Everyone get to your feet and welcome the Thunder Creek Mustangs to the field!" The announcer booms over the loudspeaker and the bleachers shake as the crowd rises, clapping and cheering. The band plays the opening notes of the fight song and we all sing the familiar tune.

I scan the field for Mack, spotting him at the end of the line of players rushing onto the field. He glances up into the stands and we lock eyes as he walks over to his place on the sideline. I take a chance and shoot him a small wave. He tips his chin up at me, the corner of his mouth lifting.

The man is fine, no two ways about it. The navy-blue Thunder Creek sweatshirt stretches taut across his chest and tonight he's wearing joggers, showcasing his very firm ass.

An ass I can't wait to hit later tonight.

"Everyone cheer for the home team!" The announcer's loud voice cuts into my fantasy as the dance team kicks and gyrates across the field.

And there's freaking Jamie, flipping her dark red hair and batting her lashes at Mack.

Of course she is.

Anything to get under my skin.

But Mack's focused on the game now as the team takes the field and he totally ignores her. Lightning Ridge has the ball first, so his sole attention is on coaching the defense. He could care less about Jamie Ware, no matter how much she wiggles her tits in his face.

We're off to a good start, stopping the other team on every play. They don't score and now we have possession of the ball.

"Let's go, Thunder Creek!" Sloane cups her hands and cheers with the crowd. Cam leans forward, elbows on his knees, his brow furrowed. Meg wrings her hands. The ball's snapped and Langley steps back, reading the field. He throws a perfect spiral to the wide receiver and we gain a ton of yards.

"Woo!" I yell. "Go, Langley!"

Every play's perfect and before long, Thunder Creek scores. We go for two and now the score's eight to nothing.

"Great start to the game, Meg." Sloane clasps her hand and Meg smiles gratefully.

"He's so nervous. I'm happy they scored. Always good to put points on the board early."

Cam nods. "For sure."

Lightning Ridge fights back hard and manages to score on the next possession. Mack's shoulders hunch forward as he stalks over to the bench, a deep scowl on his face when they kick the extra point.

My gut clenches, a rush of nervousness gripping me. I've never felt anxiety at a football game in my entire life. Usually I don't care one way or the other.

But tonight's different. I want the team—Mack—to win. This is a big game and he's been staying up late, working on plays and watching film, for weeks. I know it's not life or death or anything, but still. The team's worked hard and I want this victory for them.

We get the ball again, but Langley throws an interception and Lightning Ridge runs into the end zone and scores.

"Shoot," I mumble, worry swirling in my stomach along with the popcorn.

"Oh, Langley." Meg shakes her head, her hands working overtime. At this rate her skin's gonna be raw by the end of the game.

Mercifully, the kicker misses the extra point. But we're still losing.

"And that takes us to halftime. The score's eight to thirteen, with Lightning Ridge in the lead."

The Lightning Ridge band marches out and the halftime show begins as our team files off the field. Mack stalks away, head down, hands shoved deep in his pockets.

The man is pissed.

"It's okay, guys. It's a one score game right now. Plenty of time to win," Cam says, reassuring all of us.

"Right, exactly." I try to sound upbeat. Meg's so pale

I'm afraid she may pass out. "Meg, can I get you anything? A soda? Some candy?"

"No, thank you. I'm fine." She stares blankly at the field as the Thunder Creek cheerleaders cartwheel out for the halftime show.

A few people stop by to say hi to Cam and Sloane, and I mingle with folks I've known my entire life.

Finally, halftime's over and both teams rush back onto the field. All the coaches seem focused, especially Mack. He's flipped his hat forward, a surefire sign that he means business.

Thunder Creek gets the ball first and Langley throws a perfect spiral down the field.

"Yes! Great pass!" Cam cheers and Sloane and I high-five, bubbly excitement rippling through me.

The wide receiver's tackled near the end zone, but we gain a first down. Somehow, we don't manage to score, though, with Lightning Ridge rushing. Langley's down and Meg springs from the bleacher, her hand flying to her mouth.

Langley shakes it off, rising and limping over to the sideline. He takes a seat on the bench, unfastens his helmet. Sloane rubs Meg's back as the defense jogs out to the field.

"Let's go, Thunder Creek!" I scream, chest tight with nerves.

Mack paces, his hand covering his lips as he calls the plays. We hold them at bay, and I pump my fist in the air as the other team shuffles off the field.

I check the clock. Somehow, it's already the fourth quarter and Thunder Creek's still down by five points. Defense on both teams has been solid, keeping the score low. But now, we desperately need a touchdown.

We don't get one.

Langley's blitzed again, then he can't find an open receiver. Coach Carter calls a timeout, and the stadium's quiet as everyone stares at the scoreboard.

Finally, our team hustles back onto the field. Langley throws a quick pass to avoid getting rushed again, but the receiver's tackled before he can gain any kind of yardage.

Five minutes left in the game and we're still losing.

Mack's waving at the defense as they line up, his shoulders square. Tension's high and palpable in the cool air as Lightning Ridge makes the snap. Our defense moves and stops the ball.

"Yes!" Sloane high-fives me. "My dad's going to be happy with Mack, at least. He's made some great calls tonight."

"We've been studying film all week."

"Have you really?" Sloane's brows fly up in surprise.

"Well, he's been watching film. I mostly make popcorn and scroll Instagram on my phone. But I picked up a thing or two."

Sloane laughs. "That sounds more like the Gracelyn I know. Good to see not everything's changed since I left."

"The score is still thirteen to eight with two minutes left in the game. Thunder Creek has the ball." The announcer broadcasts the obvious, and I swear the entire stadium holds one collective breath.

This is probably our last offensive possession, our last chance to score. Sloane grabs Meg's hand to keep her from permanently damaging her skin, and Langley and the offensive line get ready. Ball in hand, he throws a quick pass to the left. The receiver gains a few yards, but not enough for a first down.

"Damn it," Meg mutters, and I huff out a quick sigh.

"Not over yet, Meg," Cam says, his voice calm and reassuring.

Langley winds back and tosses a perfect pass down the field, finding the wide receiver. I hop to my feet and cheer.

"Yes, let's go, Thunder Creek!"

The crowd erupts as we finally score, the cheerleaders chanting our victory cheer. Cam and Sloane kiss, and I high-five Meg.

"As long as we don't do anything wacky in the next thirty seconds, that should do it." Cam points to the scoreboard as the numbers flip.

If I thought I was nervous before, I was mistaken. Every muscle in my body's coiled tight as the defense takes the field one last time. Mack's waving his arms through the air, calling the play.

I hold my breath as the clock ticks down. The quarterback hurls a long pass down the field, but Mack's coverage is superior. Our guy leaps into the air, knocking the ball down.

Ten, nine, eight.

One last pass, but the quarterback can't get it done.

"And Thunder Creek wins fourteen to thirteen!" the announcer shouts, and the crowd erupts into the fight song, the bass notes of the tuba swelling and the dance team turning flips.

"Great game, Meg!" Sloane hugs Langley's mom, the color finally returning to her cheeks.

"Whew, I'm so relieved, y'all." She huffs out a breath, and Cam laughs.

"Guess this is how my parents feel every game."

"Absolutely." Meg tucks her hair behind her ear and waves at Langley, who's beaming on the sideline. "I have to get down there. Thanks for the moral support."

"Anytime." Sloane gives her arm a pat, then Meg hurries down the steps to hug her son.

"Gracelyn, I think someone's looking for you." Sloane taps my shoulder and I follow her gaze. Sure enough, Mack's peering up into the stands.

"Go ahead. We'll wait for you." She gives me a little push and I skip down the bleachers, my heart thundering in my chest.

For the first time, a guy's waiting for me on the football field of Thunder Creek High, and I couldn't be happier about it.

CHAPTER 19
MACK

"That game was wild." Sloane slips into the only available booth at Mustang's, a quiet spot in the corner. Well, quiet's a stretch. The bar's packed after we won the Homecoming game, filled to bursting with parents, alums—pretty much anyone in town over the age of twenty-one. All the kids'll be out at the lake, whooping it up and doing things I'd rather not know about. In here, the grown-ups laugh, talk, legally drink, and watch the highlights of the game on the television above the bar.

Cam scoots in next to Sloane so Gracelyn moves to the other side of the table, taking the corner spot. I slide in beside her, and Carter pauses for a second before pulling up a chair at the end of the booth.

"Lightning Ridge played well. I knew they were tough, but that game was way closer than I wanted it to be." Carter lifts his ball cap, smoothing his hair back before popping it back on again.

"Way closer," I agree. "I'm glad the defensive line

managed to stop them. If they scored there at the end, it was over for us."

"Nice job on the defense, Mack." Cam casually loops his arm around Sloane's shoulders, tipping his chin at me in acknowledgement. "Those were some good moves you used, especially in the fourth quarter. Number 87 jumping to smack that ball down? Classic."

"All those burpees coming in handy," I joke, and Cam chuckles.

"Hate those things with a fiery passion. But maybe there's a method to the madness." Cam shakes his head, grimacing. "Not doing burpees is gonna be a highlight of retirement for me, not gonna lie."

"I get it. Haven't done one since I graduated college."

Which was a long damn time ago. But I'm not about to bring that up right now, not in front of Gracelyn.

Luckily, a waitress interrupts to take our order and we quickly move away from the topic of college and aging. Something I'd rather not think about on a normal day, let alone in the context of Gracelyn.

She's never said anything negative about our age difference, but sitting here tonight with her and her friends, there's a different vibe. Amplified by the fact that *my* friend at this table is Sloane's dad.

I suppose pairings like us happen every day, especially in a small town. But it's still kind of strange and takes some getting used to.

The waitress returns with our order—we get great service, on account of winning the game—and we all raise our drinks in celebration.

"To victory." Carter clinks his bottle with mine, unspoken mutual regard flowing between us. It's nice feeling appreciated, especially when the man is a legend in his own right.

"Cheers!" Gracelyn taps my bottle with her glass of tequila, her hand resting on my thigh beneath the table. She beams up at me, a shimmery twinkle in her eye and a soft blush on her cheeks.

Don't fuck this up, Mack.

She's so enthusiastic, so innocent and unjaded. Up until now, everything with Gracelyn's been fun and flirty. Sexy. But tonight feels different, more loaded. It's probably just me being paranoid, but it's like I'm under a microscope, the bright neon bar lights burning my face.

I don't much care for the feeling.

"Mack, did you volunteer to chaperone the dance?" Sloane's voice cuts through my thoughts.

"What? Hell no. Did you, Carter?"

He shrugs. "Volunteer, no. Get volunteered, yes."

I let out a hearty belly laugh. "Oh boy. How'd you get roped into that?"

"The student council advisor called me frantic because Mrs. Potter went home sick on Thursday. I'm taking her spot."

"Sorry, man. That's rough." I take a sip of my beer, happy that it's Carter and not me going to the high school dance.

"They needed two volunteers. I offered up your name. Figured you'd be available."

I sputter on my drink, choking as the hoppy liquid flows down the wrong pipe. "What? For real?"

"Baker was supposed to take it. But Lindsey's having Braxton Hicks and he's worried about leaving her two nights in a row and for that amount of time. Doctor told her to avoid being on her feet for too long, just to be on the safe side."

"Oh, for fuck's sake." Hot aggravation whirls in my gut as my mind pulls up a vision of a dark cafeteria, high school kids screaming and doing choreographed dances to whatever trash music's popular these days. But I can't very well say no to our friend and his pregnant fiancée.

Out of the corner of my eye, I watch as disappointment flashes across Gracelyn's face. I know she wants to hang out after work tomorrow, possibly with Cam and Sloane.

Frankly, I want to spend every possible second with her too. If I have to chaperone a bunch of kids in the cafeteria, listening to lyrics I can't decipher, I at least want my girl by my side. Maybe not the most romantic date ever, but we can probably sneak in a slow dance or two. Holding her curvy little body against mine and swaying to a slow beat does sound appealing.

I spin to face Gracelyn, ignoring the loud whoosh of blood roaring in my ears and the heat licking up my neck.

"Gracelyn, will you go to the Homecoming dance with me?"

The brightest smile I've ever fucking seen lights up her face, golden beams of sunlight shooting straight through her.

"Yes! I'd love to go to the dance with you." She doesn't hesitate at all, throwing her arms around my neck and kissing me square on the lips right in front of everyone. Sloane, Cam, Carter—hell, the entire fucking bar. "This is going to be so amazing," she murmurs and I panic for a second, hoping I'm not about to let her down big time.

"Just to set your expectations low—I'm not a good dancer. Don't remember the last time I set foot on a dance floor, in fact."

"That's fine. I'll lead."

Despite my nerves, I can't help but chuckle.

"Good luck with that." Carter gazes at the two of us in amusement. "For an athlete, this guy's got two left feet. I've never seen anything like it."

"I'm sure she's danced with worse," Sloane says and Gracelyn nods, agreeing.

"For real. This is going to be so fun!" Gracelyn bounces in the tiny booth and I hope her expectations don't far exceed the reality of going to a high school dance with me.

CHAPTER 20
GRACELYN

can't believe I'm going to the Hoco dance with Mack tonight. I haven't been to a dance since college, and I've never had a date like Mack—big and strong enough to carry me, a real man. Someone I can lean on, count on. Bonus points for smelling like freshly sawed plywood and pine, a strangely intoxicating combination.

Last night after Mustang's, Sloane and I spent an hour combing through my closet for something to wear while the guys talked football. We debated back and forth between a few options, but the long black satin V-neck ultimately won. Sloane swears it shows off my curves and is the perfect dress for the occasion. Due to both time and budget constraints, I'm choosing to believe her.

Now I have to get through one last updo of the day before I race home to shower and style my own hair.

"What do you think?" I spin Avery, a junior at Thunder Creek, around and hand her the mirror. She tips her head side to side, taking in every angle.

"I like it. The butterflies are finally in the right spot."

We've been fighting about where to place the sparkly hairpins for the last thirty minutes. Thank goodness I finally nailed it because it's getting late.

"Fab! Have your mom close out the bill up front, okay?"

"Okay, Ms. Gracelyn! Thanks so much!" Avery pops out of the chair and I clean up my area, officially off-duty for the rest of the weekend.

My feet hurt and my arms ache from using the blow dryer all day, but it's nothing a hot shower won't fix.

"Bye, Mom!" I shout, dashing down the hall. "See you later!"

I only have an hour to get ready before Mack picks me up. Racing home, I hop into the shower, turning the temp all the way up to scalding. The pulsing water does the trick, easing the knots in my neck and shoulders, and I'm finally relaxed.

Much as I'd love to stay in longer, I hop out and dry off, apply lotion. Wrapping my hair in a towel, I pad to my room to get dressed. I fish through my drawer for the matching black V-string and lacy bra set and shimmy my way into the lingerie. Then I slip into the sleek satin dress, zipping it up.

Sloane's right. This dress looks good on me. The main focus is my cleavage, drawing attention away from my squishy midsection. I fasten a diamond drop necklace, along with matching earrings. Two spritzes of perfume, one on each wrist, and I'm ready for hair and makeup.

I flip the blow dryer on, turning the diffuser on my curls. After an eternity, my hair's dry and I spin the top section into a chic half-up chignon. Clipping it with a long silver hairpin, I move to makeup. I go shimmery on my eyes and add three coats of mascara for a dramatic evening look. Blush, contour, highlighter, and a swipe of nude lipstick complete the look.

Slipping on black strappy heels, I'm ready, with five minutes to spare. I snap a selfie and send it to Sloane, then pour a glass of wine while I wait.

Bestie: OMG, you look HOT!

I text her back a smiley face emoji and grin at my cell, warmth spreading through my chest.

Bestie: Have the BEST time

Gracelyn: Will do

Bestie: Keep an eye on my dad

I laugh. *Oh, how the tables have turned.* Used to be our parents worrying about us—now it's the reverse.

Gracelyn: I will. Don't worry—not much trouble you can get into at a high school dance

Bestie: IDK. There are a few teachers over there who are absolutely feral for him

Gracelyn: Well, he is pretty good looking

Bestie: Eww. That's my DAD, Grace

Gracelyn: Just saying—I can see the appeal

Gracelyn: But I understand. I'll watch out for him

Knock, knock, knock.

Gracelyn: Gotta jet. Mack's here

Bestie: Have fun! Luv ya!

Taking a deep breath, I suck in my stomach and open the door.

"Wow. You look…amazing." Mack's voice is low and husky as his eyes rake over my body, lingering on my chest. "Wow."

"Thanks. You look pretty damn handsome yourself."

And he does. I've never seen him dressed up before, not in all the time he's lived next door to my mom.

I didn't think he could get any hotter.

I was wrong.

The fancy clothes tip him into a whole new stratosphere of gorgeous. His dark blue suit fits him perfectly—it has to be custom tailored to stretch over those broad shoulders. His sandy waves are slightly gelled and brushed back from his face, his facial hair neatly trimmed, highlighting his strong jawline.

"Thanks. These are for you." Mack hands me a stunning bouquet of red and white roses tied with a chic black satin ribbon.

"Aww, sweet. Thanks. I'll put them in a vase real quick, then we can go."

I hurry to the kitchen and drop the roses into a vase, leaning in and taking a quick sniff.

Mack brought me roses.

I can't remember the last time a man brought me flowers. My heart hammers, fizzy excitement bubbling inside me.

"Ready?" I cut the lights and Mack takes my arm, leading me out to his truck and helping me into the cab.

"You mentally prepared for a night of fruit punch and noisy high schoolers?" His gravelly voice sends an electric thrill racing up and down my spine.

"Absolutely. Sounds like a great night." I shoot him a wide smile.

"You're a strange girl, Gracelyn Reynolds. But I'm glad you'll be with me."

He backs down the driveway and I relax into the well-worn leather seat, warm happiness flushing my chest.

This man could be the one for me.

One hand on the wheel, Mack reaches over and brings my hand to his mouth, brushing my fingers lightly with his lips. The warm exhale of his breath dusts my skin and I'm struck by the sweet gesture. So small, so slight, yet so tender. Hot tears prick at the corners of my eyes, threatening my three coats of mascara.

"I'm glad you asked me." I gaze over at him, the masculine scent of pine winding around me and lulling me into a Mack-stupor. The same stupor that sends my pulse into overdrive and floods my panties with even the most innocuous touch.

"Firecracker, there's no one in the world I'd rather have with me at the Homecoming dance than you." He cuts his deep green eyes at me and my breath hitches in my throat, heart pounding. That's the sweetest thing a man's ever said to me in my whole damn life.

Still, I take a slow breath, a little reminder not to get ahead of myself. I should stay grounded, realistic. Remember I'm not the star of a real-life rom-com, ready to be swept away in a glittery carriage by Prince Charming.

But damn, that's hard to do sitting next to Mack. He

looks every bit the part of my prince and I've never felt more like Cinderella in my life.

Hopefully I don't lose my strappy heel when the clock strikes midnight. I really love these shoes.

"Here we are. Let's do this." Mack parks in the school parking lot and the two of us make our way toward the cafeteria.

Music blares from speakers set up on the stage and the room's dim, the usual bright fluorescent lights replaced by strobing spotlights aimed at the makeshift dance floor. A clump of brave high schoolers moves as one in the center of the floor, while a few chaperones stand off to the side chatting.

"There's Carter." Mack points to the refreshment table.

Sure enough, Sloane's dad's standing guard next to the punch bowl, a hand shoved deep in his suit pocket. A couple female teachers hover nearby, but no one's boldly hitting on him. Not yet, anyway.

Mack and I circumvent the dance floor and join Coach Carter at the refreshment table.

"Y'all want some punch?" Coach Carter waves a hand at the giant plastic bowl of red liquid.

"I'm gonna pass. Thanks, though." Mack plucks two mini bottles of water from the table, handing one to me. "It's louder in here than Mustang's."

"What?" Coach Carter shouts and I giggle.

"Exactly my point." Mack unscrews the lid of the water and takes a long chug. "How long does this thing go again?"

"Only until ten. You'll be home before your bedtime, don't worry." Coach Carter folds his arms over his chest, surveying the dance floor.

"Isn't that the quarterback, Langley? And his mom? We

sat with her at the game." I point to the two of them standing on the opposite side of the dance floor.

"Yes, that's them." Coach Carter tips his head at the pair, both waving shyly in our direction.

"Langley brought his mom to the dance?" I scrunch up my nose at the concept. Even I wasn't that hard up for a date back in high school.

"No, she works here. In the front office. I'm sure she got roped into chaperoning too. Langley doesn't seem too happy about it either."

"Definitely not." I take a sip of water as Langley takes a huge step away from his mother, creating a wide berth. Meg tucks her hair behind her ear and glances around the room nervously. I take a chance and wave her over.

"Hey, Meg. Love your dress." I motion at her sparkly silver minidress. A bold statement for a mom of a teenager, but she looks great.

"Thanks. Langley wasn't a lot of help in the dress department." Her cheeks flush bright pink, noticeable even in the dark room.

"Boys, am I right?"

She laughs at that, her shoulders loosening a touch. I notice her sneak a sideways glance at Coach Carter and I remember what Sloane said about women being feral for her dad.

Meg Langley isn't exactly feral, but she's definitely interested.

"Excuse me, but we could use a volunteer or two over by the photo booth." An older woman with a tight gray bun taps Mack on the arm. "Would you mind?"

He shrugs. "No problem. See y'all."

Mack slides his hand around my waist and we walk over to the massive balloon arch. A photographer's snapping pics, the flash popping every few seconds. We monitor the line, making sure no one gets rowdy or flips off the camera.

Eventually, there's a lull in the action. The photographer lowers his camera, taking a quick breather.

"You two want a photo?" He eyes us, waving us over to the arch.

"I'd love one, thanks!" Grabbing Mack by the hand, I drag him into the center of the display as the photographer lifts the camera.

"That's nice." The flash pops once, twice. "Now, get closer. That's good. The gentleman needs to stand behind the lady, right. Like that. Wrap your arms around her waist and she leans back against you. Good."

Click, click, click.

"Last pose. The lovely lady rests her hand on the gentleman's chest and looks up at him. The gentleman drops his hand to her hip. Good. Hold it."

My breath catches as I stare deep into Mack's eyes, the photographer snapping away. The way Mack's gazing at me, his expression serious, sends a rush of heat to my belly and sparks light beneath his fingertips.

"You two make a great couple. Here's your photo number." The photographer hands me a paper slip with the details. "Call me when you need wedding photos."

The photographer winks at us and my cheeks flame. The next couple moves into the balloon arch and we step away.

"That was embarrassing," I whisper, moving out of earshot of the cameraman.

"He was a big fan of you." Mack shoots me a sideways glance, taking in my tight dress and my curves.

"Stop! He was not." I smack his biceps, giggling.

"Oh, yeah he was. If I wasn't there, he'd definitely be getting your number." Mack loops his arm around me possessively, pulling me in close to him.

"Good thing I already have the most handsome date in the room."

"Glad I can outperform the high schoolers." Mack squeezes my hip, a sly smile tugging at his mouth.

A slow song comes on and half the dance floor clears out, a few new faces moving in.

"Would you dance with me, Firecracker?" Mack asks.

"Absolutely."

Together we take the floor, sticking to the outer edge. Mack's hand rests at my waist and I wrap my arms around his neck, moving in closer to him. We shuffle back and forth to the beat, our feet perfectly in sync.

"What are you talking about, you're not a good dancer? You're doing great." I run my thumb back and forth on his neck, warmth radiating from his skin.

"That was kinda a lie. My parents forced me into cotillion, so I know a few of the major steps. But dancing's not my core strength."

"Well, I think you're selling yourself short. I've danced with a lot worse."

"I'll be sure to let my mother know. She'll be well pleased to hear the torture paid off."

I giggle as Mack spins me around, twirling me out before bringing me back in close to him. Resting my head on his well-defined chest, I shut my eyes and sway to the music, breathing in his clean scent.

I'm falling for this man.

He's everything I never thought I'd find. Strong, handsome, kind. A good listener, an even better lover.

I can't imagine life without him now that we're together.

The song fades out and the DJ transitions into "The Cupid Shuffle." A throng of high school kids rushes onto the dance floor, jostling us.

"And that's my exit cue. You good?" Mack stares down at me and I nod.

"Yeah. I'm good."

We leave the dance floor and Mack checks his watch. "I have to use the restroom. You?"

"I'm good. Go ahead, I'll be fine."

"You sure?"

"Yeah. I'm a big girl. I'm okay here."

"Okay." He lightly presses his lips to mine, then hustles away to find the bathroom.

Thirsty after dancing, I spin back around to the refreshment table in search of more water. Coach Carter's gone and so are all the mini water bottles.

All that's left at the table is Jamie freaking Ware.

FML.

CHAPTER 21
GRACELYN

S	*hit.*

It's too late. Jamie spots me before I can abort the hydration mission.

"Gracelyn! Fancy meeting you here." She drawls the phrase in her best Southern accent. "Didn't know you were hitting the high school dating pool now."

"Gross, Jamie. I'm not." I square my shoulders, standing as straight and tall as physically possible in these heels. I still qualify for shorty status next to Jamie and her mile-long model legs, though.

Of course, she's beyond stunning in a slinky emerald green dress cut high above the knee and baring her toned arms. The color's great on her, too, a nice contrast to her deep red hair.

Bitch.

"You came to the Hoco dance alone then? Are you on staff now? The hairstylist thing not working out?" She waves her French-manicured nails around my face, motioning at my hair.

"No. And not that I owe you any explanation, but I'm here with Mack. My boyfriend. Remember?"

"Oh, right. How could I forget? I thought y'all were such an odd couple, I assumed you'd broken up by now."

Rude.

"We didn't."

"It's just—he's so good-looking…" Her voice trails off, and she leaves the rest of the statement unsaid, hanging in the air between us.

Sizzling anger bubbles in my gut, my chest tight. I should turn around and walk away, leave her standing there open-mouthed like a dying guppy.

But it's me, so of course I can't do that.

"And?" I fold my arms over my chest, baiting her. Daring her to finish that statement.

"Come on, Gracelyn. You know and I know Mack's way out of your league. He's like a ten and you're…I don't know. Maybe a six, on a good day?"

Ouch.

Jamie's always been a bitch, but this is low, even for her.

Tears stinging my eyes, I jut out my chin. "I'm a seven and a half with personality."

"Fine. I'll give you a bump for being a good sidekick. But really, what does a guy like Mack see in little ole' you?"

"Oh-kay. We're done here. Great to see you, Jamie. Not." I spit out the words and pivot, running straight into Mack's steely chest.

"Hey, I was looking for you. You're hidden by the line dancers." Mack rubs my bare arm and I blink fast and hard, trying to fight back tears. "You okay?"

"Not really," I whisper, cocking my head in Jamie's direction.

"That bitch is still bothering you?" His voice is hard as he stares over my shoulder at Jamie.

I nod, not trusting my shaky voice. I feel so dumb, letting her get to me like this. Like she did back in high school. I thought I'd evolved, but apparently not. And neither has she, that's for damn sure.

"Want me to get her tossed?" Mack flexes his fingers, knuckles cracking, and I shake my head.

"No. That will just cause a scene," I whisper, feeling better already now that Mack's by my side.

"Hey, Mack," Jamie purrs, wiggling her fingers at him as she sidles up to us. "You look nice. Tres handsome."

Guess she picked up some French when she modeled in Europe.

Mack winds his strong arm around my waist, pulling me close to him. Supporting me. Squaring up to her, we're a united front.

"I'm only half as attractive as Gracelyn, but I tried."

Typical Jamie, she tosses her head back, laughing hysterically. Like that's the funniest thing she's ever heard in her whole miserable life.

"You're so cute," she trills, batting her fake lashes at him. Bile rises in my throat and my hands shake. I clasp them together in front of me and pray she doesn't notice the tremor.

"Great game last night, by the way. Y'all make it so easy to get out there on the field and shake our tails for you." She wiggles her hips side to side, as if she actually has a tail.

Oh, for fuck's sake.

"I had a lot of motivation. I knew Gracelyn was

watching." He winks at me and my entire body flushes, heart soaring. "Coach Carter actually needs us." His fingers grip my hip, pulling me away from the table. "Bye, Jamie." Then he ushers me away from my archenemy.

"Thanks," I murmur, relaxing the further away I get from Jamie.

"You bet. She really is terrible."

In spite of my massively hurt feelings, my lips tip into a smile.

"Right? It's not just me."

"Nope. She's giving serious mean girl vibes. And I'm a clueless dude."

"Eh, I wouldn't say you're clueless. What's Coach Carter need?"

"Nothing. I made that up to get away from her."

I smile at him, my heart swelling. "Anyone ever tell you you're the best?"

"Only my nana."

"She's not wrong."

"You ready to get out of here? There's only ten minutes left. I don't think anyone will notice if we dip out early."

"Absolutely."

With his strong arm wrapped around me, we walk out of the cafeteria, leaving behind the flashing lights and the thumping music. Ears ringing, we spill into the dark parking lot and a shiver rolls through me when the cool night air touches my skin.

"You cold?" Mack shrugs out of his jacket and eases the silky fabric over my shoulders, not waiting for my response.

"Thanks."

He helps me into the truck and we drive to my house,

country music playing softly in the background, his hand on my knee.

Back home, I unlock the door and we step inside. Mack wastes no time, unzipping my dress, unwrapping me like a precious gift. The satin garment slips to the ground until I'm standing in only heels and lingerie.

"So damn sexy." He falls to his knees, unbuckling my shoes, and I step out of them. His rough, calloused palms trace up my thighs, all the way to the hot, pulsating center. He kisses through the panties, pulling the tiny scrap of fabric down my legs. Then he resumes worshipping my body—licking through my wetness, his tongue stroking and laving, sucking on my clit. The soft prickle of his stubble tickles my skin and my eyes flutter closed, body swaying. Pushing me higher and higher, closer to the edge.

I thread my fingers through his hair, messing up the perfectly slicked style, freeing the waves.

This is the Mack I know.

More wild, unfettered.

A soft moan falls from my lips as he slides his fingers into me, finds my most sensitive spot. The one that makes me see stars, all buzzy inside.

Gripping his shoulders, I ride his face as he sucks me. Feasting like he'll never get enough. His tongue flicks at my clit and he grips my hips, holding me tight and forcing me to feel everything. The heat, the pressure. There's no escaping the waves of pleasure rolling down my spine and I spasm around his fingers.

Legs trembling, I come for him.

After a long moment, I catch my breath.

"I need you." I moan the words on an exhale, pulling him up off the ground.

Wordlessly, we stumble into the dark bedroom, kissing,

my arms wrapped around his strong neck. He reaches around and unclasps my bra, freeing my breasts.

"Fuck, Gracelyn." His thumb traces the outline of my curves, teasing the nipples into sharp points.

"Get naked." I work to unbutton his shirt, the pace frantic as I undress him as quickly as possible, the tiny round circles standing between me and more bliss. I want to see him, feel his muscles undulating as he rides me. He drops his pants and boxer briefs, pulls off his socks, while I peel the shirt from his body.

"Much better." I run my hand up and down his chest, admiring the ridges of his abs, the defined pecs.

"I agree." His eyes rake over my naked body as he walks me backward to the bed, laying me down gently before climbing on top. "I want to fuck you bare again. Nothing between us tonight."

I don't hesitate.

"Yes."

Pushing a stray hair from my face, Mack locks eyes with me, and it's as if our very souls connect in this moment. My heart pounds, each beat for him and only him.

He pushes into me, joining us together, skin to skin.

Nothing between us. No space, no air.

We are one, moving together in perfect rhythm.

Heat builds, the friction increasing. Muscles tighten, both of our bodies slick with sweat. Our breathing syncs, rough and ragged as we dance closer and closer to the edge.

"Come for me, baby," Mack murmurs, his lips soft against my neck.

His words push me over, and I shatter around him.

"Mack—" I grip the cords of muscles in his shoulders,

digging into his skin as he pistons harder and faster, going impossibly deeper, exploding inside me.

We move together as long as we can, a horizontal dance only the two of us know. Staying joined as long as possible, drawing out the bliss.

Finally, he lays down next to me, pulling me onto his chest.

Neither of us say anything, struggling to catch our breath. I feather my fingers over his chest as I wrestle with all the swelling emotions.

I love this man.

"Thank you," I whisper into the dark, so quiet I'm not sure he'll even hear.

His hand smooths over my back, tracing up and down my spine.

"Thank you, baby."

Tears shimmer in my eyes and I blink back hot tears. This night feels like a dream—the best dream—and I never want to wake up.

CHAPTER 22
GRACELYN

Mack wasn't kidding when he said football season is busy. Between work, practice, and games, the two of us have pretty jam-packed schedules. Since Homecoming, we've both been swamped and have had to squeeze in stolen late-night moments.

I'm between clients, sweeping the floor, when Mack wanders into the salon on Saturday morning.

"Hey." He sneaks up on me, wrapping strong arms around my waist and nuzzling my neck. He smells like soap and freshly cut wood, my tummy swooping at his touch.

"Hey yourself, handsome. What are you doing over here? I still have a few hours left." I lean back, giving him a quick peck on the lips.

"You sure about that?" His deep voice vibrates on my skin and a delicious shiver rolls straight down my spine. I unwind from his embrace to check the appointment calendar on my phone.

Scrolling through the rest of the day, I frown. "Weird.

This never happens. I don't have any more appointments. And I could have sworn I did, too. Sally Anne was coming in for a bridal consult."

"Guess it's my lucky day. Hang up your apron, I have something planned for us." He reaches around and unties my cape.

I bite my bottom lip and narrow my eyes. "You do, huh? This is all starting to feel a bit too coincidental."

He shrugs, the corners of his lips tipping up. "I may have asked your mother for a little help clearing your schedule."

"Mack!" I swat at his broad chest, warm happiness surging through me. "Y'all conspired together?"

"Yep. Sorry, not sorry. I know we've both been busy. And I wanted to take my girl out on a proper date." He grabs my hips, pulling me up against him. My cheeks flush as he kisses me softly on the lips, right there in the salon in front of Mrs. Smith and Mrs. Taylor sitting under the dryers.

"Aww, you're so sweet. Let me hang up my cape and we can get out of here." I sashay away, giving my mom a quick squeeze on the way out the door. "Thanks, Mama. Love you."

"Love you too, Gracie girl. Have a nice time." She beams at me and my chest aches a little. She's the best mom, always looking out for me. She'll have double the work today now, but she still wants me to go and have a good time with Mack.

"Ready?" Mack takes my hand, and I smile up at him as we head out to his truck.

"Where are we going? What are we doing?" My mind's zipping at a mile a minute, whirring through all the possibilities. Excitement zings through me as he pulls away from the curb.

"Thought we'd have a low-key day, just the two of us. Hit the farmer's market, then I'll cook us a nice dinner at my place."

"Sounds amazing." I sit back in the warm leather seat, his huge palm on my thigh, perfectly content as we drive through the neighborhood. We pass house after familiar house, some decorated for the season with oversized autumn wreaths adorning the doors.

The more time Mack and I spend together, the better everything between us feels. Like we were made for each other. He complements me—bringing the calm to my storm, while I pull out the lighter side of him that's buried way deep down.

A few minutes later, we pull up to the town square and Mack parks the truck. White tents dot the lawn, local farmers, florists, and craftspeople selling their wares.

"Oh, I love the farmer's market!" I beam at him as he takes my hand and helps me down. "I hardly ever get to come, but when I do it's always a good time. Hey there, Janie!" I wave to a woman and her toddler and she shoots me a friendly smile.

"Hey, Gracelyn. Great to see you! Love my new look!" Janie smooths her dark hair over her shoulders, and I grin.

"I cut her hair last week. It's a new style and I think it's working for her." I point out the change to Mack and he nods.

"Nice."

Looping his arm around my waist, together we walk across the grass toward the tents. About ten vendors fill the main square, with a few food trucks set up across the field.

"Let's shop, then grab a bite. After, we can head back to my place and chill until dinner."

"Perfect." I lean into him and sigh contentedly, loving how his strong body feels against mine. We pass by face after familiar face. Faces I've known since childhood, yet the entire world seems different right now. New and shiny and full of possibilities.

"I picked steaks up from the grocery and I'll grill them for us. But we need to get vegetables and maybe some bread, a dessert." Mack steers us toward the fruit and veggies at the far end of the market.

Pumpkins of all sizes, squash and zucchini, green beans, tomatoes, and a variety of lettuce spill from large wooden milk crates.

"Hello, Gracelyn. Mack." Beau Milford tips his head at us, touching the brim of his worn baseball cap. He's farmed the land on the outskirts of Thunder Creek for as long as I can remember. The farm's been in his family for generations, providing food to the local grocers in the surrounding counties as well.

"Hey there, Mr. Milford. What would you recommend today?" I survey the selection of tasty vegetables, plucking a bright yellow squash out of the crate.

"Squash is in season. Good choice this time of year. Also the best crop of apples we've had in a while." He reaches into a round wooden container and tosses a shiny red apple to Mack.

"Oh, yes! I can make a good apple crisp. Let's get some apples, and squash sounds good." I peer up at Mack, gauging his response to the plan.

"That works, as long as you're on the apple crisp. I don't know much about baking."

I laugh. "I've got you."

Mr. Milford bags up the squash and apples for us and we move on, checking out handmade jewelry, crocheted blankets, goat cheese and milk, and a nice selection of soaps.

"I think we should grab a loaf of bread, too." Mack stops at the bakery display, the table overflowing with fresh bread, homemade biscuits, and a nice selection of jams.

"Yes, love it." I snatch a loaf of sourdough from the pile.

"That would go great with this peach jam. Try it." Deb Hatter, one of my mom's clients and the local baker extraordinaire, holds out a tiny wooden spoon. Mack takes the spoon from her and lifts it up.

"Taste it, Gracelyn." Mack's husky voice, the way his eyes gleam as he slides the jam into my mouth, sends an electric ripple straight through me.

"Mmm, good," I murmur, licking the sweet jam from my lips as I hold his heated gaze. "Perfect."

Ignoring Deb Hatter, Mack dips down and kisses my sticky lips. Trailing his tongue along the seam, the lingering saccharine scent of peaches mixes with his after-shave. I moan softly into his mouth, the farmer's market falling away until it's just me and Mack standing there, lost in each other.

Finally, he pulls away, swiping his thumb lightly across my bottom lip before turning back to a flustered Mrs. Hatter.

"We'll take the jam and the bread." Mack pays, loading our purchase into the shopping bags filled with produce. "You ready to get some lunch?"

"Sure." I lace my fingers with his and together we cross the field toward the food trucks. We dodge a group of children in a boisterous game of tag, their arms outstretched as they race after each other, laughing.

"That'll be Josh and Lindsey soon." I glance over at the parents standing nearby, watching over their kiddos playing on the lawn.

Mack rolls his shoulders, his face staying neutral. "Yep. Hard to believe."

"I know. Lindsey's my first close friend to have a baby." I sigh wistfully as one of the little boys runs up to his mom and hugs her at the knees.

Mack rubs his thumb across mine. "Do you want to have kids?"

"I think so. Not, like, tomorrow or anything. But some day in the future." I bite my lower lip, suddenly feeling vulnerable. I haven't really talked to anyone about this before—my previous relationships never lasted long enough to entertain a serious conversation like this.

I glance over at him. "What about you?"

He shrugs, his broad shoulders rising. "I'm not sure I'm cut out to be a dad."

"Why?"

"No particular reason, really. I just feel like I'd mess a kid up." The laugh lines around his eyes crinkle as he squints out at the raucous game.

"I don't think that at all. I bet you'd be a great dad. You're good with the football team. Plus, you have real life skills. Any child would be lucky to have you as a father."

His face relaxes and he squeezes my hand. "Thanks, Gracelyn. I appreciate that."

"I'm not just saying that, either. You have all the best dad qualities: you're patient, relaxed, funny, and smart. And you know how to build stuff."

He chuckles as we join the taco line. "I do know how to build stuff. I'm assuming you want tacos?"

"You know it." I smile up at him as a tidal wave of happiness washes over me.

I love this man.

He's strong, yet gentle. Warm, but tough when he needs to be. And he gets me, truly gets me. Because of course I'm picking tacos.

"I love you." The words slip out of my mouth before I can stop them, a bolt of panic racing through me.

Because what if it's too soon?

"I love you too, Gracelyn." Mack snakes his hand around the nape of my neck, bringing his lips down to mine in a soft, slow kiss.

A kiss that means something.

This man is it for me.

Pure, unadulterated joy floods through me, and I'm soaring, my entire body light and airy and bright. I've never felt like this before, so free and happy.

"Thanks for an amazing date," I murmur against his lips.

"You're welcome. I know it's nothing fancy, but I wanted to spend time with you. Just the two of us." He cups my cheek with his large palm and I melt into him.

"Well, the two of us and half of Thunder Creek," I giggle as one of the kids whizzes by, laughing and screaming.

His laugh rumbles through me, vibrating against my chest. "Figured I needed to let everyone in town know you're off the market."

He winks and it's official—I've never been happier in my life.

CHAPTER 23
MACK

The next few weeks pass in a haze of Gracelyn, football, and more Gracelyn.

I don't know what it is about her, but I can't get enough.

Enough of her laugh, her smile, her fucking amazing body.

I love watching her come undone, chest flushing the prettiest shade of pink, chill bumps rising on her arms. The way she shivers beneath my touch, then begs for more.

Harder, faster, deeper.

But even more than that, I love talking to her, spending time with her. She's funny and cute and spunky.

Firecracker.

I've hardly spent any time with the guys, and they're starting to give me a hard time about it. Especially Baker.

"Yo, Mack—coming out tonight? We haven't had a chance to hang in forever." Baker raises a brow at me from across the coaches office.

"It has been a while." I huff out a breath, debating my

evening plans. I have missed a lot of boys' nights lately, and this could be one of our last chances before Baker becomes a dad.

Baker holds up his hands. "Lindsey's feeling good at the moment and I have the green light on Mustang's. So what do you say—you coming?" He shoots me a hopeful look, and I nod.

"Yeah, I'll come."

"Yes!" Baker pumps his fist in the air, a broad grin lighting up his face. "Carter's meeting us there. He had a dean's meeting, but he said he's coming."

"Okay, I'll see you over there in a few."

On the way to my truck, I text Gracelyn.

> Mack: Meeting the boys at Mustang's for a beer. I'll be home by ten

> Firecracker: Boo. I'm gonna miss you

> Mack: Sleepover tonight? My place?

> Firecracker: Tempting...

> Mack: Key's under the mat. Be naked when I get there

> Firecracker: You're awfully presumptuous. Who said I was coming?

> Mack: Oh, you're coming all right. All night long...

> Firecracker: When you put it like that...

> Mack: See you later

She sends a kissy face emoji and I toss my cell onto the

passenger seat, firing up the truck. I'm almost to Mustang's when the phone rings. Assuming it's Gracelyn, I pick up without checking caller ID.

Big mistake.

"Hello, Ulysses."

Fuck.

My throat dries up, palms instantly sweating on the wheel. There's only two people on this planet that call me by my real name, and only one of them is female.

"Hello, Mother."

"It's been an absolute age since we chatted. I assume you're coming for Thanksgiving? You haven't been home since last Christmas. Not that I'm keeping track."

Double fuck.

The last thing I want to do is spend the long holiday weekend with my family. But she's right—it has been a long time since I've been home and I suppose I do owe my parents a visit.

"Um, sure. I guess."

"Such enthusiasm, Ulysses." Her tone snarky, my guard's already rising. "What's going on in your world, dear? Since we never talk. How's the woodworking business?"

"Fine. Business is good."

"I do wish you would have pursued something less…" She pauses for a long second, choosing her words. "Working class." Her voice drops, almost as if she can't bear the phrase.

"I like what I do, Mother. And I make a good living from it, too." I exhale long and slow, trying to maintain my composure as I slide into a spot at Mustang's.

I'm going to need a beer after this conversation. Talking

to my mom always has this effect. The main reason I limit contact.

"A living subsidized by us. But it's fine. You can use your inheritance however you want, now that you're of age."

Nice dig there.

"And what about your love life? I'm not getting any younger here. I'd love a grandbaby before I die."

My hand grips the worn leather wheel and I stare at the exterior of the bar, debating mentioning Gracelyn.

"Actually, I have met someone."

"What? Really? Is it serious?" Her voice tips up, intrigue traveling straight through the line.

"Yes, really. And we're tracking that direction."

"Who is she? What does she do? She's not local, is she? Please tell me you didn't meet her on some god forsaken dating app."

I thrum the wheel, a tension headache brewing.

"No dating app. Gracelyn is a local, not that it matters. She's pretty and smart and funny."

"You must bring her to Thanksgiving, Ulysses."

Oh no. Hot dread fills my gut, temple full-on throbbing now. The last thing I want to do is torture Gracelyn with my insufferable family.

There's a reason I left Augusta. And that reason is them and what they represent.

Old money. Elitism. Exclusivity.

Everything I despise.

"I don't know, Mother. It's the holidays, she may already have plans."

"You haven't discussed the holidays? You absolutely must negotiate logistics if you're serious about this Grace girl. I deserve to spend the holidays with my son as much as she does."

For fuck's sake. My mother's getting up in arms about the division of holidays and she hasn't even met Gracelyn yet.

Maybe if I take her home with me, rip off the Band-aid, we'll start the relationship with my family on the right foot.

"Fine. I'll ask her. But no promises. Like I said—I'm not sure if she already has plans."

"Please let me know by Wednesday, Ulysses. I need to tell the chef how much turkey to prepare."

I roll my eyes, grateful I'm not on Facetime.

"Of course. I'll ask her and get back to you ASAP."

"Wonderful. I very much look forward to meeting Grace."

"Her name's Gracelyn."

"Right. Grace-lyn." She puts heavy emphasis on the ending. "I do hope to see both of you soon. Have a good night, Ulysses."

And with that, she clicks off, leaving me sitting speechless in the dark.

Oh shit.

Now I need to convince Gracelyn to come home to Augusta with me for Thanksgiving, otherwise I'll never hear the end of it from my mother and the relationship will be damaged before she's even met my family.

Holy hell.

I debate calling her right now, but this is probably a convo best had in person. Then I spot Baker and Carter walking into Mustang's—I'll have to chat with Gracelyn later.

Shoving into the bar, I immediately notice it's a lot less

crowded than the last time we were here. To be fair, it is a Monday night.

Carter and Baker have seats at the bar and beers already in hand. I sidle up, taking the spot next to Baker.

"Hey, boys."

"I was wondering if you were punking us." Baker glances over his shoulder, beer bottle raised. "Thought you weren't gonna show."

"I'm here." I adjust my ball cap, running my fingers through my hair before setting it back in place.

"Don't sound so excited, buddy." Baker frowns, shaking his head.

"It's not you two. I just got off the phone with my mother."

I know both of them will understand and sympathize with my plight, having heard all about my family over the years.

"Oh. That'll do it for sure. What's the issue this time? The club run out of Arnold Palmers or something? Wrong type of turf on the greens?"

"Worse. She wants me to bring Gracelyn home for the holidays."

"Oh shit." Baker lets out a long, low whistle. "Don't do it, man. Nothing good's gonna come from that."

I scrub the back of my neck. "I know. But if I don't take her, I'm never gonna hear the end of it."

Carter presses his lips together in a tight line, but stays silent. Something that's not in Baker's wheelhouse.

"If it were me, I'd avoid that scenario. Nothing against your parents, but I like to put off the meet-and-greet as long as humanly possible. Especially at the holidays." Baker takes another long swig of his beer and I motion to the bartender, signaling for a drink. This entire conversation's making me thirsty.

"That way, if things don't work out—and I'm not insinuating they won't, don't get it twisted—but if y'all break up, no one had to go through the special hell that is meeting the parents. Ya know?" Baker waves his bottle through the air.

"Man, who hurt you?" I tease, frowning at him.

He shakes his head. "You know what I mean, Mack."

"I do. Just giving you a hard time, Baker. But I don't think I can get out of it this time."

The bartender slides my beer across the counter, and I gratefully accept the chilled bottle. I love my parents, but that doesn't mean I want to spend the long holiday weekend at their house. Add Gracelyn to the mix and Baker's right—things could go sideways in a hurry. My mother isn't the easiest woman in the world to get along with. Everyone appeases her to keep her at bay, and there's no telling what type of snide remarks she'll make to Gracelyn. I'll have to stand up for my girl, and that will piss my mom off for sure. Honestly, I was hoping to put off the meeting with Gracelyn until we got married.

Married. What the fuck? I have no idea where that came from.

To drown out my wandering thoughts, I slug down half the beer, eyes fixated on the ball game playing on the television above the bar.

"Not to muddy the waters any, Mack. But if I were you, I'd take Gracelyn home. She's good with people. I'm sure she can charm your family. Plus, if she doesn't go, I sense your mother will be offended. Probably best to introduce them and smooth the way, since your mom's keen on the idea." Carter glances over at me, tiny frown lines etched between his brow.

Deep-down, I know he's right. I should take Gracelyn home and introduce her to my parents. Show her where I come from, why I am the way I am.

I nod, my mind made up.

"Fine. I'll take her, if she'll go. For all I know, she and her mom already have big plans."

"Doubt it. The past few years, Gracelyn and her mom came over to our house for Thanksgiving. But this year, Cam's playing football and I'm going to the game. So I won't be here."

"Hopefully Mrs. Reynolds can find a backup plan for turkey day."

Baker shrugs. "If not, you're off the hook. That there's what we call a win-win, Mack."

He's not wrong.

I shove away from the bar. "I gotta go talk to Gracelyn. See y'all tomorrow."

Plunking a ten-dollar bill on the counter, I wave goodbye to my friends as I hustle out of the bar. The sooner I get this holiday discussion over with, the better. Either way, Thanksgiving just got a whole lot more complicated.

CHAPTER 24
GRACELYN

I must've fallen asleep waiting for Mack because next thing I know, weak sunlight's spilling through the window above his bed. He's lying next to me, one strong arm wrapped around my middle holding me close. His light snore tickles my cheek with each exhale.

I shift a tiny bit and he flexes, locking his arm around me.

"Hey. You fell asleep on me last night." His voice husky with sleep, the deep tenor vibrates against my neck and an excited shiver dances up and down my spine.

Now that he's awake, I stretch my legs, waking up my entire body. "Sorry about that. I tried to stay awake, but I guess I was too exhausted. Did you have a fun night with the guys?"

"It was okay. Would have rather hung out with you, to be honest."

My heart flip-flops. "Really? That's sweet."

Lifting my face to his, I'm light and tingly all over.

I could really get used to this.

"Listen—" He traces lazy circles over my skin, the motion lulling me into a Mack-induced stupor. Calm, relaxed, malleable.

"My parents invited us for Thanksgiving. To the house in Augusta."

Every muscle tenses and my throat instantly dries up. "What? Really? You told them about us?"

Mack's eyes flick to mine. "Yeah. I mean, your mom knows all about us."

"What have you said? And what did they say?"

"I said I'm seeing someone. My mother asked if it was serious and I said yes. Then she invited us to the house for the long holiday weekend."

"Oh." There's a *shit* hovering on my tongue, but I somehow swallow it down.

"So—what do you say? Are you game?" He stares at me with an intense gaze.

"I—um…" I flick my eyes down at his bedspread, heat flaming my face. "Um…I've never met anyone's parents before. I mean, in like, an official capacity. Of course I've met parents before…" I panic-babble, words gushing out of me.

Mack presses his lips to mine, stopping the verbal mania. "It's fine, I'm sure it'll be good. And I don't care about before. All that matters is now."

Relief washes over me and I take a deep breath. "I have to talk to my mom about it. Because I don't want her to be all alone for Thanksgiving."

"Of course." He squeezes my hand. "Let me know by tonight, though, okay? My mother's a little uptight, to put it mildly. She'll want everything to be perfect for us. And apparently that takes time. Or so she says."

I laugh, wondering for the thousandth time how this is

my life. Mack, in all his gorgeousness, wanting to spend his time with me.

Nights, weekends, holidays.

Introduce me to his family.

He strokes my cheek, kissing me softly down the line of my jaw, and I know this thing between us is real, not something I dreamed up or imagined.

And for the first time in my life, I'm really and truly happy.

I want to stay like this forever.

————

Mama Reynolds does not take my Thanksgiving defection well.

"What do you mean, you're not going to be here for Thanksgiving? We're always together, every holiday!" Clutching her necklace, she twists and rubs the bright orange glass beads. "You're going to leave me here, all alone?"

Her face crumples, dark red lips turning down, and I can't help but notice the resemblance to a sad clown.

"Mama, I'm sorry." Guilt tugs at my gut. I hate the idea of my mom being alone on a holiday. But I really want to be with Mack. "I know we always celebrate together. But it's only for a few days…" I pat her back, trying to soothe her and take some of the sting out of the situation.

She's not having it.

Shaking her head, she worries the beads faster.

"Fine, Gracie. I understand. Eventually you're going to have to live your life. Leave your old mom behind. I didn't think the day would come so soon, but here we are."

Soon? I'm thirty years old, for fuck's sake.

But now's not the time to argue over the details.

"I'm sorry, Mama. I'll be home for Christmas, promise."

"Yeah, yeah."

I lean over and give my mom a hug, trying to convey all my emotions in one simple gesture. This woman has given me everything she has, everything she possibly could, and I am grateful, truly.

But I do need to live my own life. And now feels like as good a time as any to start.

Pulling back, I grip her shoulders. "Have Thanksgiving at Layla's. Or with your friend Rose. I'm sure you'll be able to find someone to spend the day with."

She tsks. "Maybe. I'll probably sit home and eat a frozen dinner in front of the TV, watching football. The holiday isn't important without family."

Geesh. Nothing like going heavy on the guilt.

"I'll ask around and see what we can work out for you, okay?"

"Sure." Her tone's flat, and she's obviously still upset. I hate that I'm letting her down, but I know in my heart that going to Augusta with Mack is the right thing for me.

"I'm sorry, Mama."

"Aww, Gracie. It's okay. Don't be sorry. You go and have a fun time with your boyfriend and don't worry about little ole me. I'll figure it out—I always do."

Now it's her turn to give me a hug, wrapping me up in her warm embrace. Just like she used to do when I was a little girl. My nose tingles and tears prick the backs of my eyes, but I blink them away.

I'm being ridiculous. It's one holiday, not the rest of my life.

But it could be.

The thought electrifies and terrifies me at the same time.

"I'm sure his family will be lovely. Make sure you don't fall in love with them, though, okay? I don't want you moving to Augusta." Mom flicks her worried eyes to mine, her brow furrowed.

"Mama. It's one weekend. I'm not moving in, promise."

"I'm holding you to that, Gracie girl. Because we have a salon to run. And I'll never find a better business partner than you."

I pop a hand on my hip, cocking a brow. "Only business partner? Not daughter?"

She throws her head back, laughing, and tension seeps from my body.

Everything's going to be okay. We're still us. Me and my mom.

"Daughter goes without saying. So—let's talk about what you're doing with your hair…"

CHAPTER 25
GRACELYN

Over the next week, I Facetime Sloane about two hundred times to get her opinion on different outfits. Mack's told me a few things about his family—I know they're a lot more formal than mine, his mom is very proper, and they live in a big house in Augusta.

I pack a wide variety of clothing to be on the safe side. I'm cramming the last pair of shoes into my bright pink suitcase when Mack walks into my bedroom.

"Whoa. That's a big bag."

I glance over my shoulder. "You think? I went with the medium-sized one, too. I have an even bigger suitcase, but didn't want to be too over the top."

He furrows his brow at me, rubbing the back of his neck. "Hmm. I'm not sure the mission was accomplished."

"You didn't tell me too much about the vibe of the weekend. Like, is this a cozy holiday where everyone kicks around in jammies all day? Or are y'all sporty? Running a 5K or something before you eat a big dinner. Do you wear matching holiday outfits?" I run through all the possibilities, listing each one off on my fingers.

"Scratch cozy holiday off the list. You will never see my mother in her pajamas, matching or otherwise."

My gut squeezes and I wonder for the thousandth time what exactly I'm getting myself into.

"Okay, so no matching jammies. What about athleisure wear? Yeah or nay?" I hold a pair of black leggings up in the air, along with a matching top.

Mack shrugs. "It's fine for the house. But if we go out anywhere, the dress code will be more formal."

Now it's my turn to scrunch up my brow.

"More formal? Like jeans? A nice blouse? What are we talking here?"

"Definitely not jeans. I never really pay much attention to what the women wear. But I'll be in chinos and a dress shirt, most likely with a jacket."

Dread churns through me as I eye my suitcase packed with all the wrong things. I misread this whole weekend, apparently. I maybe threw in one dress, to be on the safe side. Mack never told me the dress code is business formal.

"Why didn't you tell me this earlier?" I try to tamp down the hysteria creeping into my voice. We're supposed to leave in a few minutes, and I don't have any of the right clothes.

Mack rakes a hand through the waves of his hair. "Sorry. I assumed you'd know."

"How would I know?" My voice pitches up. So much for not getting hysterical. Heat floods through me and my chest tightens as I frantically unpack my bag. "I don't have any of the right stuff, Mack. And I've been packing for a week!"

"Hey, it's fine." He comes behind me, circling my waist with his arms and pulling me up against him.

"No, it's not." My voice shakes along with my hands as I toss item after item out of my suitcase. "I probably don't have anything nice enough to wear, especially for a holiday!"

"Gracelyn…" He grips my hips, spinning me around to face him. "Personally, I don't give a fuck what you wear. My favorite look of yours is buck ass naked. Wear whatever you feel most comfortable in."

I shake my head, tears stinging my eyes. This weekend's off to a rocky start already and we haven't even left Thunder Creek yet.

"It matters to me, Mack. This is the first time I'm meeting your family and I want to—*need to*—make a good first impression."

"Hey—" With his index finger, he tips my chin up to meet his gaze. "I love you. My family will love you. I get that you want to look good, and I'm sure you will. Everything looks good on you."

My heart soars as he drops his lips to mine.

Mack loves me. And I love him.

I relax into his kiss. Warm and comforting, like a worn leather coat on a chilly autumn day.

"I love you, too," I murmur against his mouth, fizzy happiness flowing through me alongside the panic. "Help me repack? Please? So we're not late?"

"Sure."

I pull away from him, mentally running through my clothing options. Mack helps me whittle the options down and half an hour later, I have my suitcase packed and ready to go.

"See? Crisis averted." He brushes a stray hair from my eyes, cupping my cheek. "All good."

I relax and let his words wash over me, sweeping away the doubt and anxiety from earlier.

"All good."

Mack zips up my suitcase and carries the luggage out to his truck while I lock up.

Five minutes later, we're on the road. He fiddles with the radio, settling on the country station. I sit back and zone out, trying not to worry about meeting Mack's family. The packing incident didn't really help calm my anxiety any. And judging by his tense jaw and the tight grip Mack has on the wheel, I don't think he's any more relaxed than me.

This could be a very long weekend.

To break the uncomfortable silence, I dig for clues about his family.

"Give me the highlights on your family."

"What do you mean?"

"The details. What's your mom like? I know she's proper, but what does she do? What are her hobbies? Basically, I want the Cliff Notes."

Mack stares straight ahead at the road, a deep furrow etched in his brow. Thrums his fingers on the steering wheel. After a long pause, he finally answers.

"You pegged my mother. Formal, uptight, prim and proper. She doesn't really *do* anything. She entertains. Plays tennis and golf with the ladies. Goes up to the club."

I bite my lip, nodding. *Super.* We literally have nothing in common. I live in a tiny-ass house and the only entertaining I do involves opening a bottle of wine. All the better if it's a screw top. I can't play tennis, never tried golf. And Mustang's is the closest thing to a social club we have in town. Kinda figuring Mack's parents belong to a different sort of thing.

"When you say *club*, what are we referring to here?"

"The country club. Or the yacht club. We belong to both."

I suck in a breath.

Shit.

Mack has a yacht? *What in the actual hell?*

"You have a yacht?"

"Not me. My family. And it's not a yacht. It's a boat. Technically, the place should be called the boat club, but that's not fancy enough, I guess."

Still.

I have a car and it's the only motorized vehicle I own. I don't even have a scooter.

"Okay." I gnaw at my lip. "What about your dad?"

"He's retired, but he used to practice law. After I quit football, he tried to talk me into joining his firm, but I politely and respectfully declined."

"He wanted you to go to law school?"

"Yeah. And I did, for two years. I dropped out during my third year and I don't think he's ever quite forgiven me."

Mack shifts in his seat, a far-away look in his eye. It's the saddest I've ever seen him and my chest aches. I quickly move away from this painful subject.

"What about hobbies?"

"He shoots, goes hunting with the guys every fall. Boats, obviously. Golf, tennis, like my mother. The usual stuff."

Um, no. None of this stuff is usual to me, but I'm not about to admit that. We're an hour away from a long holiday weekend with the family. Now's not the time for true confessions. Besides, I'm pretty certain Mack knows I don't do any of those things.

"And your sister?"

"Emma Kate. Short for Katherine. She still lives at home. Not in my parents' house, but in one of the guest houses."

"*One* of the guest houses?" My voice tips up. "There's more than one?"

I mean, damn. I don't have a guest room, let alone a house.

"Yes. It's a large property. Been in my family for generations."

"Generations?" I squeak.

"Yeah." Mack scrubs his neck, the skin flushing pink. He obviously doesn't like talking about his family, since this is the first I've heard any of this. I mean, he told me his family is well-off, but this. This is way beyond that.

Like next-level rich.

"Anyway, Emma Kate mostly hangs out. She isn't working—I think she's a social media influencer or something. I don't know." He shrugs. "She spends time with her friends, hangs out at the club. Her main goal is finding a husband."

"Oh." My stomach sinks as I mentally run through everything he's shared. The house, the boat, the family money, all the chi-chi hobbies. I doubt I'm going to have anything to talk about with Mack's relatives.

"Do they watch TV? Read? Anything nor—anything like that?" I bite back the word *normal*, not wanting to offend Mack. Because maybe I'm the one who's not normal here, I don't know.

"My mother only watches 'serious' television." He takes his hand off the wheel for a quick second, air quoting the word 'serious.' "And by that, she means the news. My father watches the news, sports, and history documentaries. Emma Kate watches her cell phone." He shakes his head again. "As far as reading, probably? I really couldn't tell you."

"Okay then…"

I grow more and more tense the closer we get to Augusta, the highway blurring as we speed toward Mack's family home. He takes the exit and nausea rolls through me, palms sweaty. I should have packed more deodorant.

He drives through town, making a right turn down a long, gravel road lined with trees. In the summer, there's probably a pretty shade canopy, but not now. We drive and drive, moving further away from town. Finally, he makes another right and pulls up to a wrought-iron gate. There's a box with a keypad and Mack punches in a code. After a few seconds, the gate slowly swings open.

We pull through and I swallow down my gasp. In sharp contrast to the dull brown trees in town, the grass here is a verdant green and stretches for miles and miles in all directions. The gravel turns to pavers and we glide over the honed brick driveway.

Finally, Mack slides up to a massive two-story, all-white house with black shutters and a huge, fancy double door.

"Oh my god. Mack. You didn't tell me your family lived in a mansion." I rub the stack of bangles on my wrist, the light jangle echoing through the cab.

"It's just a house, Gracelyn."

"It's not," I breathe, gnawing my bottom lip as I stare at the stunning architecture, the carefully manicured lawn. "It's way more than a house, babe."

He reaches over, taking my hand. "It's not who I am, Gracelyn. It's where I lived, but it's not me."

I don't know what he's yammering on about. If I grew up somewhere as fabulous as this, I'd be shouting about it from the rooftops.

"Okay." I nod, pressing my lips together.

The front door of the house swings open and a man in a dark suit steps out, but he doesn't wave. Instead, he walks across the drive and opens my door, the creak loud in the relative quiet of the afternoon.

"Thank you, hi. I'm Gracelyn." I smile broadly at the man and he nods, his expression blank.

"Good afternoon, miss." He reaches into the truck, grabbing the luggage and maneuvering it out of the backseat. "Good afternoon, sir."

"Afternoon, Bobby. Is anyone home or are they still out?"

"Home, sir. I'll take your luggage. The two of you may head into the solarium. Your mother has a tea service prepared for you after the long drive."

Tea service? For real right now? And long drive? It was like two hours.

"Thank you, Bobby."

Mack takes my hand and leads me inside. Stomach fluttery, my nerves hum triple-time as I step into the spacious marble foyer of the house. A massive floral arrangement sits on a round table in the center, directly below the most stunning crystal chandelier I've ever seen. Beyond that is a windy double staircase, spiraling up to a second floor.

"Wow." I take in the grandeur, already overwhelmed. I'm scared to breathe too loudly in here, and I'm definitely sticking to clear liquids. I don't trust myself with anything that could stain.

We move past the staircase, our footsteps clicking against the marble and reverberating in the quiet hallway.

My heart's pounding like I ran a marathon—which, let's be real, I definitely did not—and I wonder if Mack feels my racing pulse. His shoulders square, jaw tense, I have no clue what he's thinking right now. Suddenly, he feels distant, a million miles away. And I'm knocked even more off-balance.

I don't know this Mack at all.

We pass by several lavishly decorated rooms, all tastefully done in muted tones with golden accents and more light-colored furniture. I can't imagine sitting down in one of those rooms to do something as mundane as watch TV. No, these rooms are built for headier past times—studying maps or playing the harpsichord or something.

Nothing like what I do back home in Thunder Creek. The television would probably short circuit if an episode of *Real Housewives* came on.

I snicker at the thought and Mack cuts his eyes to mine, a worried look flashing across his face.

"Sorry," I murmur, pulling myself together.

"What's so funny?"

"Nothing. It's fine."

We come to the end of the hallway after walking for what seems like miles, dead-ending into a huge glass room with a rotunda and yet more white furniture. Plants artfully fill the space in carefully curated areas—vases of white calla lilies, potted orchids growing up to the sky, ferns, and potted palms. A multi-tiered silver platter filled with tiny sandwiches, macarons, cookies, and cakes is at the center of a round table, flanked by a stack of plates and flatware. A silver teapot sits next to the display, along with an assortment of beautiful teacups and saucers.

Mack's mother's sitting at the table and she stands as soon as she catches sight of us.

"Hello, darling. So glad you finally made it home. And this must be Grace."

His mother steps forward, reaching out and squeezing my upper arms. Holding me at arm's length, she inspects me, clear blue eyes raking over every last square inch of my face. I hold my breath, also studying her.

Mack's mother is stunning, not a wrinkle on her face. She could pass for twenty-five if I didn't know any better. Her blonde hair's sleek, a very becoming shoulder-length, brows artfully sculpted. Make-up is subtle and on point— slightly rosy cheeks, dark lashes, a nice pink color on her full lips. She smells like some exotic flower, the very scent expensive.

"Nice to meet you." I don't correct her on my name, instead forcing enthusiasm into my voice, an emotion I'm most definitely not feeling at the moment.

"Lovely to meet you as well. We've heard so much about you."

Really? Because until this trip, I knew next to nothing about Mack's family.

"Same." I bob my head, her long, thin fingers still clutching my arms.

"Come, sit. You all must be exhausted after the drive." She finally loosens her grip, and I inch closer to Mack.

His mother takes her seat and I follow Mack's lead, his hand hovering at my low back as he pulls the chair out for me. The one closest to his mother. I sink down into the seat as gracefully as possible, nerves thrumming wildly.

Mack's mother starts pouring the tea into beautiful little teacups, all painted with a delicate rose pattern and ringed with gold. I stare longingly at the finger sandwiches and sweets. The stress of the situation's making me hungry.

"Ulysses, my boy."

A loud, booming voice sounds from behind me and I almost drop my teacup.

Ulysses? Who the fuck's Ulysses?

My mouth opens, but I clamp it shut before I say something stupid. Only one person in this room could be named Ulysses and it's sure the hell not me.

In the last thirty minutes I've learned more about Mack than I have in the last few months.

What other secrets is he hiding?

CHAPTER 26
MACK

h fuck. Why'd my dad have to go and call me Ulysses?

I despise the name, a throwback to our ancestry that I'd love to leave behind. Far behind, in fact.

Out of the corner of my eye, I catch Gracelyn's shocked look, brows flying up.

Okay, so maybe I should have mentioned my given name.

But I hate it so damn much. One of the million and one reasons I left Augusta and never looked back.

Escaping my destiny, my mother always says.

More like my fate, if I stayed here.

"Hello, Dad." I stand and clap my father on the back, noting he's smaller and more shrunken than last time I saw him. He is getting up in years. I probably should make more of an effort to come home and spend time with my parents.

But it's so damn painful.

"This is Gracelyn." I motion at her and she rises,

shaking my dad's outstretched hand. He pumps her hand up and down three times, smiling broadly at her.

"Ah, yes. The girlfriend. We've heard a lot about you, young lady."

Gracelyn's cheeks tint pink and she smiles shyly at my dad. *Maybe the two of them can hit it off.* She'll have an easier time with him than my mother.

"Lovely to meet you, sir." Gracelyn nods at my father and he motions for her to sit.

"How was the trip, kids? Long?"

Good grief. My parents act like we drove down from Iowa or something.

"Not too bad, Dad. The traffic isn't ramped up yet. Tomorrow will probably be worse."

"Exactly why we suggested you come today. We can get in a round of golf tomorrow, then enjoy the turkey and all the fixings on Thanksgiving."

Oh shit. They want to play golf. Of course they do. I'll be fine, but Gracelyn has definitely never swung a club before. And now's sure as hell not the time to start.

"I don't know about golf, Dad…." I hedge, squeezing Gracelyn's thigh under the table. Her leg's trembling—this is going about as badly as I thought it would.

"Nonsense. We have the chef here all day preparing, along with the rest of the staff. Gives us plenty of time to hit the links!" Bypassing the tea service, he heads straight to the bar cart in the corner. He pours himself a healthy shot of bourbon, and I sorely wish I could fix myself a stiff drink as well.

But I'd never do that in front of my mother. At least not until the appropriate hour. My father gets away with it, after forty-five years of marriage. One of the few perks, I guess.

Me, not so much.

Gracelyn sips her tea, staying uncharacteristically silent.

"Ulysses, we heard from Emma Kate that your team's doing well this year." My mother locks eyes with me over her teacup, pinky outstretched like the good debutante she always was.

"They're doing so great!" Gracelyn chimes in, smiling at me, then at my mother. My mom presses her lips together in a thin line, nodding.

"Wonderful."

Silence as we all sip our tea, a bird chirping in the distance. The ice from my dad's glass clinks loudly, echoing through the solarium, and I search for safe topics of conversation.

Politics, no.

Work, no.

Anything Thunder Creek, no.

Yeah, I got nothing.

Luckily, my sister bounds into the room, sneaking up behind me and wrapping me in a huge bear hug.

"Big brother! You're home!" Her voice trills in my ear, the sweet vanilla scent of her perfume tickling my nose.

"Hi, Emma Kate." I pat her hand. "This is Gracelyn."

Emma Kate loosens her grip on me and turns her attention to Gracelyn, embracing her.

"So nice to meet you! Anyone who'd put up with my grumpy brother must be a saint." She grins and Gracelyn laughs. But it's not the sparkly laugh I love, the one that lights me up inside. This sound's more muted, lighter. Like she's not sure what to do.

"Much as I oppose the grumpy comment, I concur

Gracelyn's a saint." I squeeze her knee under the table and her shoulders relax a bit, her face softening.

"Well, I'm glad you're both here. Takes some of the heat off me for a minute." Emma Kate flounces over to the sofa and collapses against the floral cushions.

My sister's never known a day of heat in her life.

She's always been the favorite, the golden child. All my parents' hopes and dreams were pinned on me, a heavy mantle to bear. When Emma Kate came along, she was a blessing, an answer to my mother's prayers for another child. The girl could do no wrong, beginning from conception and going straight through to today.

"Uh huh," I mutter, taking a drink of the strong English Breakfast tea my mother favors.

"Did you hear that Ruthie Ann and Tate Gillivray are getting a divorce?" Emma Kate folds one leg under the other and leans forward, ready to gossip.

"I hadn't." Nor do I give a hoot, but I'd rather talk about this than other things, I suppose.

"Yep. Supposedly Ruthie Ann cheated on him with—wait for it—her personal trainer. Like, how cliché, you know?"

"Emma Kate. Idle gossip is the devil's work." My mother chides my sister, but Emma Kate merely rolls her eyes.

"It's pretty scandalous. Everyone at the club's talking about it. I heard the trainer got fired and Ruthie Ann was forced to pull her children out of the Azalea School."

"Oh my." I set the teacup down, pull two sandwiches off the tray. I offer one to Gracelyn, but she declines.

"Those poor children." Our mother sighs, acting like she can empathize with their plight. "At the holidays, too. Shame."

Gracelyn shifts in her seat, a pink flush creeping up her neck. I change the subject quickly.

"Anyway, how was the hunting trip, Dad?"

My father perks up, rattling his glass in his hand. "Fantastic. We each got a buck, plus Murphy managed to shoot a few quail. I'm having the antlers mounted. Should be up by Christmas."

Nothing says Merry Christmas like a good antler mount.

Gracelyn pales beside me and I search for yet another subject change, but I've got nothing. Every single thing that pops into my mind is so far out of the realm of everyday living, so unimportant to anyone outside of this microcosmic sphere.

"Hello!"

The hair at the back of my neck rises, my blood pressure skyrocketing.

No. This cannot be happening right now. Why the fuck is she here?

I'd recognize that high-pitched Southern drawl anywhere. In fact, that very same voice haunts me in my nightmares.

I swallow hard, mouth drier than a desert in a motherfucking drought. The voice, the strong scent of cinnamon and cloves, the full-body chills I just got without even turning around and making eye contact.

Yep, it's definitely her.

Tinsley.

My ex.

CHAPTER 27
GRACELYN

"Tinsley! So glad you're here. I was hoping you'd make it. Thought you might change your mind and go to the Maldives with your parents." Emma Kate bounces off the couch, embracing Tinsley in a warm hug.

I don't remember Mack ever mentioning a Tinsley. Maybe a cousin or something? I sit quietly, waiting to be introduced.

"Oh no, never! A week on an island with my parents? No, thank you." Tinsley flips her chestnut hair over her shoulder, then sidles over to the table. "Hey, y'all. Thanks so much for the invitation. I'm happy to be here." She glances at Mack's parents, then turns her attention to Mack.

"Hello."

An easy, simple greeting. Yet something feels off, the word heavy and loaded with an emotion I can't quite pinpoint. That and the way she's looking at him, as if she's staring straight into his soul.

"Hello." Mack's tone is flat and, unlike his sister, he doesn't jump up to hug her. In fact, he's rather cold and distant. I'm thinking *not* a cousin.

Who is this girl and why is Mack acting all weird?

A twinge of jealousy zips through me, but I work hard to ignore it.

"Tinsley, this is my girlfriend, Gracelyn."

Tinsley's glossy lips twitch, the corners barely tipping up into a smile. "Well, hello. Pleasure to meet you."

"Likewise." I nod at her, trying my best to seem friendly.

"Tinsley, dear, take a seat, have some tea." Mack's mom interrupts the introduction, pouring her a cup of tea without waiting for a response.

Tinsley doesn't seem to mind, graciously accepting the tea and dropping two cubes of sugar into the cup. She stirs the hot beverage with a tiny spoon, the soft clinking on the cup jangling my nerves.

She doesn't sit at the table. Instead, she takes a seat next to Emma Kate on the couch and sips her tea.

"Mrs. McIntire, delicious as always." Tinsley beams at Mack's mom and I swear the woman preens, glowing.

"Thank you, dear. All credit goes to the chef."

"Nonsense." Tinsley waves her hand, brushing aside the show of humility. "How long are y'all in town for? The whole weekend?" She aims the question at me, but I hesitate, waiting for Mack to take the lead.

He doesn't let me down.

"That's the plan." He takes another drink, the dainty cup doll-sized in his large hand. It's odd, seeing him in this environment. He's always been so tough and burly. This is an entirely different Mack than I'm used to.

"You ladies coming to dinner tonight?" Mack's dad directs the question at Emma Kate and Tinsley.

Emma Kate nods. "Yes, sir."

"Alright then. Excuse me while I call the club and change the reservation. And golf tomorrow?"

"Sounds great!" Tinsley claps her hands, and my stomach sinks. I'm the odd one out here. Maybe I can stay behind and illicitly watch daytime television.

Doubtful.

Mack's dad excuses himself, pouring another shot of bourbon on the way out of the room. Emma Kate and Tinsley talk with each other on the couch, not loud enough for us to hear. Mack's mom sips her tea and Mack and I sit in silence, his fingers tapping the table in a quick rhythm. Mack should probably stick to decaf the rest of the weekend.

"What time's dinner, Mother?" he asks.

"Six pm. Happy hour will begin at half past five."

"Okay. We're going go to our rooms and freshen up, get ready for dinner."

Rooms? I'm going to be alone in this giant house?

Mack stands and I follow suit, happy for an escape.

"Actually, Ulysses. Now that Tinsley's here, I'm rethinking the room situation. I believe Gracelyn will be more comfortable in the guest house. Have Bobby move her luggage, then Tinsley can take the white room."

Mack stiffens beside me. "Gracelyn will be fine in the main house."

His mom waves her hand through the air, dismissing Mack's protest. "Nonsense. The guest house is spacious and offers the best views of the grounds. She should stay there."

She shoots me a tight smile and I force a quick smile

back, trying my hardest to be friendly and cooperative. Inside, I'm panicking.

Mack's shoulders sag a fraction, a tiny sigh escaping his lips.

"Mother, as lovely as the views are from the guesthouse, I'm sure Gracelyn prefers to stay in the main house. With me."

"Ulysses, the matter's settled." Mack's mother clasps her hands together, her bony knuckles turning white. Mack sighs and gives up the fight, his lips pressed in a thin, tight line.

Together, we leave the afternoon tea party behind. His hand at my low back is the only thing keeping me moving forward right now. Chest tight, I feel like I might cry. Nothing's going as planned and we've barely been here an hour.

I gnaw my bottom lip as we move wordlessly back through the long hallway, passing room after empty room. Finally, we're back in the foyer. I desperately wish I could climb into Mack's truck and head straight home, but that's not really an option.

"Sir." Bobby appears from I don't know where, tipping his head at Mack.

"My mother requested Gracelyn's luggage be moved to the guesthouse and Tinsley's stuff moved to the white room." Mack scrubs a hand over the back of his neck, avoiding my gaze. "Please transfer my suitcase along with Gracelyn's. I'll be staying in the guesthouse as well."

"As you wish, sir." Bobby hurries up the stairs to fetch my suitcase and a cool wave of relief rushes over me.

"You're staying in the guesthouse with me? Without the consent of your mother?"

"I'm forty years old, Gracelyn. I don't need my mother's permission to do anything anymore. And I don't want you to be out there all alone."

Wow. I can't believe Mack would stand up for me like this.

"Won't she be angry?" I bite my lower lip, gnawing at the flesh.

Mack steps closer to me, taking both my hands in his giant ones.

"With all due respect, Gracelyn, I don't really give a fuck. I'm here out of duty. And I brought you as my guest. I want to be with you. If she doesn't like that, too damn bad."

I've never seen Mack so serious, so resolute, before. But I like it.

Bobby's back downstairs, both suitcases in hand. We follow him down the hallway, this time on the left side of the house. More impeccably decorated rooms, none of them currently in use. Finally, we come to a glass door at the end of the hallway. Bobby holds the door for us and we exit the main house, making a left down a pebble walkway. We walk down the path, through the gardens with a stone fountain spouting water in the center.

Sure enough, past the gardens is a beautiful pool and a guesthouse, a miniature version of the main house. Bobby unlocks the door, then hands the key to me.

"Here you go, miss. Should you require anything, please ring the main house and I'll be happy to be of service." He gives me a curt nod, then spins and heads back to the main house.

Mack shuts the door behind us, sighing. "Sorry about all this. I had no idea Tinsley would be here."

He loops his arms around my waist, pulling me close to him. I inhale his familiar woodsy scent, reveling in the safety and comfort of his embrace. Still, that nagging feeling pulls at my gut.

Who is this Tinsley girl and why's Mack apologizing?

Mack's hand drifts down to my ass, squeezing, then he drops his mouth to mine. He tastes sweet from the tea as his tongue swirls in my mouth. The tension loosens, anxiety melting away as we kiss.

It doesn't matter. We're fine.

After a long while, I pull away, unable to resist the urge to dig. "By the way, who's Tinsley to y'all? A family friend?"

Obviously she's tight with the family, popping by and spending the Thanksgiving holiday with them.

Mack bristles and that tiny bit of worry ratchets up, amplifying.

"Sort of. She's good friends with Emma Kate."

"I figured as much. Childhood friends? College besties?"

"Both." He clears his throat, his eyes flicking to the ground. "Also my ex."

"Excuse me?" I shove away from him, shocked. "What do you mean, your ex? Like, y'all casually dated? Or was it a long-term thing? When?"

"Gracelyn…"

"Mack. Or should I call you Ulysses?" I pop my hand on my hip, fiery anger bubbling inside me. It's a strong reaction, I know, but so much has been thrown at me in such a short time. Big, important things that Mack should have told me about before we got here.

"Don't, please." He steps forward and I take a step back.

"You should have prepared me for this."

"For what?" Mack raises a brow.

I throw my arms out wide. "This. All of it. The fact that you live in a Bridgerton mansion, you have a staff, you belong to multiple clubs. Your ex-girlfriend is a close family friend." I spit out the last part, the words stinging my throat. "I don't know anything about you."

"That's not true. You know me, Gracelyn. The real me. None of that stuff is mine. Not the house, or the staff, or the memberships. And I had no clue Tinsley was coming. We're done, Gracelyn. You have to believe me."

I fold my arms across my chest, heart racing. "I don't know what to believe, Mack."

All I do know for sure is my heart hurts right now—but I'm not about to admit that. It feels too real, too vulnerable, like picking at an open scab.

"Babe…" He reaches out, stroking my cheek with the rough pad of his thumb, and I waver under his touch. I concentrate on his movements, up and down, up and down.

I consciously make a decision to not hold the Tinsley thing against him. He did look shocked to see her, like it was a real jump scare.

"Fine." I open my eyes, locking gazes with him. "But is there anything else I should know? Tell me now, before dinner."

Mack swallows hard, his Adam's apple bobbing in his throat. "Tinsley and I broke up a long time ago."

He pauses and I instantly know there's more to the story.

"And?" I press, his heart racing beneath my palm resting on his chest.

"We were engaged."

CHAPTER 28
GRACELYN

"What the fuck do you mean you were engaged? And she's still a family fucking friend?" I recoil from Mack, putting distance between us. Blood whooshes loudly in my ears and black and white spots dance in my peripheral vision.

"This is unbelievable. The fact that you were engaged and never mentioned it is one thing. A massive thing." I pace the marble floor, equal parts anger and surprise surging through my veins. "But now she's here? And we have to hang out for the next few days? That's fucking weird, Mack."

He rakes a hand through his hair. "I know, Gracelyn. And I'm sorry. I probably should have mentioned the engagement thing before, I guess. But it's in the past. Like, so far back. It doesn't matter anymore."

I stare up at the ceiling in an effort to avoid his gaze and to keep the tears pooling in my eyes from spilling over. I know I'm a touch dramatic sometimes, but this is a lot of information to process at once.

I take a long, shaky breath before facing him. "I'd love to be the chill girl right now and act like it doesn't matter. Like I don't care that you loved someone before me. Enough to propose." My voice quivers and I suck in air through my nose, try to regain a sliver of composure.

"But the truth is, Mack, I do care. I'm not that chill girl. I'm emotional and a feeler and this just feels—I don't know—bad." A pang shoots through my chest and I'm hot all over.

"What do you want me to say, Gracelyn? I can't go back and change the past. All I can do is apologize for not telling you sooner."

Deep-down, I know he's right. There isn't much he can do at this point, the damage is done. My heart's a bit mangled, my ego bruised.

Still, I have questions.

I take a shuddery breath, raise my eyes to his. I need to know details.

"Who broke it off?"

Mack's jaw ticks and he shoves a hand in his pocket, drops his gaze to the marble floor.

"She did."

All the air's sucked from my lungs at his admission. I thought for sure Mack was the one who broke things off, left her behind without so much as a glance back.

But no.

Tinsley dumped him.

"Why? What happened?"

A deep furrow forms between his brows, and he shifts his weight from foot to foot. Somewhere in the distance a clock ticks—tick, tick, tick—and the noise is deafening in the silence stretching between us.

Finally, Mack clears his throat.

"We got engaged my senior year of college, and she had big plans. I was supposed to join the league and we'd get married during the offseason. After graduation, though, I didn't go pro. Things between us got rocky, but we stayed together. I started law school and we were in a decent spot. But the day I quit law school, she dumped me. Said I had no drive and she didn't sign up to spend her life with a loser." He raises his eyes to meet mine. "Exact quote."

Oof. My heart hurts for Mack, even as angry as I am.

"That was it. She gave me back the ring and I left town. We haven't really spoken since, except for the occasional run-in."

"I'm sorry." The words come out a whisper.

Mack rubs the back of his neck, shakes out his arms as if to clear his body of negative energy.

"I should have told you all of this earlier. Sit down. Please. Let me explain." He gestures at the sofa in the living room and I give in, taking a seat beside him. Even though I'm pissed, I can't help but feel sorry for him right now. Mouth turned down, worry lines marching across his normally relaxed brow, he's defeated.

Not the Mack I know at all.

"It's fine." He sighs. "All for the best. I'm glad I saw the person she truly is. Way I see it, I dodged a bullet. Tinsley was never right for me. At the time, I thought I was in love with her, but I absolutely wasn't. We were together more out of expectation."

"I never, ever felt half of what I feel for you about her. Not a second goes by when you're not on my mind. I love every little thing about you." He laces his fingers through mine and locks eyes with me, his pupils dark and deep. "You're my entire world, Gracelyn. I don't think about

Tinsley. Ever. I barely know her anymore. And I don't care to. Why would I when I have the most beautiful, sparkling, amazing woman next to me?"

Tension releases from my shoulders, the tightness in my chest loosening. Mack's right. All of this is history. Still, I'm not too thrilled I haven't heard about any of this before today.

Mack rubs his thumb up and down my fingers, his callouses rough on my skin.

"Not that it makes any of this right, how I handled things. But I hate where I come from, Gracelyn." He glances away, staring out at the pool for a long minute. "Everything about this place. My name, all the stupid rules, the etiquette, the mind games everyone plays. I didn't want any of it to touch you, touch what we have together. You mean the world to me and I didn't want my family and all of their petty bullshit to affect us."

"Mack..." I whisper, squeezing his hand. I'm still stunned by the level of things I didn't know about him, but I'm beginning to understand why he kept so much hidden.

"I didn't mean to keep secrets from you, baby. I just wanted to protect you." He meets my gaze, his eyes sad and serious.

I make a choice right then and there to choose forgiveness over pettiness.

"I forgive you. But please don't let there be a next time, Mack. Tell me—right now—if there's anything else I should know. Any more exes going to crash the party?" I purse my lips together.

He shakes his head, a wavy curl flopping onto his forehead.

"No. Only the one. You know everything now, right down to my terrible given name."

I smirk. "I'm almost afraid to ask, Ulysses—" I draw out his fancy moniker, holding in a snicker. "But what's your middle name?"

Mack groans, wrinkling his nose. "You don't want to know."

"Oh, but I do."

"Fauntleroy."

"What the hell?"

"Yeah, I know. Another family name."

"Damn. Your parents hated you, huh?" I grab him by the shirt collar and pull his mouth to mine.

He kisses me long and hard, and relief seeps through me, trickling into every crack in my heart. Filling me up and making me—us—whole again.

Mack loves me. And I love him.

We're fine.

Better than fine.

Tinsley's his past, but I'm his future.

Winding his arms around me, Mack holds me close, his forehead pressed to mine. His breath feathers over my face as he stares into my eyes, the golden flecks in his irises shining.

"Thank you, Gracelyn. For forgiving me. I'm sorry if I hurt you—that was never my intent. I love you, baby."

"I know," I whisper, my fingers curling in his shirt. "I love you too. Now give me the grand tour of this guesthouse, will you? Because I have to get ready for dinner."

The guesthouse is almost as impressive as the main house, with marble everywhere and more of the all-white color scheme with splashes of blue thrown in here and there. To coordinate with the rest of the property, I suppose.

There's a huge bedroom with an en suite bathroom,

complete with a soaking tub and walk-in shower with multiple showerheads. Plus a full kitchen, an office, and a home gym overlooking the pool.

"Too bad it's so chilly. The pool's amazing." I peer through the window at the sparkling pool.

"It's heated. We could swim if you want."

"I didn't bring a suit."

"Wouldn't stop me." Mack winks and a hot blush flames my face.

"Ulysses Fauntleroy—that's downright scandalous." I cover my mouth, pretending to be shocked at the suggestion. Even though skinny-dipping with Mack is downright tempting.

"Call me that again and I'm throwing you in that pool fully clothed." His eyes darken, and I wonder if he's joking.

"You wouldn't dare."

"Don't try me, Firecracker."

"Fine." I pout. "Only because I can't afford to mess up my hair. I won't call you that. But it is a fun name to say."

He rolls his eyes, smacking me lightly on the booty. "Listen, I need to run up to the main house and talk to my dad. Do you want to come with me now or do you need more time?"

I take a quick glimpse in the mirror. "I'm going to change into a different dress and touch up my makeup. I'll meet you at the bottom of the staircase in fifteen minutes."

"Sounds good. Call me if you get lost and I'll send out a search party."

I slap him lightly on the chest. "Very funny. See ya."

Standing on tiptoe, I kiss him on the lips before he heads back to the main house. I don't love the idea of being out here alone, but I get the feeling that punctuality's a big thing with his mother.

I quickly pull clothing from my bag, selecting a midi black dress with booties that highlights my curves. Changing into a lacy black bra and panties, I slide into the dress and switch out my hoop earrings for diamond studs. I grab my makeup bag and hurry into the bathroom. The lighting's fantastic as I apply highlighter and blush, another coat of mascara, and a quick swipe of pearly lip gloss. Then I spritz my perfume, letting it rain down on me.

Snatching up my clutch and the hostess gift I brought— a nice bottle of Veuve—I race out of the guesthouse. The sun's sinking and a cool breeze blows through the trees, the leaves rustling in the wind. I follow the path up to the main house, slightly more relaxed now that I've hashed things out with Mack.

I'm almost to the house when I hear the soft giggles and hushed voices coming from the other side of the decorative hedge. I slow my footsteps, inching closer to the sounds. The faint scent of cigarette smoke tickles my nostrils and I hold my finger to my nose to suppress a brewing sneeze.

"She's not really his type. Well, except for the huge tits."

The voice sounds like his sister.

"Agreed. I bet he motorboats in those things."

"Eww, gross, Tinsley. That's my brother you're talking about."

Tinsley, obviously, with her deep Southern accent.

"I'm just saying. Mack's always been a tits-and-ass kinda guy."

Ears burning, I'm struggling to breathe. I should keep

walking, but I'm afraid they'll hear me and think I was eavesdropping.

"She's really quiet. I wonder if the two of them ever talk." Emma Kate's voice drifts through the hedge.

"Probably not. They probably just have sex. They can't have much in common. Your mom told me she's a hair-stylist." Tinsley sneers the word, making my profession sound shameful. Like I'm a common criminal or something.

"She does have really great hair. And makeup."

Thanks, Emma Kate. At least I have that going for me.

"I just don't know what Mack sees in her. She's so—I don't know—regular."

For the second time today, tears sting my eyes. This trip's going worse than I ever imagined and all I want to do is leave. Go home to Thunder Creek and hide in my bed under the covers for a good long while.

Maybe forever.

There's a shuffle from across the hedge, the *snick, snick* of perfume being sprayed. The heady scent of clove carries on the wind, then the crunching of footsteps as Emma Kate and Tinsley walk away.

I clutch the gift bag, my throat dry and chest tight.

I'm never going to fit in here.

Buzz, buzz.

I shift the bag onto my wrist and fish my cell from my clutch.

Mack: You lost?

With shaky hands, I text back.

Gracelyn: No, on my way. Be there in a sec. Had to run back and get the gift

Shoving the cell back into my clutch, I square up my shoulders and hold my head high.

Mack's ex isn't going to scare me off. I'm going to go in there and charm the pants off the whole damn family. By the end of this weekend, we're all going to be besties. I may even invite Emma Kate to be in the wedding, who knows?

I take a deep breath and walk straight into the ring of fire.

CHAPTER 29
MACK

Never have I ever endured a more painful dinner at the club than the one tonight.

Things started badly and spiraled down from there. The second I set foot inside the stuffy clubhouse—all oak, scotch, and old money—people rushed up to greet me.

Not the current me, carpenter and high school football coach me.

Nope.

The old me. College football star and eldest son of the McIntires.

Worse, Tinsley standing with the family sent all the wrong signals. Guess the town's collective memory is long.

"Mack, so good to see you, my boy!" Dr. Franklin, my former pediatrician, hops up from the brown leather couch in the main lobby and slaps me on the back. "Tinsley." He tips his graying head at Tinsley, and she beams at him like she's Miss damn Augusta or something.

"Hello, Dr. Franklin. You're looking mighty fine this

evening." She bats her lashes at him, and Gracelyn stiffens beside me.

"Why, thank you."

I swear Dr. Franklin blushes at the compliment. Before I get a chance to introduce Gracelyn, he spins to my father and launches into a long diatribe about malpractice insurance.

"We should check in." My mother glances at her watch, tapping the sparkly crystal-encrusted timepiece. "I hate being late for our reservation."

"I'll do it," I happily volunteer. Anything to stay under the radar.

With one hand hovering at Gracelyn's low back, we move away from the family.

"Wow. This place is historic, huh?" Gracelyn peers up at the light oak-planked, vaulted ceiling as we walk toward the dining room.

"Yes. One of the oldest country clubs in the South. Lots of out-of-date traditions abound."

"I sense you're a big fan."

"Huge. Love the men-only dining room and the mandatory dinner jacket rule."

"Seriously? That's a thing?"

I nod. "Yep. Welcome to 1950."

The college-aged blonde at the hostess stand smiles widely at me, teeth sparkling white under the light from the chandelier.

"McIntire." I give the name and she bobs her head.

"Of course, Mr. McIntire. I recognized you when you walked up. We have your table ready whenever you are."

Good grief.

The hostess gathers the menus, ducking behind the

stand to grab silverware. Gracelyn leans in, her floral cologne winding around me as she whispers in my ear.

"How does she know who you are?"

"There's photos somewhere around here."

"Here?" Gracelyn scrunches her nose. "In the clubhouse?"

I shrug. "Won the father-son golf tournament two years in a row back in college."

"Oh my gosh. You're a local celeb." Gracelyn grins, fanning herself. "I didn't know I was dating a celebrity."

"I assure you, you are not."

"Are you ready, Mr. McIntire?" The hostess gazes up at me through her long, fake lashes.

I hate when people call me mister. Makes me feel a hundred years old.

"Yes." My mother answers for me, the rest of the family appearing behind us.

"Right this way."

The hostess leads us through the bar area into the main dining room. No less than five people stop me on the way, chatting and saying hello to me and my dad. By the time I make it to the table, everyone's seated. My mother at one end with a spot for my father at the other. Tinsley's next to my mother and Emma Kate's beside her. There are two open spots left for Gracelyn and me. I hesitate for a moment, trying to decide where Gracelyn would rather sit —next to my mother or my father. My hand's on the back of the chair next to my dad when my mom chimes in.

"Grace, dear. Have a seat next to me." She pats the menu at the place setting beside her, and I swallow down my grimace.

Okay then. Decision made.

I pull out the chair and Gracelyn slides in, plucking the napkin from beneath the menu and spreading it over her lap.

A waiter appears and offers us water, then a sommelier stops by with the wine list.

"Yes, we'll take a bottle." My dad peruses the chunky folio of wines. "How about this one? The Cab from Sonoma?"

"Excellent choice, sir. I'll bring it right out." He scurries away and I chug my water, suddenly parched.

"I trust the guesthouse is acceptable." My mother peers at Gracelyn, one of her brows arched.

Thankfully, she either doesn't know I moved out there too or is brushing over it for the sake of peace. More than likely the former, but I'm not going to bring it up.

"Yes, thank you. The guesthouse is lovely." Gracelyn smiles at my mom, but she's already glancing down at the menu. Gracelyn ducks her head quickly, cheeks flushing.

Damn, this is fucking painful.

Mercifully, the wine materializes, and we all raise our glasses in a toast.

"To time with family—and friends who feel like family." My dad nods first at Tinsley, then at Gracelyn, and my gut twists. I'm not sure how much more of this I can take. Hopefully, Gracelyn didn't notice the slight. She seems preoccupied with the menu.

"What's good here?" she asks, setting her wineglass down.

"Everything," Emma Kate says. Always so very helpful.

"I like the duck. Or the steak." I point to both selections on the menu, and Gracelyn shoots me a grateful look.

"So, Gracelyn, what's your family doing for the holidays?" Emma Kate swirls her wineglass around, the red liquid sloshing dangerously close to the edge.

"Um…my mom's having Thanksgiving with her friend." Gracelyn fiddles with the stack of silver bangles on her wrist.

"Oh. It's only the two of you then?" Emma Kate forges on, digging for details like the nosy little sister she's always been.

"Yes, just the two of us." Grace shifts in her chair, leaning back a touch.

"No annoying brother then?" Emma Kate scowls across the table at me.

"No. I always wanted a sibling. But that never happened."

"Consider yourself lucky," Emma Kate says, rolling her eyes at me. I know she's teasing, but Gracelyn's face falls. I quickly change the subject.

"Emma Kate, read any good books lately?"

She snorts, covering her mouth with her hand to catch any errant spray. "God, no. I haven't read a book since college."

I kick Gracelyn's foot under the table, and she glances over at me, lips tipping up slightly.

"Have you, Mack?" Tinsley locks eyes with me across the table, her pupils wide and dark, and my gut clenches.

"Only if you count the high school playbook. I've been pretty busy."

"You found time to date." Tinsley runs her finger along the rim of her glass, then takes a slow sip of wine, her gaze searing into me.

I glare across the table at her, my muscles tight and my

body cold. This night's already been long and insufferable, and Tinsley's presence is only making it worse. I'd love to take off my jacket, but that's not allowed in the main dining room. Instead, I down the rest of my wine in one long slug.

The waiter appears, cutting the tension. Everyone places their order, wineglasses are refilled. A few people stop by the table to chat, clapping me on the back and talking about the football glory days.

From the corner of my eye, I watch as Gracelyn tries to join the ladies' conversation. But Emma Kate and Tinsley start talking about a few of their sorority sisters. That leaves Gracelyn with my mother.

Not ideal.

"You and your mother work together?" My mom steeples her fingers.

"Yes, ma'am. We own a popular salon in Thunder Creek." Gracelyn's cheeks turn pink and she's animated for the first time since we got to the club.

"That's nice. What's the name of the shop?"

"Plumb Perfect."

"How quaint." My mother gives Gracelyn a tight smile and a nod.

"It's a sweet little spot. I enjoy what I do."

"That's lovely. Ulysses always says the same thing. Although we do wish he would have done more, with all the advantages he's enjoyed."

I tense, one fist clenched beneath the table. Ever since I moved to Thunder Creek, I've been hearing about what a disappointment I am.

It's exhausting.

But now's not the time for yet another confrontation. I

gloss over the jab, pretending I didn't hear. The food arrives and conversation slows, all attention on the entrees.

I'm cutting into my filet when I feel a slight bump against my leg. Then a bare foot snakes up my ankle, rubbing beneath my pants.

Is Gracelyn playing footsie with me at the club with my mother sitting next to her?

I sneak a quick glance over at her, but she's engrossed in her Cobb salad. Stabbing a leaf of lettuce with her fork, she's not paying any attention to me at all. I lift my eyes and Tinsley winks at me, so quickly I'm positive no one else saw.

What the hell?

Jerking my leg away, I ram my knee against the table. Hard. Glasses wobble and silverware rattles on the plates.

"Oww." I massage my bruising kneecap, trying to ease the pain.

"Ulysses, are you alright?" My mother's eyes widen with concern.

"Yeah, just a Charley horse. I'll go walk it off." I shove away from the table, eager to get some fresh air.

"I'll come with you. I need to use the ladies' room." Tinsley stands before I have a chance to protest or escape alone.

Wonderful.

Gracelyn bites at her lip, shooting me a worried glance.

"I'll be fine." I squeeze her arm reassuringly.

"You need me to come with you?" Her voice tips up.

"He used to get those things all the time, Gracie. He'll be fine," Dad says, ripping off a piece of bread and cramming the carb into his mouth.

"Okay."

I pat Gracelyn's arm one more time, then limp out of

the dining room with Tinsley hot on my heels. She inches closer to me, our arms brushing, and I step further away. When we pass the restrooms, I anticipate her ducking in, but she doesn't.

"Thought you had to go to the bathroom?" I jerk my head at the restroom door.

"And I thought you were giving me a signal that you wanted to talk to me."

I shove my hand in my suit pocket, jaw tense. "No. What I want you to do is leave me the hell alone."

"Oh, c'mon, Mack. You can't still be upset over what happened between us." She flips her long hair over her shoulder. "That was ages ago."

"I'm not upset. In fact, I don't care at all. It's over and done with as far as I'm concerned."

Hand tracing her collarbone, she presses in closer to me. "You can honestly say you don't have any feelings toward me still?" She brushes her fingers over my dress shirt, trailing across my pec, and I jerk away.

"Oh, I have feelings. But they're not positive ones."

Tears shimmer in her eyes and her lower lip quivers. "Really? I remember all the fun we had together. The night we swam in the fountain, then you took me to your dorm and made love to me." She feathers her hand over my forearm and my stomach roils, steak and wine and anger churning together.

"Tinsley. I'm not interested in this walk down memory lane with you. I'm not interested in you at all. I'm with Gracelyn now and I'm happy."

Her face hardens, jaw tensing and dark eyes going cold.

"You're making a huge mistake, Mack. How can

someone like you be with someone like her?" Tinsley's voice rises, her harsh words echoing off the high ceiling.

"Mack? You okay?"

I spin to face Gracelyn, guilt flooding through me as I back away from Tinsley.

How much did she hear?

CHAPTER 30
GRACELYN

don't think I'm winning Tinsley over. And I don't think I care, either.

I thought Jamie was bad.

Turns out, Tinsley's her even-more-evil twin.

I'm almost one-hundred percent sure she just told Mack I'm not good enough for him. Which is most likely true, but still. Rude of her to point that out.

Besides, what's it to her? She doesn't want him anyway.

"Hey, Gracelyn. Yes, I'm fine. Let's go back to the table." Mack takes my arm, looping his elbow with mine, and we practically jog back to the dining room.

"What was all that about?" I squint up at him, not sure I want to know.

"She wanted to rehash old times. I wasn't up for it." Mack frowns, his worry lines pronounced.

"Oh." I want to know more, but we're already back at the table and Mack's pulling my chair out for me, the waiter fanning the black linen napkin over my lap.

"You good, son?" Mack's dad asks over his fork.

"Yes, sir. Fine." Mack resumes eating at a rapid pace, his plate almost clean. Tinsley's still not back.

"I'm going to check on Tinsley." Emma Kate tosses her napkin on the table. "I'm done eating anyway."

"Oh for heaven's sake. I've never had so many disruptions at a meal," Mrs. McIntire mutters, but Emma Kate ignores her. She hustles away from the table, leaving me and Mack alone with his parents.

We eat in silence for a few more minutes, the mood strained. Suddenly, all the water and wine hits me at once and I have to pee. Desperately.

"I hate to do this, but I need to use the restroom." I don't bother waiting for a response, hopping up and half-jogging to the bathroom.

I burst through the door, already lifting my dress to make a sprint to the first available toilet. The restroom is spacious, a large enough spot to throw a party, complete with multiple rooms. All I care about right now though is finding a toilet.

Sprinting through an ornate sitting room, I finally find the toilets and shove into one of the private stalls. I lock the heavy door and pee in complete peace.

The stalls are fancy, with gold bath fixtures and intricately carved wood doors reaching all the way to the floor. Not like in cheaper places, where you can see the feet of the person peeing next to you.

I'm almost finished when I hear a faucet running, followed by two now-familiar voices.

Oh shit. Tinsley and Emma Kate are still in here.

It's fine, everyone pees. I'll just wash my hands and leave, like a normal potty break.

"I can't believe your brother, Emma Kate."

Tinsley, and she sounds like she's crying.

"I mean, we were engaged! I thought he'd still care about me, at least a little."

"I know, I know." Emma Kate shushes her like she would a small child, her voice calm and soothing. "He's a man, Tins. They don't know what they want."

"Right?" Tinsley's voice rises, and she laughs harshly. "I mean, obviously, judging by what he brought home."

Ouch.

My face burns and I start to sweat. I don't know if it's from shame or being locked in the stall, but my hair's sticking to my neck and I'm hot all over.

"She's so…so…"

So what, Tinsley?

Perversely, I'm dying to hear.

"Average. Like, not special. What does he possibly see in her?"

She does have a point, although it sucks to hear the words out loud. I've asked myself that a million times.

"You don't think he's going to marry her, do you, Emma Kate?" Tinsley sounds horrified at the mere idea of me marrying Mack.

"I doubt it. They haven't been together that long, I don't think. And like I said, she doesn't seem like his type. If you know what I mean…"

I have a pretty good idea she's talking about my weight and not-so-slender figure. Another wave of hot mortification rolls over me, my feelings impossibly hurt.

"Well, you're his sister. Put in a good word for me. I thought I was over him, but maybe not. Seeing him with *her*—" She snarls the word *her* like I'm a vampire or a smelly swamp monster. "—is making me rethink everything."

"You know I will, babe. Come on, my mom's probably pissed we've been gone so long."

The water shuts off and I wait until the door creaks open, then slams shut.

Silence.

Then I wait another solid thirty seconds, just to be on the safe side.

Finally, I crack the door open and peer out. The bathroom's empty except for me.

I stand at the sink, staring at my reflection in the mirror. Tight ringlets curl around my face from the humidity, my cheeks flushing bright pink with heat and humiliation. The skin on my neck's blotchy and my hands tremble.

Tinsley still has a thing for Mack.

What if he still harbors feelings for her, deep down? What if he's not sure how he feels? About her or me?

My heart aches as I kick around the possibility that maybe Mack and I aren't meant to be. Tinsley and Emma Kate do have some things right—I'm different than other girls he's dated. Less sophisticated, less thin and fit, and apparently a whole helluva lot poorer.

Maybe Jamie and Tinsley and the rest of the world see what I'm too delusional and lovestruck to see.

That Mack and I don't belong together after all.

Mack avoids a confrontation with his mother, sneaking into the guesthouse after we "retire" for the night. We snuggle together in the dark, the low howl of the wind rattling the windows. He pulls me in close, his cock rock-hard against my back.

"You interested?" He nuzzles my neck, but I shake my

head. I'm way too upset about everything that happened today to even think about having sex.

"Not tonight."

Sighing, his warm breath dusts my skin. "You okay?"

"Mm-hmm." I don't trust my voice to say more. Not after the convos I overheard today, first in the garden, then in the ladies. Chest tight, I can barely breathe, let alone speak.

He strokes my arm and tears sting my eyes. I blink rapidly, trying to get the offending liquid to dissipate.

The move backfires and the tears streak down my face into the fluffy cloud of a pillow, seeping into, and most likely staining, the five million thread count pillowcase.

Dammit.

I cry quietly, but my body must shake because Mack stirs, lifting up on his elbow.

"Hey—are you crying?" He gently spins me to face him and I shake my head no, furtively swiping away the tears.

"Firecracker…" He pulls me against his chest, folding his arms around me and holding me close, my body shuddering as I cry harder.

I sniffle into his bare chest. "I'm…I'm sorry."

Mack strokes my hair. "Shhh. No, I'm sorry. My family's horrible."

"N-n-n-ooo," I protest. A total lie. Because yes, they absolutely are.

"Yes, they are, babe. Why do you think I moved away?"

Despite how awful I feel, Mack still manages to make me giggle, my chest lightening a touch.

"Is there anything specific I need to address? Whose ass do I need to kick tomorrow? Or maybe tonight? I can rush in there and haul them out of bed."

I laugh hard at that, drying his beautiful pecs with the sheets. "Not tonight. And no, I'd rather leave it alone."

He frowns at me, his hand running down my spine. "You sure? If it was my mother, I can talk to her."

"It wasn't. Not really. Nothing in particular." Tinsley's name dances on the tip of my tongue, but I don't have the energy to go there. Not right now.

"Okay. If you change your mind, holler, and I will absolutely kick some ass. Got it?" He swipes the last remaining tears from my cheek, so soft, so tender, I almost start crying again.

"Got it. Night, Mack."

"Night, Firecracker. Sleep tight."

We fall asleep together, twisted up in each other's arms, a united front.

CHAPTER 31
GRACELYN

Try as I might, I don't manage to get out of the golf outing. Even after confessing how terrible I am at sports.

"Gracie, you can drive the cart. C'mon, it'll be fun!" Mack's dad ushers me out of the house amidst my protests.

And that's how I end up being Mack's golf cart driver and caddy. Emma Kate and Tinsley have another cart, and Mack's parents share a third. We're only on hole five and I'm already bored out of my mind.

Playing golf—or rather, spectating—makes watching paint dry seem downright exciting.

The cart girl motors by and Mack's dad flags her down, buying a round of drinks for everyone. I opt for a bottled water, as does Mack. Tinsley, Emma Kate, and Mack's mom all order mimosas, and Mack's dad gets two shots of bourbon to throw in his iced tea.

Pretty sure the alcohol's not going to improve anyone's

golf game. Maybe that's how Mack managed to win two back-to-back tournaments. Everyone else was drunk.

At least the sun's shining because the air's chilly, especially with the light breeze. I'm a little bit cold, despite my chunky sweater and cream leggings.

"Atta boy!" Mack's dad whoops as he stripes his ball straight down the fairway. "Look at 'em go!"

I have no idea where the ball lands, but he seems happy about it. Must have been a good shot.

Mack's mom hits next. Her ball flies a decent way, but she shakes her head and curses under her breath. Clearly not happy about the shot.

"Emma Kate, go on. We haven't got all day." Mack's dad waves at Emma Kate. Tinsley elbows her, stopping her cell phone scroll.

"Sorry, Daddy." Emma Kate pops a cute little pout and sidles up to the tee box. She hits the ball firmly and there's a nice thwack, which I take means good things.

"Beautiful, darlin'. Tinsley?"

Tinsley hops right up, driver in hand. Sashaying past us, she swishes her ass back and forth in her tight white pants, directly in Mack's line of sight. She bends down and tees up her ball, moving like a limber cat stretching in a patch of sunlight. Leaning over the club, she wiggles her round ass side to side for a solid fifteen seconds.

"Hit the ball already," Mack mutters under his breath and I snicker.

Tinsley steps away from the ball, not taking the shot. She lowers her designer sunglasses and shoots me a withering glare.

"Quiet, please."

I hold up my palm. "Sorry."

Then she goes through the whole process again, this time even slower.

For fuck's sake.

After an age, Tinsley finally hits the damn ball. It flies through the air, landing in the middle of the fairway.

"Great shot, Tins!" Emma Kate cries.

"Yes, nice ball." Mack's dad bobs his head in appreciation, and Mack's mom smiles.

Of course Tinsley's great at golf. Of fucking course she is.

Mack unfolds himself from the cart and crosses to the tee box. Tinsley bends over as he gets closer, giving him a full, unbridled view of her ass.

Yeah, we get it. You have a nice ass.

Mack averts his gaze, stepping around her and stabbing the ground with his tee. Tinsley brushes against his arm, swiping her tee from the ground.

"Sorry. Don't want this to be in your way." Then she spins on her heel and swish-swishes away.

Lips pressed together in a tight line, Mack's brow furrows in concentration. He takes a practice stroke, then drives the ball further than everyone else.

"Impressive." Tinsley trills the word and a tiny bit of vomit rises in my throat.

"Let's hit it, kids. We've got a group behind us." Mack's dad hitches his thumb at the impatient foursome glowering behind us.

Mack's dad takes off and I follow, depressing the pedal all the way. We pick up speed going downhill and I let off the gas pedal, hoping to coast.

All of us slow down as we approach the fairway and I cut the cart to the right, trying to get close to Mack's ball. Unfortunately, I hit a patch of white gravel as I near his parents' cart. I slam on the brakes and the cart slides twenty feet. I'm an inch away from rear-ending his mom and dad. Mack braces himself as a puff of white dust blossoms around us and we screech to a halt.

"Good God almighty, son! What's going on back there?" Mack's dad adjusts his hat, shaking his head, and Mack's mom scowls at us. The look's practically her entire personality at this point.

"Sorry," I say sheepishly.

"It's fine, babe." Mack pats my thigh, Emma Kate and Tinsley snickering in the background.

I can't even drive a golf cart right. Who am I kidding? I'm not a country club – golf – tennis – yacht girlie. I'm a small-town—tequila-drinking—bar girlie who occasionally has sex in the back of a pickup truck beneath the stars.

This isn't me at all.

Everyone hits their shots, then Mack's back in the cart.

"You drive." I scoot over, motioning at the plastic steering wheel.

"No, you've got it."

"No. I don't."

"Let's go!" Tinsley shouts, revving her cart behind us.

"Fine." Mack sighs, sliding behind the wheel. I fold my arms over my chest and try to think happy thoughts.

Nothing comes to mind.

"I'm going to bounce at the middle, okay?"

"At the turn?" Mack glances over his shoulder, artificially green grass whizzing by.

"Yeah. At the midpoint. Halftime. Whatever." I shrug, not sure of the technical jargon and not caring, either.

"Okay. Bobby can run you home."

"It's fine, I can walk."

"Gracelyn, it's over a mile."

"I need the exercise."

"Says who?"

"Tinsley." The names pop out of my mouth before I can stop myself.

He eases off the gas pedal and the cart slows. "Did she say something to you?"

"Forget it."

"Hell, no, I'm not forgetting it."

"Mack—" I squeeze his strong biceps. "Please, don't make this an issue."

"Gracelyn, what did they say?"

I drop my gaze to the ground, wishing I could melt into the cart path somehow and disappear.

Forcing conviction into my voice, I square my shoulders and turn to face Mack. "Do not say anything to her. I'm serious. That only makes me look like a crybaby. Besides, no one said anything to my face. I heard her talking behind my back. To Emma Kate."

"That bitch," Mack growls, his jaw ticking.

"I agree. But I still don't want to make a big deal about it. I'm just gonna walk home. It's fine."

"I'll come with you. I don't want to play golf anyway."

"No. Have a fun time with your parents. I'll be fine."

Mack pulls his cell phone out of his pocket. "I'm calling Bobby."

I cross my arms over my chest. "Fine. I'd probably get lost anyway."

His thumb hovers over the dial button. "You sure you don't want me to come? We could have some alone time, if you know what I mean?"

I smack him in the arm. "I know what you mean. And no, stay. Spend time with your family."

Make all this worth my while.

I don't say it, but I sure the hell think it.

At halftime—excuse me, *the turn*—I make my excuses and wave goodbye. The only one I'm sad to leave is Mack, but I figure his parents will be a Tinsley buffer. She wouldn't dare make a move on him in front of them.

Bobby drops me off at the guesthouse and I wander in and crash onto the bed, stare up at the coffered ceiling.

Even the guesthouse ceiling is fancy here.

Buzz, buzz.

Bestie: How's it going?

Gracelyn: TOTAL DISASTER

Bestie: NO!

Gracelyn: YES

I tap her icon, longing to hear a familiar voice. She answers on the first ring and my throat tightens.

"Hey."

"Gracelyn!" She's so sweet, so comforting, so Sloane, that I almost start crying.

Somehow I manage to hold it together.

"What's going on? What happened?"

"Sloane, it's been awful. Absolutely awful." I tuck my legs up under me, readying for a long, consoling chat.

"His mother?"

"Yes. But his sister hasn't been great either. And wait for it—his ex showed up."

"No!" Sloane gasps.

"And not just an ex-girlfriend. He was engaged!"

"What?!?" Her voice tips up into a shriek. "Mack—my dad's friend Mack—was *engaged*?"

"Yep. A long time ago, right after college. Her name's Tinsley and she's terrible."

Terrible Tinsley does have a nice ring to it.

"Gorgeous, too, which makes it worse." I lean back against the pillows. "Thin and perfect. Great skin, nice hair."

"Gracelyn, you're more gorgeous, I'm sure. You have the best hair in the whole wide world. And your skin's always dewy and perfect. Plus, you're funny and witty and the nicest person on the planet. That girl's got nothing on you."

My chest squeezes as Sloane glazes me glossier than a Krispy Kreme donut hot and fresh from the fryer.

"Thanks, bestie. I love you. And I wish you were here because Tinsley is Jamie 2.0, I swear."

"Yikes."

"I know. I could totally use the backup. Not that Mack's not backing me up. He totally would. But I don't want him to."

"Why?" Sloane asks the innocent question and I gnaw at my lip, considering.

"I don't want to drag him into the mean girl shit. It's fine."

"No, it's not, Gracelyn. Let him shut it down." Her voice is firm and she almost convinces me.

Almost.

"I can't, Sloane. It'd be too embarrassing. I overheard them talking about me. Twice. Once in the garden and another time in the ladies' room. I'll look like a tattletale if Mack mentions it."

"Probably..." Sloane's voice drops as we both consider my options.

"Not probably. Definitely. I'm not a snitch."

She laughs, and my shoulders loosen a touch. I miss my best friend so much right now it actually physically hurts.

"Are you in Atlanta with Cam for the game?"

"Yes. He plays this weekend. But most of the team came up early, to beat the holiday traffic."

"Nice. What are y'all doing for Thanksgiving?"

"Going to the hotel restaurant. My dad's pumped."

I chuckle at this. "Don't know why. Your mimi always cooks the dinner."

"She recruits him. Every year, like clockwork."

"I miss you, bestie." I can't hold in my sigh.

"I miss you, too. It'll all work out, Gracelyn. Things always do." Sloane's voice is calm and comforting, and I relax a little, trying to believe her.

"Aren't you the sage one, now that you're almost wifed up?" I tease, a touch of jealousy rippling through me. Sloane and Cam are so happy. I want a fraction, a glimmer of what the two of them have.

"Just quoting my bestie. I believe I was retching over a toilet when you uttered those words of wisdom."

"Damn. Sometimes I'm too smart for my own good."

Sloane giggles and we say our goodbyes. I click off, feeling a teensy bit better than I did before.

CHAPTER 32
MACK

'm seething mad the rest of the round and my score reflects that. I drive the ball great, besting my typical yardage through power fueled by rage. But I can't putt for shit, all my focus on Gracelyn and how to make her feel better.

The situation's worse with Tinsley shaking her ass in my face every two seconds, giggling and acting stupid.

Like I'd get back with her, particularly after what Gracelyn told me.

"Why so grumpy, Mack?" She knocks her knee against mine, having volunteered as tribute to squeeze into the third row of the SUV with me.

"I'm not grumpy." I slide my knee away from her, squaring my shoulders up and facing away from her. Trees whiz by as Bobby motors toward the house and I'm struck by the fakeness of everything around me—the landscape, the massive houses, the people.

I can't wait to be back home in Thunder Creek with Gracelyn.

"Sure seems like it to me." Tinsley swipes at my knee again and my hand darts out, encircling her wrist.

"Stop it, Tinsley. I'm not amused."

Her eyes flash with something—anger, hurt. I don't know what and I don't care.

"Fine. You're being a real asshole."

"Probably why we broke up."

She pulls her wrist away, folding her arms across her chest. We ride the rest of the way home in silence, my family none the wiser.

"Cocktails at six, Ulysses. Be sure to tell Gracelyn. I do hope her headache's better." My mother lifts her sunglasses, sliding them atop her head.

"I'll give her the message right now."

Taking my escape route, I hustle out to the guesthouse. Knocking on the door, I shift from foot to foot. I hope Gracelyn's up to drinks and dinner with the family. It will be hard to explain her absence away if she's not.

Gracelyn flings the door of the guesthouse open, wrapping her arms around my neck and pulling me inside. Pressing her mouth to mine, she kisses me long and slow and it's the best part of the whole miserable day.

"Hey, handsome. How'd you play?"

"Terrible." I slide my hands down to her ass, lifting her up. She wraps her legs around my waist and I carry her to the bathroom.

"Shower with me." I nuzzle her neck, inhaling all her goodness, her wholesomeness.

I love this girl.

"Here?" she squeaks, catching my eye in the mirror. "At your parents' house? What if they have cameras? Rich people always have cameras."

I chuckle, setting her ass down on the counter and

lifting off her top. "No cameras, babe. Pretty sure that's illegal. My dad was a lawyer, remember? He takes that kind of shit seriously."

"Oh, right."

Reaching behind her, I unclasp her bra and slide the straps off her shoulders. The lacy material falls to the ground and I dip down, kissing each of her rosy nipples.

"I love your tits."

She smiles, twining her fingers in my hair as I suck at the sharp points. "I know."

"I love your ass, too." I glide my hands beneath the waistband of her pants, pulling them down to expose the tiny scrap of fabric passing for panties. "So round and firm."

"It's not that firm."

I smack her cheek. "Yes, it is. You have a fucking beautiful body and I'll hear nothing negative about it."

She blushes as I work the globes of her ass, sliding her pants all the way down until she's naked for me.

"Fucking perfect." I kiss up and down her chest, down her torso. Lick across her clavicle, all the way down her arms to the tips of her fingers, sucking each one into my mouth. A soft moan falls from her lips as I drop down to my knees and spread her legs, my tongue trailing through her wetness. Her eyes slip shut as my tongue circles her clit, flicking the swollen bud.

After a few seconds, I pull away and turn on the shower. Water pounds the tile and the room fills with steam as I quickly strip. Taking Gracelyn by the hand, I pull her under the warm stream of the rainfall shower head. Rivulets of water stream down her body, running over her breasts, dripping down her stomach, her thighs. She wraps her arms around her middle, and I remember the first night we hooked up. How she wanted to keep the lights off.

"Hey—" I tip her chin up, shielding her face from the spray of water with my body. "You're beautiful, you know that?"

She nods, but doesn't smile or say anything. Anger at Tinsley rolls through me, my body tensing. But I shove that away for now, instead focusing on the gorgeous woman standing in front of me.

"Gracelyn, you are stunning. Every last inch of you." My fingers trace over her cheek, her shoulder, down her arm. I splay my palm across her belly, her hips, pulling her to me by her ass I love so much. "I want to spend the rest of my life—all the rest of my days—worshipping this body God gave you. I can't get enough of you and your curves."

"Stop…" She rolls her eyes, blushing in the billowing steam.

"No, ma'am, I will not stop. You are fucking breathtaking and I need you to hear it, believe it." I stroke her cheek, but she averts her gaze, staring at the wall tile.

"Mack, I appreciate you saying that. But you don't have to. I know I'm not thin. I'm average, nothing special." Her lower lip quivers as the words fall from her mouth and my heart twists in my chest. *How can she believe that about herself?*

"Gracelyn, every single inch of you is amazing. You are not average. You're way, way beyond that, beautiful. And I'm honored that you would share your sensational body with me."

I seize her lips in a hot, possessive kiss, slip my tongue into her mouth, our tongues tangling together.

This is my girl. And I need her to know it, to feel it.

Everything about her is soft and comforting. She feels

like home, like a safe, happy place to snuggle into every night.

"I love you," I murmur, my hands massaging her perfect peach of an ass. "So much. All of you." I reach down and loosen her arms, pulling them away from her belly. Dropping to my knees, water pounds my back as I kiss all over her stomach. Her fingers wrap around my neck and she leans into me, her body softening.

"I love you, too," she whispers, barely audible over the splashing of water.

Slurping warm droplets from her skin, I lick and suck until she's quivering beneath my lips and my knees ache from the hard tile. Standing, I claim her mouth in another long, hot kiss. Then I drop my hand between her thighs, hot and slippery with her arousal. Spreading her wide, I play with her clit, her skin flushing pink.

"So wet and ready for me. Beautiful. And all mine." I sink two fingers into her pussy, flexing to find her G spot. Sucking in a sharp breath, her muscles tense around my hand as I stretch her.

"Such a good fucking girl. My girl. Do you want my cock? Or do you want to come all over my fingers first?"

"I want your cock, Daddy." She nips at my lip, gazing up at me with shiny droplets of water on her lashes and a playful glint in her eye. Her self-consciousness melts away as I wrap my arms around her and bring her closer.

A growl rumbles from deep in my chest, my cock impossibly hard for her. I love it when she calls me that. I seize her lips in one more hot, greedy kiss, then spin her around to face the shower wall.

"Hands above your head, baby girl, and brace yourself against the tile. I want to feel your perfect peach of an ass on me and I don't want you slipping." I nip at her earlobe, sucking drops of water from the skin. Chill bumps rise on her neck, her nipples hardening to sharp points.

She lifts her arms above her head, placing her palms flat on the white tile. I smack her right cheek, then her left, and she squeals. The high-pitched sound bounces around the small space and I grin, watching her ass pinken for me.

"That's good, spread your legs, baby. Just like that." She moves her legs apart, a gorgeous, curvy starfish.

"You're fucking stunning, Gracelyn." I press my chest to her back, run my hands over her warm belly, cupping her round, full breasts. My erection bobs on her spine, begging to sink into her hot, tight pussy. But I want to bring my girl close to the edge first, so fucking close she's shaking for me.

I fondle her breasts, pinching at her nipples and rolling them between my fingers. She's breathing faster, her chest rising and falling in quick pants. I twist one of the buds and she bites at her lip. Twisting the other, her muscles clench as she presses her ass up against me.

"Fuck—" she hisses as I release, blood flowing back into her tight buds. I rock my hips against her ass and she wriggles, seeking friction.

"Tell me what you want, gorgeous," I murmur into the tender skin of her neck, teeth grazing the flesh.

"I want you to fuck me, Daddy."

That's all I can take. I line my dick up with her entrance and push in. Not slow and gentle, but with one hard upward thrust. I impale her with my cock and she gasps in surprise, her muscles clenching around me.

"That's it, baby girl. Take all of Daddy's big, hard cock." I pull out, then thrust into her again. She pushes back against me, shimmying her ass against my pelvis. "Fuck, yes."

I pull out and drive into her again and again, our bodies slapping together, wet and warm and slippery. Pressure builds low in my gut, the familiar tingling sensation at the base of my spine growing and building. She keeps her grip on the wall, her face pressed against the tile as I pound into her.

One hand gripping her hip, the other circling her wrist, I drive into her tight channel. Her muscles tense and clench, milking my cock as she spasms. Crying out, she crashes over the edge and I follow her lead, exploding. I spurt my seed into her, over and over again until my dick's limp.

Pulling out, I kiss all the way down her neck, the straight line of her spine, to her tailbone then back up again. I spin her around and drop my lips to hers. She wraps her arms around my neck, water spilling down around us.

"You are so fucking perfect, baby. All of you."

"I love you," she murmurs.

"I love you, too, baby."

I hold onto her like that for a long, long time, enjoying the feel of her soft curves against me, the warmth of the water and steam wrapping around us. I wish we could stay like this forever, just the two of us in our little cocoon, where we're safe and happy.

Everything about this moment—about us—feels right.

But things are never that simple, especially with the McIntire family involved.

CHAPTER 33
GRACELYN

Thanksgiving day's bright and sunny, a picture-perfect crisp autumn day. The air's brisk with a slight wind, leaves blazing orange and red, and the smell of a wood-burning fire hangs in the air.

"We have cocktails outside around the fire before dinner. Family tradition." Mack laces his fingers with mine as we walk up to the main house.

I spent the last hour selecting the perfect holiday outfit—black dress number six wins. A cute wrap dress with a ruffle hemline, I accessorize with diamond studs, a delicate pave drop necklace, and booties, topping the entire ensemble with a soft gray cashmere wrap. Mack assures me the outfit's suitable, but butterflies still zoom around my tummy. They seem to have taken up permanent residence there. I suck in a quick breath, trying to get a hold of my nerves.

Even after two full days here, I'm still not comfortable. Tinsley has a lot to do with that, but it's difficult to unravel the situation. Emma Kate hasn't exactly been welcoming, and I doubt I've left an amazing impression on either of Mack's parents.

I have a lot of work to do to win over the McIntire family.

Maybe today will be the day. A cozy holiday celebrating food and family.

"Gracie, Ulysses. Happy Thanksgiving!" Mack's dad bellows across the lawn as we approach the back of the main house.

Just like Mack said, the family plus Tinsley stand around a crackling fire in the freestanding brick fireplace. A sofa and chairs flank a teak coffee table, set with a fancy spread of hors d'oeuvres. Piles of meat and cheeses, olives, and nuts, tiny finger sandwiches, and caprese skewers fill the table, along with crystal glasses and an open bottle of champagne.

"Happy Thanksgiving, Dad." Mack hugs his father, then his mother, and I follow suit. I try to act natural, even though the gesture's stiff, considering we're practically strangers.

"Happy Thanksgiving, Brother." Emma Kate squeezes her brother, then gives me a light hug. "Gracelyn."

I hug her back, patting her awkwardly on the back while sucking in my stomach. No need to give her more ammunition.

Tinsley murmurs her greeting, but doesn't attempt to hug or touch either of us.

Fine by me.

As far as I'm concerned, she needs to keep her grubby little debutante paws off my man.

One of the staff presses champagne flutes into our hands, and Mack's dad raises his glass to the sky for a toast.

"To a great holiday season." He nods at each of us, then downs his bubbles in one long slug. Seconds later, he has a refill.

"Cheers." Tinsley taps her glass to Emma Kate's and the two of them exchange a knowing glance. Some secret eye signal I can't decipher.

Whatever.

I have no desire to be in the mean girls club.

"Thanks so much for hosting, Mr. and Mrs. McIntire." I smile warmly at Mack's parents and his mom nods, sipping her champagne.

"Our pleasure. I always love seeing my Ulysses." She beams at her son, and I take the micro jab in stride.

The breeze picks up, the hem of my dress fluttering around my legs, and chill bumps pepper my bare arms. It's colder out here than I realized. I move toward the fire, eager for the warmth. Mack's right behind me, but then his dad waves him over to discuss a college classmate of his.

I don't want to seem clingy, so I stay rooted in front of the fire sipping my drink. Michael Bublé croons from invisible speakers hidden among the landscaping somewhere and I let the gentle notes wash over me, soothing my frayed nerves. One of the staff rushes out to the garden and Mack's mother excuses herself to tend to the impending culinary crisis.

Leaving me alone with Tinsley and Emma Kate.

Super.

"So, Gracelyn. What are your plans?" Emma Kate swirls the golden liquid in her flute round and round, staring at me over the rim of the glass.

"For Christmas?" I take a quick sip of the drink, the cold liquid sliding down my dry throat.

"More like long-term. Your plans for my brother."

I choke and sputter, the last drops of wine burning my esophagus.

"What do you mean?"

"Don't act coy, Grace." Tinsley narrows her eyes at me. "Are you planning on marrying him?"

My tummy seizes, clenching hard, and I swear my dress shrinks two sizes. Suddenly, I can't breathe, the supple fabric digging into my waist. Face on fire, I shuffle from foot to foot.

"I mean…I don't know. Maybe?" I answer honestly.

"Figure he'd be a real catch for someone like you." Tinsley lowers her voice, making sure only the three of us can hear.

I've had just about enough of her negative energy, blistering anger ripping through me. I can't hold back any longer.

"What do you mean, someone like me exactly?" I spit out the terrible phrase, the same one I've heard several times this trip. Vague enough to fly under the radar, a subtle insult.

"You know." She cocks her head, smoothing her long brown hair over her shoulder.

"No, Tinsley. I honestly don't." I work to keep my voice even, but the struggle is real. I'm extremely pissed off now. "Say what's on your mind and let's get this out into the open."

"Wow, okay. You don't have to be so hostile." Tinsley holds up an open palm, pretending she's innocent. A real fucking peacemaker.

Emma Kate steps closer to Tinsley, making it clear that it's two against one here. Them versus me.

"I'm not being hostile, Tinsley. But I'm tired of the

innuendo, the snickering behind my back. If you have a problem with me, go ahead and say it."

"Fine." She juts out her chin, her cheekbones high and angular. A perfect face, stunningly beautiful.

Too bad her attitude doesn't match.

"I think you're after Mack for his money. I don't know how you landed him, what kind of magical spell you cast. Nothing about the two of you makes sense. I mean, look at him." Her eyes dart to the corner of the garden where Mack's deep in conversation with his father.

And she's right.

The man is freaking gorgeous, in his tailored button down and navy blazer, the luxe fabric stretching over his broad shoulders. The soft waves of his hair feather in the breeze, stubble shading his square jaw. He could pass for a GQ model posing at an outdoor photo shoot. My pussy flutters as he shoves his strong hands into his pockets. Hands that play my body like a finely tuned instrument, pulling out all the right notes. Those full lips that kiss my insecurities away, leaving behind sweet, sweet pleasure.

How the hell did I manage to land Mack?

I'm not rich or beautiful, polished or pedigreed. I didn't attend a prep school with uniforms and a sprawling wide-open campus. I don't have a fancy car or boat and I sure as hell don't belong to any membership-only clubs, unless you count the local beauty supply store.

All I have to offer Mack is my heart. Why would he settle for that?

Not when he could have all this.

An expansive estate with a thin, beautiful wife, a few cute babies sometime down the line. Running around on the lawn, laughing, his parents bursting with pride. And his wife and Emma Kate could be besties, spending spa days together and going on couple vacations.

That's never going to be me.

I take a deep, shuddery breath and pull myself together. Tinsley may be right about some things, but I have to set the record straight. I'm not a gold digger.

"I'm not after Mack for his money. I didn't even know he had money until we came here."

"Uh-huh, right." Tinsley rolls her eyes, pursing her full lips together.

"I swear. He never breathed a word about it."

"You expect me to believe you didn't know my brother has a trust fund?" Emma Kate chimes in, hand on hip.

"Believe whatever you want." I spit out the words, crossing my arms over my chest. "But I had no idea. Not sure if either of you've ever visited your brother in Thunder Creek in all the years he's lived there. But if you had, you'd know I'm telling the truth. Mack lives next door to my mom. It's a nice house, but it's nothing like this. He drives an old aqua pickup truck—he prefers you call it vintage—the same one his grandfather left him. He runs a successful carpentry business out of his garage. This —" I gesture at the lawn, the striking outdoor fireplace, the massive main house. "All of this is not the Mack I know."

Emma Kate and Tinsley both stare at me dumbfounded, mouths slightly open like two stunned goldfish.

"Now if you'll excuse me." I set my champagne glass down on the table and walk toward the house. I need to duck into a bathroom and compose myself before facing Mack's parents at the dinner table.

Stepping into the safe haven of the main house, I run straight into his mother.

"Hello there, Grace. Everything okay?" Her eyes flick

over me, sizing me up and surely noticing my blotchy neck. Confrontation always mottles my skin, giving me away.

"Yes, I'm fine, thank you."

Mrs. McIntire wraps her arm around my shoulders. "I'm glad I ran into you. I've been meaning to get you alone."

Oh shit. Now what?

I gulp, but force a smile onto my face. "Oh?"

"Come." She leads me down the hallway, past room after room. I swear I could spend a month here and still get lost in this maze of untouched spaces.

Finally, she ushers me into a quiet, jewel-toned room, with forest green wallpaper and twin matching brocade sofas. Oak shelves line the walls, filled with books I'm certain no one currently alive and in residence has ever read. At the far end of the room, illuminated with soft gallery lighting, is a full wall of trophies, ribbons, and photographs.

An homage to Ulysses Fauntleroy McIntire III.

"Oh wow." I survey the bronze trophies, each engraved with Mack's name.

All-state champion.

Defensive Player of the Year.

MVP.

College all-star

A photo of a young high school Mack in a suit and tie on college signing day, giddy as he commits to Georgia. Mack in his college jersey, holding a football and grinning at the camera. Mack and his team after winning the rivalry game against Florida, trophy raised high above his head.

"Ulysses was always a very talented athlete. We thought for sure he'd turn professional after college." Mrs.

McIntire sighs, her hair swishing across her shoulders. "When that didn't happen, his father and I still held high hopes for our son."

A tiny furrow forms between her otherwise smooth brow. "He was a decent student. He only needed three years of school to practice law with his father. We had absolute faith in him."

I nod, my throat dry and scratchy. *Why is she telling me all this?*

"We thought for sure we'd be grandparents soon, too. He and Tinsley dated through college and we had the wedding practically planned."

Heat flames my face, the wind sucked from my lungs. It's like his mother just sucker punched me without lifting a diamond-encrusted finger.

"The day they broke up was devastating. Absolutely devastating."

The tell-tale sting pricks at my nose and the back of my throat. I'm frozen to the spot, don't dare make eye contact with her.

"We all loved Tinsley. Plus, we knew she came from good people and her heart was in the right place. She has her own family money, she doesn't need ours." Mrs. McIntire spins to face me, her blue eyes cold. "Ulysses can be—how should I say this—" She taps the pads of her fingers together, searching for the words. "Rather obtuse about people and their motives. Not that I'm saying yours are bad…"

Uh-huh.

I swallow hard, running my thumb over the smooth stack of bangles on my wrist.

"Ulysses is my only son. He inherits much of this kingdom. We hate to see him squander his many blessings." She presses her lips together in a tight pinch, frowning.

So now he's squandering his blessings on me?

I've had more than I can bear.

Taking a shuddery breath, I nod. "Yes, ma'am, I understand. Your son is an amazing man." My voice wobbles and tears prick at my eyes, but I refuse to let this woman see me break.

"I love him very much. For who he is, not what he has. For the record, I had no idea about any of this. He never breathed a word about his family fortune."

Or his family, but I figure now's not the time to mention that.

"Thank you for sharing this with me." I gesture at the Ulysses shrine. "He's incredible."

I back away from the wall and his mother, slowly at first. As I get closer to the door, I pick up speed. Then I turn and hurry away as quickly as I can, putting distance between me and Mack's family.

This is never going to work.

I don't fit in here. Don't *want* to fit in here.

This may be Mack's world, but it will never be mine.

Jogging down the hall, I burst out into the garden and run down the path to the guest house.

I need to go home.

CHAPTER 34
MACK

"Where's Gracelyn?" I glance around the garden, but I don't see her anywhere. She's not sitting and chatting with Emma Kate and Tinsley. Can't say I blame her there.

She's not in front of the fire, nibbling cheese and crackers and sipping wine.

She isn't talking with my father.

And she's not with my mother and me.

"I'm not sure, dear. Perhaps she went to the bathroom." Mom twirls the drink skewer holding the bleu cheese-stuffed olive in her martini, avoiding my gaze, her posture ram-rod straight.

I guess we've moved onto the stiffer drinks now.

"I should try to find her." I sidestep my mother and go into the house. The clattering of pots and pans sounds from the kitchen as the chef and staff put the finishing touches on Thanksgiving dinner. A few people move through the hallway, carrying dishes for the feast.

No sign of Gracelyn anywhere.

I walk down the hallway, checking each room I pass. They're all empty. Room after room, each one quiet and unoccupied. I peer into the library and spot two empty champagne flutes on one of the round side tables.

Stepping into the space, I quickly glance around. Nothing but empty sofas, unread books, and a bunch of stupid trophies my parents insist on displaying to impress their friends.

So embarrassing.

Where the hell's Gracelyn?

I'm worried now. The last time I saw her was over forty-five minutes ago at least. My dad yammered on and on about some kid I vaguely remember from school who started practicing law down in Florida and made a fortune chasing big pharma. Like I give a shit.

Maybe Gracelyn's in the bathroom.

I hustle down the hall, knocking on the powder room door. No response. I open the door to check she's not passed out or something.

Empty.

After checking every bathroom on the main floor, panic sets in. *Where could she be?*

I pull out my cell and shoot her a quick text.

Mack: Where are you? Worried

I stare at the screen, willing her to respond. No dots pop up and swirl, the message only marked as Delivered.

Hurrying out of the main house, I jog down the path to the guest house. It's the only spot I haven't checked outside of the upstairs and she has no reason to go up there.

I knock on the guest house door and wait. She doesn't

answer, so I turn the knob and push inside. The house is still and quiet, and no lights are on.

"Gracelyn?" I call her name, striding through the house in search of her. "You here, babe?"

My voice booms in the emptiness.

"Gracelyn?" I call for her again as I enter the kitchen, a hint of panic edging my voice. I spot a note on the table and grab the paper with a shaky hand.

> *Mack,*
>
> *I'm sorry to leave like this, but I couldn't stay. After a lot of thinking, it's best if we spend some time apart and reassess our relationship. I think we may be too different after all. We'll talk about it later—I don't want to ruin your family holiday.*
>
> *Please pass my regrets to your family, along with a thank you for their hospitality.*
>
> *Happy Thanksgiving and again, I'm sorry.*
>
> *Love,*
>
> *G.*
>
> *P.S—I took your truck because I couldn't get an Uber. I'll come pick you up this weekend. Maybe Bobby can drop you in town and I'll meet you there?*

I toss the note back on the table, slamming my fist down hard.

"Dammit!"

Pulling my cell out of my pocket, I mash Gracelyn's

number and wait. I get sent straight to voicemail. I call again and leave a message.

"Gracelyn, it's me. When you get this message, call me. Please." My voice is low and desperate, but I can't help it. Bolting out of here without saying goodbye isn't Gracelyn's style. I need to know what happened, who hurt my girl.

Anger surging through me, I charge back to the main house, gravel crunching under my feet. The garden's empty, Michael Bublé singing only to the decorative hedges. Appetizers are gone, all the dishes cleared away. Cocktail hour's over.

I square my shoulders and stomp into the main house. Voices carry down the long hallway. My guess is everyone's gathered in my mother's favorite sitting room, the one adjacent to the dining room used only on holidays and special occasions. Not to be confused with the regular, everyday dining room.

Blood roaring in my ears, I loosen my shirt collar and head in the direction of the voices. Sure enough, my mother, sister and Tinsley are relaxing on the sofas in the peacock blue sitting room, while my father freshens his drink at the bar cart in the corner.

"What happened?" I growl, not bothering with any niceties. "What did y'all say to Gracelyn?"

"Huh?" Dad blinks at me over the ice bucket. "What are you talking about, son?"

I shove one hand in my pocket, knuckles flexing in the small cotton cave.

"One of you—maybe two of you—" I peer over at Tinsley and Emma Kate, "must have said something to her. Because she's gone."

Tinsley gasps, her hand flying to her mouth. Like she

actually cares Gracelyn left. It was probably her plan all along.

"Really? She just *left*?" Emma Kate's voice tips up in shock. "Before we even had dinner? That's so rude."

Anger boils in my veins as I spin to face my little sister. "That's the rude part? Y'all have been beyond rude and inhospitable to her ever since we got here."

Emma Kate sits up straight, crossing her feet at her ankles demurely. "That's not true. I personally made it my mission to talk to her any chance I could." She presses her manicured nails to her chest and acts affronted. "Not my fault she didn't have much to say." Shrugging her shoulders, she feigns innocence.

"Yeah, right. The Gracelyn I know always has a lot to say. What did you talk to her about? Cotillion? Your sorority sisters? Did you ask her anything about her life, her interests? Doubt it."

"We did, Mack. Swear." Tinsley backs up Emma Kate, smoothing her hair over her shoulder and fluttering her lashes. "We tried."

"By talking bad about her behind her back?" I spit out the words, heat creeping up my neck.

"What? No." Emma Kate shakes her head, but doesn't make eye contact with me. She's always been a terrible liar.

"I know you did, Emma Kate. You and Tinsley talked shit about her every chance you got. And guess what? She heard you. So nice job. And she didn't want me to mention it because she's mature and wanted to get along with everyone. But the way you treated my girlfriend is wholly unacceptable."

Emma Kate blushes a bright pink, all the way to the tips of her ears. At least she has the decency to be embarrassed.

Tinsley, not so much.

That bitch sits on the sofa examining her fucking nails and pretending she did absolutely nothing wrong.

"And you, Tinsley." I level my gaze at my ex. "How dare you say anything bad about Gracelyn and the way she looks? She's a better person—more beautiful inside and out—than you'll ever be."

Tinsley touches her slender throat, her face pale. She opens her mouth to speak, but nothing comes out.

I spin to face my mother. "And don't act all blameless, Mother. You could have embraced Gracelyn, welcomed her with open arms. Instead, you invited my ex for the holiday —" I jerk my head at Tinsley, "then shoved Gracelyn into the guest house, away from the rest of the family. You made jabs about her career—which she's very good at, by the way— and made her feel less than. If I don't call or visit enough for your liking, the only person you have to blame is yourself."

My mother's lips press into a hard, thin line and she frowns. "Now, Ulysses. That is just not the truth."

"It is, Mother. It is the truth. Whether you want to admit it or not. The reason I don't come home is because this isn't me." I sweep my arm across the room, gesturing at the expensive paintings, the blown glassware from Milan, the priceless first editions. "All this stuff. It's too much. I feel trapped, suffocated by this lifestyle. Maybe if y'all were warm and open, it'd be different. But this visit shows me that's never going to happen."

"I'm sorry you feel that way, Ulysses." My mother's voice wavers a little and tears shimmer in her eyes, glistening in the glow of the lamp. "We've always done the best for you, tried to give you everything. And this is how you repay us? With ingratitude?"

"No, Mother. I'm not ungrateful."

Raking my fingers through my hair, I take a deep breath and forge ahead. "I appreciate having the means to live how I want, on my own terms. But those terms have never been enough for you." I glance up and meet her gaze. "And that's the problem."

My father stares at me from across the room, nodding his head in agreement. He's wise enough to stay out of it, for fear of retribution from my mother. I understand his position, but it would be nice to have back-up every once in a while.

"Now if you'll excuse me, I'm going to find the woman I love." I take a deep breath, my conviction growing stronger. "The woman I want to spend the rest of my life with. Because she understands and appreciates me for who I really am, not who she wishes I would be."

My chest lightens as I say the words out loud.

I love Gracelyn. I want to be with her. I want to make her my wife.

"Dad, I'm going to need to borrow a car."

He sets his glass down on the bar cart and hustles across the room, ready to spring into action.

"You've got it." Looping his arm across my shoulders, he ushers me out of the silent sitting room and toward the garage.

The four-car garage attached to the main house stores my father's collection of modern cars.

"Any one you want, son." He gestures at his fleet, driven mainly around town when he feels like a quick escape from my mother. "My personal favorite is the Maserati. It's got some pick up."

"Perfect."

My dad presses the key into my palm. "Take good care of her, son."

"I will. I'll bring her back without a scratch."

"I'm sure the car will be fine. I was talking about Gracelyn."

He winks, slapping me on the back, and for the first time in ten years, I think my dad gets it. Gets me.

"Thanks, Dad." I hug him, my heart full. "I appreciate it."

"Give me a minute and I'll have the chef fix you a to-go plate. For you and Gracelyn. Happy Thanksgiving, my boy."

"Thanks, Dad. Happy Thanksgiving."

CHAPTER 35
GRACELYN

I cry the entire drive home.

For myself. For the relationship I left behind. For the future I had planned that's never going to happen.

All the pent-up emotion of the last few days seeps out of my body, leaking down my face in streams of hot tears. My nose runs and mascara tracks down my cheeks, but I'm past caring. Somehow the release of all the tension and the bullshit feels strangely good.

Cathartic.

Still, my chest aches and my heart hurts at losing Mack. He's a good man—the best man—but we don't work. The two of us don't make sense together. After spending time in his world and understanding where he comes from, I get it now.

His mother's right.

He needs more, deserves better, than me. He's Ulysses Fauntleroy McIntire the third, for fuck's sake.

And I'm just Gracelyn Ann Reynolds the zero. I'm not even Anne with an 'e.' Just plain old Ann.

He could have any girl in the whole wide world. A beautiful girl like Tinsley or Jamie. Someone tall and thin, with great cheekbones and a perfect figure. A woman he's proud to have on his arm, eager to show off to his friends and family.

Why would he pick someone like me? Short and curvy, with skin that mottles at every reaction like a freaking emotional chameleon. I'm cute enough, I guess, but I'm no international model or pageant winner.

I maybe could win Miss Congeniality. If a judge feels generous and you get bonus points for good hair.

Cranking the truck window down, I pop my arm out as I take the exit for Thunder Creek. The cool, fresh air of my hometown flows through the cab and I suck it in. Rolling past the familiar places—the local grocery, the drugstore, the Burger Basket—my body relaxes, the tension unraveling from my muscles.

Then I drive past my mom's street—Mack's street—and a sharp pang shoots through me, stabbing me in the chest.

I should have trusted my gut and not fallen for someone as great as Mack.

I knew I could get hurt and still my dumbass went for it.

Stupid, stupid Gracelyn.

Always wanting what she can't have. Starting way back in grade school and I've never learned my damn lesson.

I'm average, regular. A seven on a good day, as Jamie oh-so-helpfully pointed out at the Homecoming dance.

Why do I always try to score the tens of the world?

Why would Mack squander his blessings on someone like me, as his mother so delicately put it?

The short answer: he shouldn't.

I'm a big mistake, whether he wants to admit it or not.

I can't let Mack throw away his shot at happiness, ruin his relationship with his family over me. I'm not worth it.

Pulling into my lot, I park Mack's truck and cut the engine. I close my eyes and breathe in Mack's lingering scent, the leather soft beneath me. Much as I love the man, I know I have to let him go.

A lone tear splashes onto my cheek, squeezing through my closed lids. How I have any tears left, I don't know. My chest aches and I'm sad. So, so overwhelmingly sad.

Letting Mack go is the right thing to do.

Hauling my weary body from the truck, I wheel my suitcase up the walkway and unlock the door. I step inside my cozy little townhouse and make a beeline for the sofa, not bothering to turn on a light. Pulling the fuzzy blanket down from the back of the couch, I wrap the material tight around me. A warm, safe cocoon.

More tears leak from my eyes and I cry myself to sleep, feeling oh so sorry for myself.

The next thing I know, it's dark outside and a loud pounding is coming from outside. I blink, heart racing as I regain consciousness.

"Gracelyn, it's me. Open up." Mack's deep voice carries through the thin wood of the front door. "I know you're home. Please. We need to talk."

Unwinding myself from my blanket cocoon, I shuffle to the door and crack it open. And there's Mack, still in his dress shirt and pants. He must have lost the blazer some-where along the way. His hair's disheveled and the tiny crinkles around his eyes are more pronounced, even in the dark.

"Hey." I open the door wider, wiping the sleep from my eyes.

"Hey." A quick flash of relief dances across his face. He shoves one hand in his pocket. "May I come in?"

I shrug. "Sure."

I owe the man that much. Breaking up with the love of my life via a handwritten note left on the kitchen table isn't very cool.

Mack slides past me into the townhouse and I catch a hint of his woodsy scent, the cologne I love so much. The smell almost undoes me, my resolve already weakening. Being near him like this is dangerous.

Also, my new reality.

Because how am I going to avoid him in a town as small as Thunder Creek? Especially when he lives next door to my mother and my job.

Shit.

Not only is this the most painful thing I've ever done, it's also going to be damn near impossible.

Shutting the door, I shore up my resolve before turning around to face him.

"Gracelyn—" he says at the exact moment I say, "We need to break up."

"What?" His face falls, a deep furrow in his brow.

"We. Need. To. Break. Up." I say each word slowly, carefully, making sure he hears and understands the simple language.

"No." He shakes his head, sandy waves flopping onto his forehead. "No, we don't."

"Yes." I nod, wrapping my arms around my body to keep from reaching out and touching him. "Yes, we do. I'm not the right girl for you, Mack. That was pretty damn obvious this week."

"No." His lips press into a tight, thin line.

"Yes. Your family hated me, Mack. The way I look, how I act, where I come from and what I do. I'm not good enough for them." My voice cracks and I drop my gaze to the ground, tears filling my eyes. "Or for you."

"Stop, Gracelyn. Don't even talk like that." He steps forward, trying to wrap his arms around me, but I move out of reach. I don't trust myself to touch him and not fall right back to where we were. Being this close to him physically hurts, and I'm not sure how long I can endure the pain.

"It's true, Mack. You know it. Don't deny the facts."

"Gracelyn, I need you to hear me right now." He inches forward and tips my chin up with his finger, forcing me to look him in the eyes. "You're more than good enough for them. You're better than them. In every way that matters. Your pure heart, the way you treat others, how much you love your family and friends. How much you love me. That's what matters. All the other stuff is superficial bullshit."

My lip quivers and the tears spill over, splashing onto my cheeks. I love Mack, more than anything, but I'll never fit in with his family.

Swiping away the tears, I straighten my shoulders and stand tall. "I love you, too. But I'll never fit in there, Mack. The family stuff is always going to be there. They hate me. I don't want them to hate you too. For choosing me." My voice drops to a whisper and Mack sighs.

"Gracelyn…"

He brushes his thumb across my wet cheek, and this time I let him wrap his strong arms around me. Bringing me close, I press my face to his chest and sob. Chest heaving, I let out all the disappointment and sorrow I have left.

This is goodbye and I want to savor every last second I have with Mack. His arms around me, holding me to him.

"Shh, baby. Don't cry. Fuck them." He kisses the top of my head, stroking my hair lightly.

"I can't not care, Mack. Your parents, your sister. They matter. They'll never accept me."

"So what? I'm a grown-ass man. I don't need Mommy and Daddy's approval anymore. We can go to the courthouse on Monday and get married and no one could stop us."

I tense in his arms.

Married?

"Or if you want to have a wedding, that's fine too. We can have one right here in Thunder Creek. We don't have to invite them. I. Don't. Care." He punctuates each word, his voice firm.

"Mack..." I lift my head, staring up at him. "You should care. They're your family."

"Maybe I should. But I don't. If that's how they're going to treat the woman I love, I'd rather not be associated with them."

Woman he loves.

I'm that woman. The woman Mack loves.

We've said those three little words before—lots of times now—but hearing him say it like that hits me deep in my soul.

"But what about holidays? When we have kids? Are you going to keep them away from their grandparents? I would love to believe life is as simple as you're saying, but it's not. I wouldn't feel right cutting them off. From you or our future children."

He frowns, lips pressed together so hard the flesh turns white. "We never need to see them on the holidays. And if we're blessed with children, maybe they'll come around and stop acting like assholes."

I raise my brow. "Wouldn't count on it."

He scrubs a hand over his neck. "Yeah, you may be right about that. But we can cross that bridge when we get to it. All that matters right now is you and me and being together."

I sigh, wanting to believe him. Buy into the fantasy he's creating. Us against them, where we win every time.

"That's not reality, Mack. Much as I want it to be true, that won't work."

"Why, Gracelyn? I've lived like that for the last ten years. Why should anything change now?"

"Because your mother and sister have a point. You're Ulysses Fauntleroy McIntire the third. You deserve someone better than me." I swallow hard over the painful truth.

"Shut up. Right the fuck now. There's no one on this Earth that's better than you, Gracelyn. You're sassy and funny and kind. Beautiful and caring. It's me who doesn't deserve you. I'm just a washed-up old football player who builds stuff for a living. Nothing great."

"Stop." I bat at his chest. "You're amazing and you freaking know it. Plus, you have a trust fund."

"That you don't give two rips about. You love me for me and that's what matters."

He does have a point.

I've never cared too much about money. As long as I can pay my bills, I'm happy.

"So what do you say? Will you please take me back?"

Mack gazes down at me, his jade eyes pleading. I debate for a long second, rational me and emotional me feuding.

"Yes. I'll take you back."

Mack's face breaks into a gigantic smile, wider than I've ever seen, and he picks me up and twirls me around the dark living room.

Wrapping my arms around his neck, I press my lips to his in a hot, slow kiss. I know we haven't solved all our problems—and we probably never will. But for now, I'm choosing him and me and happiness.

After kissing for what seems like hours, he finally sets me down.

"You hungry?"

"Huh?"

"Are you hungry? My dad had the chef prepare a Thanksgiving dinner to go for us."

My hand flutters to my chest. "Really?"

"Yeah. My dad's on board with us. He really liked you."

Well, that's a start. "That's so sweet. I liked him, too. How'd you get here, by the way?"

"Borrowed my dad's Maserati."

Of course he did.

"We can take it for a joyride later. Let's eat. Now that I've got my girl back, I'm starving."

My girl.

I could get used to the sound of that.

CHAPTER 36
GRACELYN

Now that we're back home in Thunder Creek, everything between me and Mack's back to normal. Better than normal, in fact.

We're together every possible minute and haven't spent one night apart in the last two weeks. He swears he's fine with how everything went down and doesn't care about the family feud, but I can't shake the bad vibes. I'm a people pleaser down to the very last fiber of my soul and I hate being the reason Mack's not speaking with his parents.

Which he isn't, to my knowledge. Well, his mother at least. His dad's definitely on our side, but he's keeping a low profile since he has to live in the same house as her. A big house, for sure, but they still share one roof.

I'm sweeping the floor of the salon after my last client of the day when the door chimes announcing a customer. My mom's already gone—she has Mahjong on Tuesday nights with her friends—and I'm positive I don't have another client booked. It's too early for Mack to come around. And Sloane's back down in Florida with Cam.

"We're closed," I call down the hall, waiting for the door to slam shut or someone to acknowledge my words.

Instead, there's the soft fall of footsteps and in walks Mrs. McIntire in all her posh, old-money glory. Hair upswept in a chic chignon, she's quite fashionable in wide-leg trousers, an off-white blouse, and tweed flats. She's totally out of place in my hometown.

Heart racing, I grip the broom so tight my knuckles turn white.

"Like I said, we're closed." I have no idea why she's here and absolutely nothing to say to her.

"I'm not here for a haircut, Gracelyn."

I figured as much.

"Mack's not here."

"I'm not looking for him."

"Oh." I swallow down my nerves, my throat tight, fervently wishing I'd taken up Mahjong when my mother offered.

Too late now.

Instead, I'm stuck in a staring contest with Mack's mother.

"I'm here to see you, Grace. To apologize."

For the second time, Mack's mom sucker punches me in the gut. But this time, it's at least good.

"I shouldn't have insinuated you were dating Ulysses for his money. That was wrong of me. I could go through a long litany of excuses for my behavior, but the truth is I've always worried about him getting caught up with the wrong types of people. I never gave you a chance and for that I'm truly sorry."

"Thanks." I run my hand up and down the broom

handle, my bracelets tinkling softly in the silent salon. "And I'd love to say it's fine, but honestly, you really hurt my feelings." I gnaw my lower lip, feeling extremely vulnerable.

"I may not have a lot to offer financially, but I do love your son. With my whole heart. And he loves me. We want to be together and would very much like your blessing. It would make Mack happy, I'm sure. But I won't put up with that kind of treatment ever again." I stand taller and straighter, my posture perfect. Mrs. Johnson, my ballet teacher from grade school, would be proud.

"I understand. I'm sorry for how everything transpired and that you were hurt." She tucks an invisible strand of hair behind her ear and shifts from foot to foot. It's the first time I've seen her look anything but poised and at ease.

"I've brought you a small gift as a token of my regret. Please accept this with my apology." She steps forward, pressing a black velvet jewelry box into my hand.

I immediately shove the square box back at her. "I couldn't."

"Just open it. Please." Hands clasped, she all but begs me to open the gift.

With shaky hands, I pry the box open. A pair of huge sparkly diamond studs wink up at me, glistening beneath the salon light.

"Oh. Wow." My mouth forms a perfect 'O,' heart racing. "They're very beautiful."

"Thank you. The earrings are a family heirloom. They belonged to Ulysses' grandmother."

I snap the box shut. "I can't possibly accept these."

I try to give the jewelry back, but she holds up her palms. "Please. She'd want you to have them. *I* want you to have them. Nana asked me to give them to Ulysses' bride. I don't think I'm being rash giving them to you now."

My heart hammers, blood roaring in my ears.

Bride.

His mother believes Mack's going to propose.

To me.

Gracelyn Ann Reynolds, without an 'e.'

And I think she may be right about that.

"I—I don't know what to say."

"You don't have to say anything, dear. Those earrings belong to you now. Take good care of them. And of my son." Her eyes glisten with tears, and I almost feel sorry for the woman. Even with all her money, her pedigree, the country club friends, the ginormous mansion and the staff, she can't have the one thing she wants.

The true love and respect of her son.

Maybe, over time, they can find their way back to each other.

Stepping forward, I reach out and grip her forearm. "Thank you. I will."

With a sad smile, she pats my hand, then pivots to go.

"Gracelyn—" She glances over her shoulder. "Take care. Hopefully we'll see you and Mack again soon."

Then she sashays out of the salon, leaving behind only the slightest hint of her expensive perfume.

CHAPTER 37
MACK

'm walking out of football practice when I spot the SUV. A Mercedes with blacked out windows and matte rims. Those rims are special order, and I'm betting these particular wheels traveled all the way here from Augusta.

What in the hell is my mother doing in Thunder Creek?

In the decade I've lived here, she's never visited. Not even once.

Damn, we were on a good streak too.

I sidle up to the idling SUV, tapping on the rear passenger window. The black glass slides down and there's my mother. Sitting in the backseat, ankles crossed, with Bobby at the wheel.

"Hello, Mother."

"Hello, Ulysses."

"To what do I owe this pleasure?"

She frowns at me for a split second, then fixes her face, moving back to neutral. A few high school kids walk by, laughing and joking. They wave to me as they pass.

"Bye, Coach."

"See you tomorrow, Coach."

I shoot the kids a wave, then turn back to the problem at hand. My mother.

"Is there somewhere more private we can chat?" She narrows her eyes at the kids, goofing around in the parking lot.

I tip my head to the sky, debating.

"I could use a beer." I duck my head into the car. "Bobby, follow me."

Bobby nods and I hustle to my truck and hop in. Figure if my mother's going to stop by, she should have a tour of Thunder Creek, starting with Mustang's.

Firing up the truck, I pull out of the lot and drive over to Mustang's, carefully following all the rules of the road. Wouldn't want Bobby to lose me.

This is going to be fun.

Thursdays are popular nights at Mustang's, the local college kids taking full advantage of the beer specials. I find an open spot and Bobby circles around, dropping my mother at the door. She climbs out of the SUV, her lips pressed in a thin line as she surveys the neon sign and the bucking horse.

I doubt my mother has ever visited such an establishment before, probably viewing this type of place as way beneath her. No doorman here, she shifts uncomfortably from foot to foot.

Taking my time, I sidle across the parking lot. Thoroughly enjoying the look of displeasure settling on my mother's unlined face.

Good.

She's getting a little taste of her own medicine.

I open the door for her and she crosses the threshold,

the sour stench of stale beer and peanuts hitting hard. The music pumps, groups of college kids dotted around what will soon become the dance floor. I see an empty booth toward the back and usher my mother over to the spot.

"After you." I gesture at the pleather seat and she slides in, her nose wrinkled as the seat scrunches beneath her.

"This is—" she surveys the scene. "Interesting."

I hold in a snicker, handing her a sticky plastic menu. "I wouldn't recommend the wine, but suit yourself."

A waitress appears, saying her hellos and complimenting me on our latest win of the season. Against my advice, my mother orders a house chardonnay, and I order a beer. The waitress takes off to fetch our drinks and I sit back in the booth, relaxed in my own environment.

"So, what's up?"

"Ulysses…"

My skin crawls at the use of my given name here, but I bite my tongue. She's already uneasy. No need to rub salt into the wound.

"I came to apologize. For the whole Gracelyn situation." She casts her gaze down to the table, her mouth scrunched tight.

"Which situation are we talking about? The inviting my ex thing? The shunting of my girlfriend to the guest house? Or are we addressing the fact that you called Gracelyn a gold digger?" My voice is harsher than I intend, but I've put up with my mother's bullshit for a long damn time and frankly, I'm sick of it.

"Yes." Her voice is quiet, her shoulders slightly slumped.

My mother never has anything other than perfect posture.

"Thanksgiving was a total disaster. Gracelyn never

wants to go back to your house again, and I can't say I blame her. The way you and Emma Kate and Tinsley acted was abhorrent." Anger gurgles up inside me again, even this many weeks later.

The waitress reappears, breaking the tension. She sets our drinks down, then bustles away. My mother lifts her glass and takes a sip, her nose scrunching up in distaste.

I warned her.

I take a long slug of my beer, appreciating the chilled beverage as it slides down my throat, giving me liquid courage.

"Gracelyn's important to me—special enough to bring home—and the three of you made her feel awful. Less than."

My mother swirls the straw-colored liquid in her glass, avoiding my gaze.

"I know."

Well, damn. I didn't think she had it in her to admit a mistake.

"I know, Ulysses, and I'm here to make amends. With you and with her. I gave her Nana's earrings today."

"What?" My voice tips up in shock.

"The diamonds your grandmother wanted your bride to have. I gave them to Gracelyn."

Every muscle in my body tenses, yet a heavy weight lifts off my shoulders. A weight I didn't even realize I was carrying until right this second.

"You gave Gracelyn Nana's earrings?"

My mother nods. "I did. I know you're going to propose. Nana wanted your bride to have those diamond earrings."

I let out a long, slow breath. I always loved my nana

and she loved me. The real me. Mack, not Ulysses Fauntleroy McIntire III.

Just Mack.

My mother recognizing that Gracelyn deserves those earrings is huge.

Fucking monumental.

My heart cracks open a tiny little bit, just enough to see my mother for the first time in a very long time.

A mom wanting to reconnect with her son.

Even if that means coming down to Thunder Creek and meeting me on my level. A level she's not comfortable with and never will be.

"Thanks." I reach across the table and grab my mother's hand. It's warm and soft and smaller than I remember.

She lifts her eyes to mine, shiny beneath the pendant light above the table.

"I really am sorry, Ulysses. I hope this can be the beginning of something good. I've missed you."

Squeezing my mom's hand, I nod. I doubt we'll ever be the matching PJ family, sitting around the kitchen table playing UNO until midnight.

But this feels like a pretty great start.

CHAPTER 38
GRACELYN

Christmas is a week away. I have one last appointment before I hang up my stylist apron for the holiday break.

Of course, the appointment's running late.

Dammit.

All I want to do is go home and take a nice hot shower, wash away the knots in my shoulders then snuggle on the couch with Mack. He promised he'd watch a cheesy holiday movie with me—his words, not mine—and I'm *so* ready for it.

The door chimes and I check my watch. Fucker's ten minutes late. I'm not even certain who's showing up. My mom booked the appointment last minute, before she headed out the door for a White Elephant gift exchange with her book club.

"About damn time..." I mutter under my breath, spinning to face the tardy client.

And there's Mack, in jeans and a button down, looking fine as hell.

"Well, hello there, handsome. You're not my 6:30, are you?" I peek around his shoulders, trying to see if anyone else came in behind him.

"I am. But I don't need a haircut. Close up shop—we have plans." He shoots me a grin, all white teeth and gorgeousness, and heat unfurls in my belly.

I love this man.

Who would ever have thought my mom's broody next-door neighbor would be hella romantic?

I hurry to close up, clicking off the lights and locking the door. Mack grabs my hand and together we walk down the steps.

"Where are we going? What are we doing?" I'm practically bouncing with excitement as we walk down the sidewalk to his truck. I love surprises.

"Thought it would be fun to catch the lights in town. See the Christmas tree. I know how much you love the holidays."

He helps me into the truck, then we take off into the night. He turns on the radio, Parker McCollum singing about being my man, and I sink back into the comfy leather seat, happy and content. We drive through the neighborhood, every house lit up with holiday lights, a few lawns sporting those gigantic inflatable snow globes. Nobody does Christmas better than Thunder Creek.

Mack takes a left turn, then another left, until we're in the center of town. He parks at the square and together we walk across the lawn toward the giant Christmas tree.

Sparkling with white lights, the tree's massive and beautiful, strung with gold and silver tinsel and decorated with red, green, and gold ornaments. The shops around the square are decorated too, each storefront strung with glittering lights.

"I love the holidays." I rest my head on Mack's broad shoulder, snuggling into his warmth. "They're so magical."

He kisses me on the top of my head, his arm wrapped around my waist.

"They are. Oh, look—that gift is for you." He points at a giant box beneath the tree, with a huge gold bow and a tag reading *Gracelyn*.

"You planned this." I swivel my head toward him, eyes narrowed.

He shrugs. "Maybe. Grab the gift."

I bend down and pick up the beautifully wrapped box.

"Go on, open it."

Holding my breath, I tear through the shiny red paper. I lift the top and find another, much smaller box, wrapped in identical red paper with the cutest little gold bow.

Mack's hand at my back, I rip through the tape of the smaller gift. The red paper falls to the ground, revealing a plain box. I raise the lid and gasp.

Inside sits a beautiful, sparkly Princess-cut diamond ring.

"Mack—" I breathe, lifting my gaze from the jewelry.

He's on one knee, reaching for my hand.

"Gracelyn, I love you. You are the most genuine, loving, bubbly person I've ever met. You make the sun shine brighter, the wind blow lighter, and the days feel better, just because you're there by my side. Where I want you to be today, tomorrow, and all the rest of our days. Gracelyn Troublemaker Reynolds, will you do me the honor of becoming my wife?"

He fixes earnest jade eyes on me, wide and serious.

I'm speechless, the breath sucked from my lungs.

I love this man with all that I have, all that I am.

"Yes, Mack. Yes. I would love to be your wife."

With a steady hand, he plucks the ring from the box and slides the glittery diamond onto my finger. A perfect fit.

Rising, he kisses me long and slow on the lips, right there in the square with the Christmas tree in the background.

This is the most perfect moment of my life and I've never been happier.

I take a deep breath, inhaling the heady scent of the tree and Mack and all his goodness.

I love this man with all my heart and I can't wait to be his wife.

Everything is going to work out.

Gracelyn and Mack.

Together, we'll call the shots and live happily ever after.

Want a peek into Gracelyn and Mack's future? Subscribe to my mailing list and you'll get instant access to an exclusive bonus scene!

CHAPTER ONE

Bree

Pacing the terrazzo floor of Terminal Three at LAX, I scowled with annoyance at my silent phone.

Crickets.

Pax, my soon-to-be-ex-boyfriend, was ignoring my barrage of angry texts.

Two days ago I'd seen a suspicious tweet from a twit named Keely: *Had the best night w/ @PaxJones!* But my breaking point was an Instagram pic of Pax kissing a rando girl smack on the lips.

It could have been a scene from his upcoming movie,

but I didn't think so. He'd told me he was in Montana, filming scenes for his next big film, a Western flick starring him as a gorgeous-but-lonely cowboy. But the background in the photo appeared to be the Pacific Ocean, and even though I'd never been to Montana, I was pretty certain that's NOT what it looked like.

I immediately did some digging and sure enough, that asshole was in Laguna Beach, staying at the Ritz. And he definitely wasn't alone, judging by the amount of Veuve and spa treatments charged to his room.

"Final boarding call for Flight 4356 to Atlanta, GA. All remaining passengers should board at this time."

I hesitated, took a deep breath. If I was going to flee LA and the paparazzi, I had to get on this plane. Any second now, the disastrous headlines could hit:

Relationship expert Bree Hart is no 'expert' when it comes to her own love life

Superstar Paxton Jones leaves so-called 'dating doctor' for B-list actress

Relationship guru Bree Hart left brokenhearted by actor Paxton Jones

Gah. I so did *not* want those headlines to hit. My dating podcast was finally trending, and I'd just made it into the Top 25 in the Relationship Category. This could devastate my career. Never mind my heart—Pax had already broken that several times.

I'd been trying (unsuccessfully) to dump Pax for the last 24 hours. Timing was everything and I wanted to break up with him before the media got wind of a cheating scandal. Then I'd disappear for a bit, under the guise of visiting my sister. Pax could step out with someone new, and I'd fade into the background, yesterday's news.

But, per the usual, Pax was even making breaking up

difficult. He wasn't answering my texts or calls, probably because he was too busy with his new sidepiece.

"Seriously. This is the last and final boarding call." The ticketing agent shot me a pointed look. I was the only person still standing at the gate.

Taking the not-so-subtle hint, I wheeled my suitcase over to the kiosk and presented my ticket.

"Have a safe flight."

"Thanks," I said, juggling my shoulder bag and luggage.

As I made my way down the ramp, my shoulder vibrated. Crap. That could be Pax, finally calling me back. I rooted through my bag and managed to fish out my phone.

"Hello? Hello?"

Silence. I checked the screen. One missed call and it was from Pax.

"Damn it!" I immediately hit his name, calling him back. One ring, two rings, three, four. Pax's voice came on the line, *"You know what to do. Leave me a message."*

"Hey, Pax, it's me, Bree. So, I saw your Instagram and it looks like you're with someone else. Not going to lie, I'm pretty upset and it's really uncool that you're not even answering my texts. But whatever. Obviously, you've moved on. I'm not going to stall here or anything, I'm just going to come right out and say it. We're—"

"Good-bye."

Seriously? Even Pax's *voicemail* was too busy for me. I dialed him back. I needed to get this off my chest this instant, so I could move on with my life and avert career disaster.

Ring, ring, ring. *Beep. "Sorry, but the voicemail box is full.*

Call back later." And with that, I was automatically disconnected.

"Ugh!" I cried, shaking my phone. "All I want to do is dump you!"

I slammed my phone back into my purse and looked up. Two flight attendants flanked the doorway to the plane and they were both staring at me.

"Boyfriend problems," I explained, a hot blush creeping over my face. They both nodded knowingly.

"Girl, who doesn't?" The attendants whispered something to each other, then glanced back at me. The one on the right ushered me over and checked my ticket.

"You're in Seat 2B now," she said, winking as she took my ticket. "We ladies need to stick together. Enjoy your flight."

"Thanks," I said, smiling in gratitude. "I will."

Breaking up with Pax would have to wait until I landed. I intended to take full advantage of first class while I had the chance.

———

As soon as the plane touched down in Atlanta, I powered up my phone to a string of missed texts from Pax:

"Babe. It's not what you think w/ Keely. But if you want to pump the brakes, that's cool."

"Life is too short to be unhappy."

And my personal fave:

"Could you still pick my laundry up at the cleaners? Thx."

Asshole, I thought, collecting my rollaboard and deplaning. *What did I ever see in that jerk? He couldn't even bother to call, just left me a bunch of texts, like a freaking middle schooler.*

I sighed and shook my head, exasperated at my terrible choice in men. Like most of my clients, I blamed it on my parents. If my dad hadn't skipped out on us when I was only eight, maybe I'd be better at this relationship thing. Probably not, but maybe.

Making my way over to the rental car area, I signed my life away for the opportunity to motor around the greater Atlanta area in a mid-sized Chevy Malibu. I collected the keys, dashed off a quick text to my sister, Brooklyn, and hit I-85, happy to be away from the prying eyes of the paparazzi.

————

Three minutes after I arrived at my sister's, she tasked me with afternoon chauffeur duty for my niece. Destination: Pee Wee football practice. Fine by me—it kept me busy and, frankly, I didn't have much else to do.

"Alexa, do you have your mouthguard? Water bottle?" I asked, popping the car door open for her.

"Yes, Aunt Bee, see?" She held up her pink mouthguard and water bottle as proof.

"Great. Then let's go." I shoved her mouthguard into my handbag and clicked the lock button on my key fob, although I highly doubted anyone would steal my car.

After all, we *were* in Peachtree Grove, Georgia. AKA, Smalltown, USA, home of the Peach Cobbler Festival and approximately 10,000 people, most of whom were born and would die in Peachtree Grove. My sister and her husband were two of the few "newcomers," meaning they'd only lived here for the last five or so years. (They wouldn't be considered "locals" until Alexa had children, probably.) Brooks moved when Alexa was a baby so her husband, Dr. Craig Williams, could be closer to the hospital at Emory, where he was both a prominent doctor and a professor. When she'd first described Peachtree Grove to me, I thought she was exaggerating, but then I came to visit. It was definitely a shock to my jaded LA system. No flashy cars or movie stars here. Just high school football. Which, by the way, is an actual, legitimate season. Seriously. It's *printed on calendars*, like the 4th of July and Easter. In Peachtree Grove, Friday is for football, Saturday is for football, and Sunday is for church and football. Weekdays are for work and football practice. Rinse and repeat.

Which I guess is why my niece loves football. And why I now found myself standing on a plushy field with tons of other pee wee players and their parents, looking for the head coach of the—what did Brooks say the name of Alex's team was?—oh yes, the Lions.

Holding my hand to my forehead, I shielded my eyes from the sun. Even with sunglasses on, it was still too bright to see across the field. Ah, September in the South.

"Is that them, over there?" I pointed to a group of about ten kids on a big square marked with a #4 sign, two fields over on the right. "That might be the coach, wearing the blue shirt." His back was to us, but his jersey said "Coach." An excellent tipoff. I *so* had this aunt thing down.

"Yeah, that's my friend Cole." Alexa nodded, then took off in a sprint towards the group, deftly dodging clumps of boys, all Alexa-sized.

"Wait up!" I called, doing my best fast walk across the fields. It was futile; she was already way ahead of me. *I should have worn sneakers. Oh well, at least I'm not wearing heels and I go to the gym.*

When I finally caught up to Alexa, I was a little out of

breath and perspiration beaded on my brow. Flipping my hair over my shoulder, I fanned myself with one hand. I slid in with the group of moms hanging out on the side-lines, just behind the man in the blue Coach shirt. Alexa and all the other kids were in a big cluster, facing the coach.

"Okay, guys, it looks like everyone's here," the coach announced in a loud voice, doing a quick once-over of the Pee Wees.

"What's your name?" He pointed at Alexa.

"Alexa Williams," she said in a soft voice. The other kids chittered away, while Alexa stared down at her sneakers and kicked at a clump of grass.

"Hmmm, I don't see that name on my roster." The coach went down the names on his clipboard. "Oh, here. Alex Williams?"

She nodded up at him with wide blue eyes.

"I'm her aunt." I gave a little wave and stepped forward to clear up any misunderstanding.

The coach turned towards me and my breath caught in my throat.

Coach was drop-dead gorgeous.

He reached his hand out to me and I shook it, noting he had very large, strong hands. He was super tall, probably 6'3", and had deep marine eyes with long, dark lashes. Dark hair, cropped short, and he looked like he'd be ripped.

"Does she go by Alex or Alexa?"

"What?"

"Your niece. Does she prefer Alex or Alexa?" he asked, nodding in her direction.

"Oh. Um, Alex. Or Alexa. I think she likes Alexa." My

voice trailed off as my cheeks burned. *Really, Bree? You don't even know which name your niece prefers?*

"I like Alex," Alexa piped up. "Call me Alex."

Coach grinned over at Alexa, showing off perfectly straight, white teeth. A dentist's dream.

"I'm Ryder, by the way. Ryder McCauliffe." He smiled at me and I noticed he had very cute dimples and a nice square jaw. This man was fine.

"I'm Bree. Bree Hart. Alexa's, er, Alex's aunt," I corrected myself, shoving my hands into my back pockets. *Super awkward.* "I'm gonna just stand over here," I motioned to the group of mingling parents, chatting with each other and ignoring me. "And watch."

"Sounds good, Bree." He grinned at me again as I backed away toward the sideline, torn between wanting to crawl into a hole and die or watch this beautiful man coach Pee Wee football.

Coach Ryder turned towards the Pee Wees. "Does everyone have their mouthguards?" Eleven kids nodded yes, while Alexa shot me a pointed look.

"Oh yes, I have that!" I fumbled in my bag, produced the mouthguard.

Running back out to the field, I handed it to my niece, willing myself not to trip or otherwise further embarrass myself. I felt Ryder's eyes on me. Swiveling back around, I wished fervently for the safety of the sidelines. I was clearly out of my league here.

"Okay, so guys, how many of you have played football before?" Coach Ryder asked the kids. All twelve hands shot up in excitement.

"Great! We're gonna be a great team then. And on my team—your team—we all have to follow a couple rules.

My number one rule is be safe. How do you think we can do that?"

I filed that away; I'd have to tell my sister as soon as we got home. Safety first here at Pee Wee football!

Oh shoot, I never called her to tell her we got to the field. Grabbing my phone, I tapped out a quick text:

> Made it. We're all good. And Coach is HOT

I hit send and listened to Ryder talk about rule number two, be kind and show good sportsmanship.

> Brooklyn: What's coach's name?

> Bree: Ryder McCauliffe

> Brooklyn: THE Ryder McCauliffe?

> Bree: ????

> Brooklyn: You know. Former NFL Wide Receiver for the Dallas Cowboys. High school hotshot. Played at UGA, then drafted by Dallas. First round

> Bree: Um, obvi I did NOT know or maybe would have taken more than like 10 secs to get ready

> Brooklyn: You're definitely calling things off with Pax, right?

Bree: Yes. I mean, I tried. I *think* we're broken up

Brooklyn: He's single, you know. Wink-wink

Bree: I didn't ask

Brooklyn: You didn't have to. I'm your sister

Bree: Am I that transparent? Geez, I hope I have a better game face than that

Brooklyn: His kid is probably on the team

Bree: Wha-what?!?!

Brooklyn: Yeah, cute kid. Think his name is Charlie. Or something like that

Bree: So you're telling me this hot pro baller is a Single. Dad.?!?!

Brooklyn: Yep. Look around. How many very attractive women are attending football practice right now?

I glanced around and did a quick mental survey. There were several blondes in tight spandex leggings gathered together, another pretty brunette on her phone (snapping a photo or two?), and one intense dad with a clipboard, taking notes.

Bree: Yes, loads

Brooklyn: He's a local celeb. I'm sure women throw themselves at him. All. Day. Long.

Bree: I can see why

Inwardly, I groaned. Of course they would. And I'd embarrassed myself already, within the first two minutes of meeting the guy. Mental head smack.

"And our last team rule is to have fun. Because if we do all of those things, we'll be winners! Now I want you guys to put your hands in here, like this," Ryder demonstrated, dropping his hand into the middle of all the kids, "and on the count of three say 'Go Lions! Roar!' Ready? One, two, three!" All the kids yelled out "Go Lions" and did their best roar, which was adorable. Cue heart melt. I glanced around and noticed several of the moms videoing the speech. Oh brother. This guy was a freaking saint.

Ryder had the kids run some drills, so I took the opportunity to find my way to the bleachers and do a quick Google search. A few taps and I had the dude's (Wikipedia) life history:

Age: 32

Height: 6'4" (I shorted him an inch. Shame on me.)

Weight: 220 lbs

Position: Wide receiver

Stats: Football superstar at Peachtree Grove High School, helping lead the team to state victory with 18 touchdowns his senior year. Recruited by University of Georgia (2004-2008), where he played first string Wide Receiver all four years. Team went on to win

Nationals. First round draft pick in 2008. Signed with Dallas, #18, where he continued to play wide receiver position. Five successful seasons as starter for Dallas, including one trip to Super Bowl. Shoulder injury in sixth season left him benched. Retired in 2014.

No mention of personal life, relationship, kid. A few more taps, though, and I had additional dirt.

Ryder McCauliffe and Dallas cheerleader Shayna Bowman tie the knot in lavish multimillion-dollar wedding

Ryder McCauliffe and Dallas cheerleader wife welcome son

Dallas Wide Receiver Ryder McCauliffe and cheerleader wife on the rocks

Dallas cheerleader Shayna McCauliffe files charges of domestic abuse against former pro player-husband Ryder McCauliffe

Former Dallas Wide Receiver McCauliffe calls it quits with cheerleader wife

Sounded like a train wreck. I clicked through the articles, taking in as much info as possible.

There were a few photos of Ryder when he was playing for the team, looking about the same as he did now.

An article about his shoulder injury, sustained during game eight of his sixth season with Dallas. Separated shoulder, requiring multiple surgeries. He sat the bench the rest of the season, then was cut from the team.

Then it looked like his life pretty much fell apart. Domestic abuse charges filed, but he was later cleared of all charges. Divorce looming, nasty custody battle.

From what I read, it seemed like Ryder had full custody and the articles alleged possible substance abuse by Shayna. I zoomed in on every photo of her. She was pretty. Very cheerleader. Chesty. Dark, straight hair, wide smile, curvy in all the right places. Perfect abs. *Just like me,* I thought wryly. Dumb to even compare myself, we were nothing alike. She was taller than me, curvier than me, definitely bustier than me. I had long, blondish hair with a slight wave, her hair was stick straight, and in most photos she had bangs.

It seemed like she was in it for the money. As soon as Ryder got cut from the team, she started the separation proceedings, which led to the divorce. *Bad situation for his kid*, I thought.

Just for fun, I did a quick Google search on Shayna McCauliffe. The same articles popped up, plus her LinkedIn page, describing her as a Dallas Cheerleader/Lifestyle Expert. Interesting plot twist, considering the drug allegations. There was an article about her dating one of the League owners, as well as the Defensive Coordinator. The girl got around, and she definitely had a type. Rich, with athletic being a bonus.

There was only the one mention of their son, Charlie, in the article about his birth. None of the Shayna articles mentioned the child at all and there were zero photos of him. Seemed like Ryder did his best keeping his private life private. I respected that. It was one of my (many) issues with Pax.

"Aunt Bee! Aunt Bee!" Across the field, Alexa jumped up and down, waving me over.

"Coming!" I waved back to her and bounced off the bleachers, taking the steps as quickly as I could. Most of the other moms were already gathered around Ryder, hanging on his every word. I hoped whatever he was saying wasn't critical; I wanted to make sure I got all the information for Brooks. She'd get an email about it, though, right?

Just as I was closing in on our team's huddle, a sharp pain hit me in my left knee. Next thing I knew, I was flat on my back in the soft grass, staring up at the blue sky. *Hmmm, very few clouds today…*

"Are you alright?"

I blinked several times; I wasn't sure if the blurriness was from the sun beaming directly into my eyes or from the blow to the back of my head. Eventually, Ryder's eyes came into focus, tiny wrinkles of concern forming around them. *Cute…*

"Uh, yeah, I think so." I tried to sit up, but Ryder put his hand on my shoulder, gently keeping me still.

"Wait a few seconds. Trust me on this, lots of experience getting tackled." He winked and my cheeks flushed crimson.

"K," I murmured. "Um, what happened? Did I really get tackled?"

"Yeah. A nine-year-old laid you out. Not sure you're gonna make the first-round draft picks this year. You may need a little more work on your game," he chuckled, guiding me up by my elbow.

"How's that feel? Are you dizzy at all?" He gazed deep into my eyes, trying to gauge my concussion risk, I supposed.

"Aunt Bee, are you okay?" Alexa stood by my side, furrows creasing her brow.

"No, not dizzy. I'm fine. I'll be okay, Alexa." I waved my hands to brush off their concern and demonstrate my fineness. I bent my knees to try to stand and involuntarily let out a tiny whimper. "Ouch," I whispered under my breath.

"Let me take a look, I'm a physical therapist by day." He poked and prodded my knee, bending it this way and that. "You're going to need to ice that when you get home. That will minimize the swelling."

"Swelling?" I asked in a panicky voice.

"Yeah. That kid ran straight into your knee." He pointed to the side of my left kneecap. "You'll probably be okay, but it's going to bruise and you could have a microtear. Why don't you come into the clinic tomorrow and I'll take a closer look, reassess the situation?" Ryder tilted his head, waiting for my response.

"I'll be fine." I waved my hand again, brushing off his concern.

"I insist. Plus, I have a knee brace, or at the very least, a wrap to decrease swelling." He touched the side of my knee to demonstrate the wrapping motion and a tingle ran up my leg. That was a good sign, no numbness or loss of feeling. And clearly my libido hadn't sustained any injury.

"Okay, I'll come in," I said.

"Great. I'll give you my card and you can drop in around lunchtime. We're usually pretty slow then."

"Cool. I mean, great, thanks." I blushed, stumbling over my words. Maybe I did have a slight concussion.

Some of the other moms were shooting me dirty looks, like I'd ruined practice, and the kids were getting rowdy since the coach wasn't looking.

"You better get back." I nodded my head towards the group.

"Let me help you up." Deftly, Ryder leaned in and scooped me up, wrapping one of his arms around my waist and putting almost all my bodyweight onto his strong shoulders. The kids cheered; several of the blonde moms rolled their eyes. *So much for good sportsmanship*, I thought.

He gave them a wave with his right hand and together we limped to my rental car, Alexa trotting behind. My close proximity to Ryder helped block out the shooting pain in my knee. He smelled fantastic, crisp and clean, despite having run practice in eighty-five-degree weather. I'd been right about his hands—they were large and strong, supporting me at my waist. His pec muscles were straining underneath his shirt, yet he moved effortlessly through the parking lot, as if I weighed nothing. I tried not to swoon.

"This is it." I nodded at the white Malibu, fumbling in my purse for the keys. I had to lean into him to get to my purse and I fully appreciated his strong, muscled chest against my side. He gripped my waist tighter while I searched, so I wouldn't topple over.

"Here they are." I dangled the keys, unlocked the car.

"Are you alright to drive?" Ryder asked, concern clouding his eyes.

"Yep, perfectly fine," I nodded, stifling a wince. He opened Alex's door first, then mine, easing me down gently into the seat. His face was so close to mine, I saw his five-o-clock shadow. My breath hitched and we locked eyes for a moment. A frisson of heat shimmered down my body as I gazed at the darker navy flecks in his eyes.

"Sure you're okay?"

"Right as rain," I sing-songed in my most cheerful voice, nodding.

In reality, I could barely hear him over the thumping of my racing heartbeat. No, I was definitely *not* okay.

I was crushing hard on Peachtree Grove's most eligible bachelor, Ryder McCauliffe, former pro football player and hot-as-hell single dad.

Read RUSHING INTO LOVE now!

ALSO BY KARA KENDRICK

SEAGLASS BEACH SERIES

Unmistakable

Unstoppable

Unrivaled

Undone

PEACHTREE GROVE SERIES

Rushing Into Love

Turning Up the Heat

Chasing After Forever

THUNDER CREEK SERIES

Out of Bounds

Calling the Shots

MAN OF THE MONTH CLUB: STARLIGHT BAY

New Year's Renovations

Love in Bloom

Stars & Sparks Forever

My One & Goalie

MAN OF THE MONTH CLUB: SYCAMORE MT.

Snowbody But You

MAN OF THE MONTH CLUB: CANDY CANE KEY

Reeling Him In

Lights, Camera, Christmas

MAN OF THE MONTH CLUB: MAGNOLIA POINT

Brides & Birdies

HOLIDAY NOVELLAS

Christmas in Cayman

Mr. Right Under the Mistletoe

My Charming Holidate

Snowed In With the Scrooge

BILLIONAIRE SERIES

Charming the CEO

Flirt Like a (Fake) Groom

HEART OF A WOUNDED HERO SERIES

Soldier On: Heart of a Wounded Hero

WILD BROTHERS SERIES

Forever Wild

Find them all at www.karakendrick.com

Kara Kendrick writes fun and flirty small-town romance destined to give you all the feels. A reformed English major, she also has a master's in counseling and was an elementary school counselor in her pre-mom life.

She loves the beach, wine, and rock-hard abs, not necessarily in that order. When she's not dreaming up Happily Ever After's, you can find her chasing after her boy-girl twins, working out semi-hardish, or walking her adorable Shiba pups with her husband, who's not too bad himself.

Let's be friends! Sign up for the VIP newsletter and be the first to hear about upcoming releases, promos, and giveaways.

If you enjoyed reading this book, please help spread the word by leaving a review on Amazon, Goodreads, Bookbub, Facebook Reader Groups, Booktok, Bookstagram, or wherever you talk spicy romance books!

To stay in touch, visit www.karakendrick.com

ACKNOWLEDGMENTS

Deepest gratitude to all the people involved in helping me put this book out into the world:

My alpha readers, my sisters and mom; Valentine Grinstead and the entire Valentine PR team; Nicole McCurdy at Emerald Edits; Beth Hale, line editor; Chelsea Kemp, cover designer; Rachel Hill, beta reader; and my social media team, Cassie, Jackie, and Chelsey. And a huge thanks to my ARC team and all the bookstagrammers and bloggers who took a chance on me.

Last, but never least, thank you to my home team—Lance, Luke, and Kinsey. I love you all and am so grateful for the opportunity to pursue my passion. Xoxo.